Applause for L.L. Raand's Midnight Hunters Series

The Midnight Hunt
RWA 2012 VCRW Laurel Wreath ~~ ~~ ~~er~~ *Blood Hunt*
Nigh~~ ~~

"Raand has built a ~~ ~~ ~~ ~~olves, vampires, and other paranorm ~~ ~~ ~~ ~~ ~~ ~~ ~~readers a complex plot filled with wond ~~ ~~ ~~ ~~as insight into the hierarchy of Sylvan's pack an ~~ ~~ ~~ ~~ns. There are many plot twists and turns, as well as erotic ~~ ~~x scenes in this riveting novel that keep the pages flying until its satisfying conclusion."—*Just About Write*

"Once again, I am amazed at the storytelling ability of L.L. Raand aka Radclyffe. In *Blood Hunt*, she mixes high levels of sheer eroticism that will leave you squirming in your seat with an impeccable multi-character storyline all streaming together to form one great read." —*Queer Magazine Online*

"*The Midnight Hunt* has a gripping story to tell, and while there are also some truly erotic sex scenes, the story always takes precedence. This is a great read which is not easily put down nor easily forgotten."—*Just About Write*

"Are you sick of the same old hetero vampire / werewolf story plastered in every bookstore and at every movie theater? Well, I've got the cure to your werewolf fever. *The Midnight Hunt* is first in, what I hope is, a long-running series of fantasy erotica for L.L. Raand (aka Radclyffe)."—*Queer Magazine Online*

"Any reader familiar with Radclyffe's writing will recognize the author's style within *The Midnight Hunt*, yet at the same time it is most definitely a new direction. The author delivers an excellent story here, one that is engrossing from the very beginning. Raand has pieced together an intricate world, and provided just enough details for the reader to become enmeshed in the new world. The action moves quickly throughout the book and it's hard to put down."—*Three Dollar Bill Reviews*

Acclaim for Radclyffe's Fiction

In *Prescription for Love* "Radclyffe populates her small town with colorful characters, among the most memorable being Flann's little sister, Margie, and Abby's 15-year-old trans son, Blake…This romantic drama has plenty of heart and soul."
—*Publishers Weekly*

2013 RWA/New England Bean Pot award winner for contemporary romance *Crossroads* "will draw the reader in and make her heart ache, willing the two main characters to find love and a life together. It's a story that lingers long after coming to 'the end.'"—*Lambda Literary*

In **2012 RWA/FTHRW Lories and RWA HODRW Aspen Gold award winner** *Firestorm* "Radclyffe brings another hot lesbian romance for her readers."—*The Lesbrary*

Foreword Review Book of the Year finalist and IPPY silver medalist *Trauma Alert* "is hard to put down and it will sizzle in the reader's hands. The characters are hot, the sex scenes explicit and explosive, and the book is moved along by an interesting plot with well drawn secondary characters. The real star of this show is the attraction between the two characters, both of whom resist and then fall head over heels."
—*Lambda Literary Reviews*

Lambda Literary Award Finalist *Best Lesbian Romance 2010* features "stories [that] are diverse in tone, style, and subject, making for more variety than in many, similar anthologies…well written, each containing a satisfying, surprising twist. Best Lesbian Romance series editor Radclyffe has assembled a respectable crop of 17 authors for this year's offering."—*Curve Magazine*

2010 Prism award winner and ForeWord Review Book of the Year Award finalist *Secrets in the Stone* is "so powerfully [written] that the worlds of these three women shimmer between reality and dreams…A strong, must read novel that will linger in the minds of readers long after the last page is turned."—*Just About Write*

In **Benjamin Franklin Award finalist** *Desire by Starlight* "Radclyffe writes romance with such heart and her down-to-earth characters not only come to life but leap off the page until you feel like you know them. What Jenna and Gard feel for each other is not only a spark but an inferno and, as a reader, you will be washed away in this tumultuous romance until you can do nothing but succumb to it."—*Queer Magazine Online*

Lambda Literary Award winner *Stolen Moments* "is a collection of steamy stories about women who just couldn't wait. It's sex when desire overrides reason, and it's incredibly hot!"—*On Our Backs*

Lambda Literary Award winner *Distant Shores, Silent Thunder* "weaves an intricate tapestry about passion and commitment between lovers. The story explores the fragile nature of trust and the sanctuary provided by loving relationships."—*Sapphic Reader*

Lambda Literary Award Finalist *Justice Served* delivers a "crisply written, fast-paced story with twists and turns and keeps us guessing until the final explosive ending."—*Independent Gay Writer*

Lambda Literary Award finalist *Turn Back Time* "is filled with wonderful love scenes, which are both tender and hot."—*MegaScene*

By Radclyffe

Romances

Innocent Hearts

Promising Hearts

Love's Melody Lost

Love's Tender Warriors

Tomorrow's Promise

Love's Masquerade

shadowland

Passion's Bright Fury

Fated Love

Turn Back Time

When Dreams Tremble

The Lonely Hearts Club

Night Call

Secrets in the Stone

Desire by Starlight

Crossroads

Homestead

Against Doctor's Orders

Prescription for Love

The Color of Love

Honor Series

Above All, Honor

Honor Bound

Love & Honor

Honor Guards

Honor Reclaimed

Honor Under Siege

Word of Honor

Code of Honor

Price of Honor

Justice Series

A Matter of Trust (prequel)

Shield of Justice

In Pursuit of Justice

Justice in the Shadows

Justice Served

Justice for All

The Provincetown Tales

Safe Harbor

Beyond the Breakwater

Distant Shores, Silent Thunder

Storms of Change

Winds of Fortune

Returning Tides

Sheltering Dunes

Visit us at www.boldstrokesbooks.com

THE COLOR
OF LOVE

by

RADCLY*f*FE

2016

THE COLOR OF LOVE

© 2016 By Radclyffe. All Rights Reserved.

ISBN 13: 978-1-62639-716-3

This Trade Paperback Original Is Published By
Bold Strokes Books, Inc.
P.O. Box 249
Valley Falls, NY 12185

First Edition: July 2016

THIS IS A WORK OF FICTION. NAMES, CHARACTERS, PLACES, AND INCIDENTS ARE THE PRODUCT OF THE AUTHOR'S IMAGINATION OR ARE USED FICTITIOUSLY. ANY RESEMBLANCE TO ACTUAL PERSONS, LIVING OR DEAD, BUSINESS ESTABLISHMENTS, EVENTS, OR LOCALES IS ENTIRELY COINCIDENTAL.

THIS BOOK, OR PARTS THEREOF, MAY NOT BE REPRODUCED IN ANY FORM WITHOUT PERMISSION.

CREDITS
EDITORS: RUTH STERNGLANTZ AND STACIA SEAMAN
PRODUCTION DESIGN: STACIA SEAMAN
COVER DESIGN BY SHERI (GRAPHICARTIST2020@HOTMAIL.COM)

Acknowledgments

Love comes in all sizes, shapes, colors, and combos—of age, ethnicity, cultural heritage, gender identities, sexualities, social strata, and more. The color at the center of this book is green and seems fitting in a time when difference is feared, and a great many people think building walls, physical and metaphorical, will cure what ails us. Those of us in the LGBTQ community know a lot about breaking down walls and out of closets and fighting to be visible. Preserving the rights and freedoms of others is essential to preserving those same things for us. So goes one, so go we all, sooner or later. This book is a love story about two women, about home and family, and about the boundaries that must fall for us to preserve our love and our lives.

Many thanks go to: senior editor Sandy Lowe for the inspiration and hard work, editor Ruth Sternglantz for endless attention and expertise, editor Stacia Seaman for her unique skills, Sheri Halal for a super cover, and my first readers Paula, Eva, and Connie for encouragement and aid.

And as always, thanks to Lee for the best colors of all—green grass and blue skies. *Amo te.*

Radclyffe, 2016

To Lee, for rainbows

CHAPTER ONE

At ten to nine, Emily settled into one of the leather and mahogany captain's chairs at the round oak table in the library on the second floor of the Winfield Building and looked out the tall leaded-glass windows into the Flatiron District. A light, late snow fell, delicate and subtly powerful. So far the dusting was pleasantly picturesque, painting the sidewalks and marquees in a fleeting lacquer of white, and not enough to snarl traffic in Manhattan. She'd been in her office before six and hadn't minded the walk from her apartment in Chelsea. Spring was around the corner, snow or not.

She sipped her Earl Grey and waited for the others, soothed as always by the faint lemony scent of furniture polish and the seductive aroma of parchment. She never used the renovated conference room on the first floor, with its bright lights, steel and glass tables, sleek modern chairs, and absolutely no soul. This room had soul. The shelves were filled with history—history she was part of now—books discovered, sponsored, birthed by the Winfield Literary Agency for a hundred years. She hadn't been born into this world, but she'd been born with the love of words and she'd found her home.

Home. A flood of melancholy washed through her even after all this time. Almost ten years since home had become a place of sorrows and loss. She brushed the fleeting sadness aside, even while knowing it would return. The past was never truly gone, and she didn't want it to be. She had forged a new life, but memories, even painful ones, could still bring moments of joy. She did not regret hers.

Right now she had a very busy day ahead of her, and she looked forward to it. She sipped more tea and scanned the agenda on her tablet.

Acquisitions, launches, marketing and ads, budget, contracts. Business items to some, but excitement to her. Behind every bullet point a book was waiting.

At five to nine, Ron Elliott arrived, looking neat and polished as he always did in an open-collared, blue button-down shirt and flawlessly tailored black trousers. His chestnut brown hair draped over his forehead in a subtly artful accentuation of his dark brows and piercing blue eyes. He was handsome in the way some men could be beautiful and masculine at the same time. If she'd been interested in men in a personal way, and if he hadn't been gay and happily married, she would have picked Ron as the perfect match. He loved the work the way she did—as more than a job. He hadn't even complained when she'd been moved ahead of him into the senior agent position when she was younger and had less time in than him. He claimed he really only wanted to spend his time on acquisitions, and she believed him. Some days she envied him, when her carefully scheduled half-day of reviewing the slush pile went to hell in a handbasket with an unanticipated fiscal crisis, a frantic author with a missed deadline, or an impossible publisher request to advance a pub date.

"New haircut?" Ron sat opposite her at the round table.

Emily fingered the loose curls that just touched her shoulders and feathered back from her face. "Just a few inches off."

"Looks good. Now you could almost pass for twenty instead of twelve."

"I do have a mirror, you know. The twelve thing hasn't been true for at least five years. And you're the only one who ever thought so anyhow."

Ron grinned. "Just make sure to have ID if we ever go out clubbing again—or, miracle of miracles, you say yes the next time someone asks you for a date."

Emily shook her head and concentrated on her tablet. Ron was just about her best friend, but he was also one of those people who thought everyone should be as happily married as he was. She couldn't convince him she was far too busy and had too much to accomplish to need anything else. Anyone else. Maybe someday, when she was sure Pam's future was secure. Right now, her life was going according to plan—*her* plan, and that was all she wanted. No more surprises, no more disappointments.

At 8:59, the senior members of the agency arrived. Her team—two acquiring agents in addition to Ron, their interns, the marketing director and his intern, and the budget supervisor.

"Morning, everybody." Emily received a chorus of *morning*s and one barely audible groan. Clearly, one of the interns was not a morning person, but that would change if they wanted to make it in the rapidly transforming and ever-competitive world of literary discovery. Greetings completed, Emily jumped in.

"Okay, we've got three months to the launch of the summer season—so where are we in terms of ads, promotions, and tours? Ron—why don't you start."

Ron ran down his six forthcoming titles with reports from the corresponding publishers' marketing divisions, recaps of conversations with the authors, and summaries of his agenda for pushing his titles out to reviewers and bloggers ahead of release. Emily listened but didn't take notes. Ron was always on top of his list. For nearly an hour, the other agents in turn reviewed the forthcoming titles of the authors they represented, strategies were revised, and projected costs were approved, amended, and revised.

"We should be in good shape," Emily said, scanning the notes she'd made and projecting the timelines for the intersecting campaigns in her head. "Ron, Terry, you've got to keep on top of Heron—they're going to let the Emery and Rosen titles fall to the bottom of the list if we don't push, especially now that they've moved up the release of Baldwin's mystery."

"On it," Terry said.

"Already talking to them about it," Ron echoed.

"Good. Any author issues we need to know about?" Acquiring books and promoting them was only part of their job. Once the manuscripts were contracted and handed off to the publishers, a great deal of hand-holding was required to get their authors, especially the new ones, through the long, arduous process of editing, cover design, and advance promotion before the books went to press.

"All my chickens are happy," Terry said.

"Race Evans doesn't like his cover," Ron said. "I can't say I really blame him, but it's right for the market and we got Sellers and Saylor's art department to come as close as we could to what he was hoping for."

"Hopefully he'll be happier when he sees the sales." Emily cast one more look around. Everyone seemed satisfied and on point. "All right, then. I'll see you all Wednesday for production."

She stayed seated while the others left, adding a few more notes. She had fifteen minutes before a phone call to a client about acquiring their manuscript, her favorite kind of call. The author was usually excited, and she was happy to be adding another new title to their list.

When her cell rang, she checked the number and answered immediately. "Hi, Vonnie."

"Hi, Emily," Vonnie Hall, the president's personal secretary, replied. "Can you come on by? She wants to talk to you for a few minutes."

Emily frowned and checked her watch. "Is it urgent? I have a phone conference in five."

"I'll let her know you'll be half an hour."

"Thanks."

Thirty minutes and one about-to-be-signed contract later, Emily tucked her phone and tablet into her shoulder bag and climbed the winding wooden staircase to the fourth floor and made her way down the plush carpeted hall to the office at the far end. The top floor housed the senior agents' offices and looked as Emily imagined it had a century before with its vaulted tin ceilings, ornate hanging light fixtures, and recessed alcoves framed in dark, carved wood. Above the gleaming walnut wainscoting, framed portraits of generations of Winfields adorned the pale green, floral-patterned wallpaper. In the muted light, the eyes of the men and one woman followed her. With each step, she felt as if she moved back in time, although there was nothing outdated or antiquated about the woman she was about to see. Like Emily, Henrietta Winfield simply appreciated history.

Vonnie Hall, a trim, flawlessly presented woman in a red suit with thin ribbons of black along the collar and cuffs, guarded the door to Henrietta Winfield's inner sanctum with the ferocity of a she-wolf and the smile of an angel. She greeted Emily with genuine pleasure. "She'll just be a minute. She's finishing a phone call."

"Sure," Emily said. "How are you? Is Tom on his way home yet?"

Vonnie's smile blazed at the mention of her husband, still deployed with the National Guard. "He's in Germany, thank the Lord. He ought to be home in about ten days."

"I'm so glad."

A light on Vonnie's phone blinked and she gestured toward the closed door behind her. "Go on in."

"Thanks." Emily shifted her shoulder bag a little higher, skirted Vonnie's desk, and stepped into Henrietta Winfield's domain. The room was twice the size of the library she'd just left but resembled it with its filled-to-capacity bookshelves on two walls, the comfortable leather sofa and chair in the seating area, and the big wooden library table that served as a desk. The president of the Winfield Agency sat behind it now in a dark brown leather swivel chair.

At five-four and a hundred and ten pounds, Henrietta should have been dwarfed by the size of the table and the expansiveness of the room, but she filled the space—any space—with a palpable energy. When Emily had first met her seven years before, she'd been twenty-two and fresh out of school, and had felt as if she'd walked into the path of a hurricane. Despite being five inches taller and nearly forty years younger than Henrietta—HW, as everyone called her in casual conversation—she still sometimes had to run to keep up with her. Henrietta was energetic, trim, and formidable. She was also Emily's mentor, role model, and closest friend.

Henrietta, her shining black hair cut casually short, without any gray and naturally so, nodded hello. As was always the case, she wore a business suit, this one a gray pinstripe with a white open-collared shirt and a plain gold necklace showing at the throat.

"Hi," Emily said. "Sorry I couldn't make it sooner, but I just finished a call with a client."

"That was the fantasy you were telling me about the other night at dinner?"

Emily shook her head, although she shouldn't be surprised. HW's memory was prodigious and enviable. "That's the one."

"Is the author signing?"

"She is."

"Excellent. I agree with you—we're going to see a resurgence in high fantasy in the next year. Can you get this one positioned with one of the brand divisions?"

"I think so." Emily doubted Henrietta had called her in to discuss a relatively straightforward contract, but she waited patiently.

"Sit down. This will take a minute."

Emily's heart jumped. Something about the way Henrietta was

looking at her sent a chill down her spine. When she'd been a young intern working directly for HW, she'd been the recipient of a few hard stares, an occasional quiet but unforgettable admonishment, and a thousand more words of encouragement. Henrietta Winfield was the best at what she did, and she'd held the reins of her company in a firm grasp through economic and industry upheavals that had decimated other agencies. If she was unhappy, Emily couldn't fathom what might be the cause. She sat, feeling the pulse beat in her throat.

"I've just been on the phone with our attorneys," Henrietta said without preamble. "There's a better than even chance we're going to lose our H-1B approval at the end of the year."

Emily caught her breath. If that happened, her application for permanent residence would be in limbo—or terminated. "Why?"

"Because the idiots who make the laws, or listen to the people who elect them, are hysterical about immigration issues right now and they're cutting all the quotas. We are not tech, and that's where most of the allocations go."

Emily knew that, but she'd been in the United States since she'd enrolled at Harvard as an undergraduate. Singapore had a very good working relationship with educational institutions in the United States and obtaining a student visa had been easy. Then when she'd been accepted as an intern after a year of graduate school, she'd moved into H-1B status. Other than being a supreme hassle in terms of paperwork and documentation, her visa had never really been a problem.

"But if—" Emily swallowed. "Am I going to lose my job?"

"Not if I can help it," Henrietta said, a fierce light in her eyes. "The entire thing is ridiculous, and we're working on it, but I wanted you to know."

"Of course, yes." Emily's mind reeled. She couldn't lose this job—this was more than a job, it was her passion, her future, and if she had to return to Singapore...she couldn't. She'd never find the kind of job there she had here, and even if she could, she'd never earn the same. The cost of living was even worse than New York City, and with Pam's expenses...she'd never manage.

"I don't want you to worry." Henrietta laughed shortly, her voice catching as she coughed. She drank from a glass on her desk and grimaced impatiently. "I know that's a ridiculous thing to say, but we've worked our way through miles of red tape more than once.

Unfortunately, this time we have to deal with multiple agencies, federal at that, and it might take some time."

"I—" Emily cleared her throat. "I'll do anything necessary. I love this job, you know that."

Henrietta's expression softened. "Of course I do. You also happen to be very good at it. We've never really talked about it, but someday, I expect you'll have a much larger role in the company."

"I can't imagine being anywhere else, doing anything else."

"Well, I don't plan on retiring anytime soon," Henrietta said, "and there's time for us to talk about that when this visa business is straightened out. We need to get you that green card and be done with it."

Emily sighed. "Believe me, I know."

"Well, I've set up a meeting with our attorneys for the end of the week. We'll talk about all of it then."

"Thank you." Emily swallowed around the lump in her throat. She wouldn't panic. They had time to straighten it all out. She'd keep her job, she'd be able to take care of Pam. Her plans would all be fine.

"Emily," Henrietta said, rising from behind her desk and starting toward her. "You don't need to worry. I'm not going to let—" She stopped abruptly, one hand reaching for the side of her desk. Her expression registered surprise and then she gasped, "Oh."

"I'm sorry? What?" Emily said. "Henrietta? Henrietta!"

Emily jumped up as Henrietta Winfield slumped to the floor.

CHAPTER TWO

Derian tossed the keys to the Maserati to the uniformed attendant who raced from beneath the portico of the Hôtel de Paris to intercept her before she had even turned off the engine. With a wave of thanks she strode up the wide red-carpeted stairs and into the lobby of the grand hotel. Despite the enormity of the space with its polished marble floors, high decorative arched ceilings, plush carpets, and many seating areas carefully designed for privacy as well as comfort, the decibel level was higher than usual. Early crowds already filled the streets, cafés, and hotels for the upcoming race. She cut her way rapidly through the milling people to the single bank of elevators in the rear that led to the exclusive racecourse suites. She punched in the security code and within seconds was whisked to her level and the doors to the elevator slid silently open. The hallway was a stark contrast to the bustling lobby—quietly proclaiming confidentiality and discretion even though all of the suites along the wide hallway were undoubtedly in use. Grand Prix time was synonymous with party time in Monte Carlo, and the race was only three days away.

She inserted her entrance card at the Garnier suite and walked into a party well in progress. A wall of sound accosted her, dozens of voices laughing, calling to one another, conversing animatedly. The drapes had been pulled back from the floor-to-ceiling French doors opening onto one of the balconies overlooking Casino Square and the course, and the late-afternoon sun streamed into the room, bathing the faces of the partygoers in soft golden light. The beautiful people glowed with good health, good fortune, and bonhomie.

Derian wondered if their appearance of happiness was as false as what she sometimes felt, and just as quickly pushed the thought aside. Such slivers of dissatisfaction only plagued her when she was weary, and she'd had a long night at the gaming tables. She'd been winning, as she did more often than not, and the satisfaction of beating the odds had kept her mind and body energized. Now she would have been happy to take a long, hot shower and relax in the corner of the white leather sofa with a brandy and an audiobook, but the sun never set in Monte Carlo during Grand Prix season, the partying never stopped, and no one escaped. If she'd wanted to escape the never-ending bacchanal, she wouldn't be here to begin with.

Shedding her black blazer, she tossed it over a hanger in the closet next to the door, rolled up the sleeves of her white silk shirt, and made her way around behind the wet bar set up at one end of a living room that was as large as some hotel lobbies. She sorted through the array of high-end liquors, two-hundred-dollar bottles of champagne, and vintage wines until she found the single malt. After pouring an inch of scotch into a short crystal glass, no ice, she sipped the smoky liquid and let the burn spread through her and blunt the edges of her simmering discontent. She wasn't in the mood to look too closely at why she'd had an itch between her shoulder blades for weeks now, reminding her at the most inopportune times that she was bored or restless or simply tired of racing across the Continent following the circuit and chasing a high that never quite satisfied. Whatever it was would pass, and she could go back to living on the thrill of the next race, the next encounter, the next woman.

Speaking of women, she watched with appreciation as a buxom redhead in a very revealing form-hugging emerald green shirt, skintight black silk pants, and needle-thin heels stalked toward the bar. She didn't know her, and she would've remembered a face like that—wide luscious mouth, high cheekbones accentuated with artful makeup, and a curly, flowing mane of hair glinting with gold and flaming reds that gave her a sultry, leonine appearance. She stopped opposite Derian on the other side of the wet bar and slowly appraised her.

"My, my," the redhead said in a low voice that vibrated with a hint of French and teasing promise, "Michigan certainly is hiring attractive bartenders these days."

"What would you like," Derian said, not bothering to correct her. "To drink? Or…"

"Or?" Derian smiled. Everything in life was a game, and none she liked better than the first few moments of establishing the playing field with a new woman. "Is there something else I might be able to do for you?"

The redhead chuckled and wet her lips with the tip of a pink tongue. "Darling, there are so many things you could do for me. What time do you finish here tonight?"

Instead of answering, Derian poured a glass of cabernet from a bottle of PlumpJack reserve someone had opened and left standing on the bar. Shame to waste a great wine on philistines, but she hadn't invited most of the people crowding her rooms. The guest list had been Michigan Tire's call. She handed the glass to the redhead. "You look like red wine—full flavored and unforgettable. This one is savory and mysterious, it lingers on your tongue as only the finest tastes can do. I think you'll like it."

Color flared in the redhead's throat and she kept her eyes locked to Derian's as she closed her fingers around the stem of the glass. Brushing her thumb across Derian's knuckles, she lifted the wine slowly to her mouth. Her lips parted, caressed the rim of the glass, and she tilted the liquid into her mouth. She ever so slowly swallowed and made a low purring sound in her throat. "Very nice indeed."

"I'm delighted you like it."

The redhead cocked an eyebrow. "You're not the bartender, are you?"

"I can be, if you'd enjoy that."

"I already am. Who are you?"

"Derian Winfield."

"Ah," the redhead said, not missing a beat. "Then I have you to thank for this wonderful soirée."

"Me and Michigan Tire," Derian said.

"Yes, you're one of the sponsors of their team, aren't you?"

Derian found her scotch, took another sip. "That's right."

"I'm surprised you're not driving one of the cars."

Derian grinned wryly. "I thought I would, once upon a time. But it's very hard work and I have an aversion to that."

Laughing, the redhead held out her hand. "I'm Françoise Delacorte. Delighted to meet you—Derian."

Derian lifted her hand, kissed her fingers. "Françoise. My pleasure."

"So is it *Dare* as in daring?" Françoise held on to Derian's hand, her lips pursing as her gaze slid down Derian's body. "It suits you very much."

"No." Derian extracted her fingers gently. "It's pronounced the same, but it's *D-e-r-e*."

"Are you then, just the same? Daring?"

"Some people think so."

"Do you only gamble on cars and cards?"

Derian glanced out over the room at the sea of faces, some of whom she recognized, most she didn't. She always sponsored a big party for donors, sponsors, and VIP friends of the team at each stop on the circuit. MT handled the invites, and she paid. She didn't see anyone she wanted to talk to. The malaise settled in her chest again, the weariness of repetition growing harder to ignore. She set down her glass. "I like a challenge—at the tables, on the course…in the bedroom."

"Mmm. So do I." Françoise took another swallow of wine and set the glass aside. "We are well-matched, you and I."

"I think you're right," Derian said, sliding around the bar, "and I'd very much like showing you."

"I think that's a wonderful idea."

"Will you be missed for a time?"

"Not right away."

"Good." Derian took Françoise's elbow. "This way."

She guided Françoise to the far side of the room and unlocked the door to her private rooms. The bedroom occupied a corner of the suite with the king-sized bed positioned to give its occupants a view into the square. When she closed the door, the sounds of the revelry faded. Turning Françoise to face her, she kissed her, sliding one arm around her waist, and took her time exploring the soft surface of her moist lips, tasting the earthy aftermath of the wine on her tongue. Françoise was an experienced kisser, and she melted into Derian's body, one hand stroking up the back of Derian's neck and into her hair. What Derian liked best about kissing a woman, about taking her to bed, was the way her mind shut off and her body took control. When she was focused on giving pleasure, she no longer recognized the distant pall of emptiness that lingered on the edges of her consciousness.

Françoise was a beautiful and seductive woman, but Derian was having a hard time losing herself in the taste of her mouth and the press of her breasts against her chest. She could see herself as if she stood a few paces away, watching the familiar scene play out, the familiar ending unreel. The challenge, the victory, the cries of passion, and, inevitably, the parting played through her mind as predictably as the endless cycle of parties, races, and risk that defined her life. The long, empty hours until the scene played out again stared back her, as accusing as her own eyes in the mirror. What was she doing, where was she going, and when would she stop running?

Questions she did not want to ask, or answer.

Derian kissed her way down Françoise's throat, slowly cupping her breast and squeezing gently. Françoise arched against her, a small sob escaping as her fingers tightened in Derian's hair.

"Yes," Françoise murmured. "So very good."

"Come, let me show you how much better," Derian said, taking her hand and tugging her toward the bed. Once beside it, she unbuttoned Françoise's shirt and slipped her hand inside to rub her thumb over the peak of the nipple pressing upward through the thin silk of Françoise's bra.

"Your hands are wonderful." Françoise tilted her head back, eyes closed, lips parted on a long shuddering sigh. Her fingers raked through Derian's hair and tightened on her neck. "Please, I want them everywhere."

Obediently, Derian opened the remaining buttons and gentled the silk off Françoise's shoulders, pushed the sleeves down her arms, and let it fall away. This was a dance she knew, choreographed for pleasure and predictably assured. At last the heat of Françoise's skin, the smooth satiny sensation of flesh yielding to her touch, consumed her. Immersed in the command of Françoise's quivering body, still fully clothed, Derian eased Françoise down onto the creamy sheets, opened her silk pants, and bent over her to kiss the center of her abdomen. When she rubbed her cheek against the downy skin and licked lightly at the juncture of Françoise's thighs, Francoise cried out and arched upward, presenting herself to be taken.

"Soon," Derian whispered.

"I cannot wait." Françoise's voice broke on a husky sigh. "I am too ready."

"You are too beautiful to hurry." Derian kissed once between her thighs and Françoise sobbed. "And I want to savor you."

Derian undressed her completely and, when she was naked, straddled her with her legs framing Françoise's hips. She braced her body on an arm and stroked Françoise's throat, trailing her fingers down to her breast. "Look at me."

Françoise's eyes were hazy with need, her breath short, body vibrating. "Yes, please. I want to watch you take me over."

Derian took her time, relaxed and certain of her skill, her caresses practiced, her kisses perfected. She knew how to please a woman, enjoyed it immensely, almost as much as she enjoyed the respite from thought. When she stroked between Françoise's thighs, when she played her fingers gently over the delicate valley, when she slid inside, every movement was timed, intentional, designed for the pinnacle of pleasure. When Françoise's gaze clouded over and her lips parted on a silent scream, Derian registered a sense of satisfaction and success.

When Françoise's choked sobs trailed off and her body slumped, Derian stretched out beside her, head propped on her hand. She traced Françoise's nipple with a fingertip, fascinated as it pebbled in response. She didn't expect Françoise to reciprocate, didn't need her to. Her goal had been to pleasure Françoise, and she was confident she had been more than successful.

"You are a marvelous lover." Françoise caressed Derian's face, her voice husky and her eyes hazy with satisfaction.

"Thank you," Derian said, meaning it. Françoise's openness, her vulnerability, her trust were a precious gift.

"If you have a need—" Françoise began.

"I am more than satisfied," Derian murmured, giving Françoise a slow, lingering kiss. She didn't lie. She didn't want anything else. "You are what I wanted. All I wanted."

"Then I should go," Françoise said with a sigh. She gave Derian a final caress and sat up. "My escort will be looking for me."

"Of course." Derian rolled over and leaned back against the pillows, watching Françoise dress, enjoying the way her body disappeared with each article she donned as much as she had enjoyed disrobing her. She knew the planes and contours of her flesh now. She was like a beautiful landscape Derian had touched, claimed, and would forever own in some small way. Aimlessly, she stroked her stomach through her silk shirt, felt the stirring between her thighs, anticipated satisfying it later. Her cell phone rang and she pulled it from her pants pocket. She checked the number and set the phone on the bedside table.

Françoise regarded her with a raised eyebrow. "No one important?"

"No. Not in the least." She had no intention of taking a call from the family attorney. As much as she liked her childhood friend, Audrey Ames had taken sides when she'd gone into the Ames family business of representing Winfield Enterprises. And that side was not Derian's.

Françoise sashayed closer, leaned down to give Derian a very impressive view down her shirt, and kissed her, her tongue dancing over Derian's for an instant. "I hope I will see you again before the race moves on."

"Yes," Derian said, committing to nothing. Once was usually all she wanted with a woman. So much safer that way. Her cell rang again and she sighed. Audrey wasn't usually so insistent and just left a message. "I'm sorry, I should take this."

Françoise tapped her index finger against Derian's mouth. "And I should go. Thank you again, Derian, my darling."

Derian took the call, watching Françoise disappear. "Bad timing as usual, Aud."

"Dere, you need to come home."

"It's three days before the race." Derian sat on the side of the bed and slipped into her shoes. "You've already got my proxy vote, just send it in as usual—"

"Derian, it's Henrietta."

A fist slammed into Derian's midsection and the room wavered before her eyes. "I'll be on the next plane."

CHAPTER THREE

Emily jerked awake to the swooshing sound of the ICU doors opening. She blinked the mist of sleep from her eyes and jumped to her feet. Her vision swam. She'd lost track of how long she'd been sitting in the too-bright alcove just up the hall from the intensive care unit, waiting for word of Henrietta's condition. Too many cups of coffee, too many packets of crackers from the vending machine. Her stomach roiled, her throat ached from the tears she'd swallowed back, and her head pounded. Vonnie had kept vigil with her the first few frantic hours, sharing the burden of leaving discreet notifications regarding Henrietta's sudden illness and organizing the staff who'd been left in the lurch when the EMTs had stormed in, rapidly assessed Henrietta's terrifyingly motionless form, and bundled her up and out of the building in what felt like seconds. Odd, now that Emily thought back to those first hours, that Vonnie had no phone number for Henrietta's family. Emily had only spoken to the Winfield attorney when she'd called the emergency contact number listed among the agency's files. And then no one else had reached out to her for information, or even to Vonnie, Henrietta's personal secretary. Perhaps the close family were out of town and had called the ICU directly to speak with Henrietta's caregivers. Of course, that must be it.

Vonnie had finally gone home hours before to take care of her family. For a time, Emily had shared the stark waiting area, made no more welcoming by the presence of a coffeemaker in one corner and a television on the wall, with an elderly man whose dazed expression tore at her heart and a weeping husband and wife who had stumbled out into the hallway to talk to an exhausted-looking resident in wrinkled green scrubs before disappearing. Then she'd been alone, waiting for she knew not what because she could not bear to leave, clinging to the hope that soon someone would come who could tell her of Henrietta's fate.

Now a handsome middle-aged, black-haired man with a commanding air strode brusquely past her little warren. His double-breasted charcoal suit was impeccably tailored, his black oxfords shined to a high gloss. A large gold watch glinted on his left wrist. Even if Emily hadn't recognized him, she would have known him. Taller than Henrietta, his jaw heavier, his eyes far harder than Henrietta's, he still bore an unmistakable resemblance to her.

Emily jumped up. "Excuse me." When he didn't respond, she rushed into the hall after him. "Excuse me! Mr. Winfield?"

The man halted, spun around, and glanced at her without the slightest expression in his icy blue eyes. "Yes?"

Throat dry, she stepped forward and held out her hand. "I'm sure you don't remember me, I'm—"

"I'm sorry. I have nothing to say at this time—"

"I work for Henrietta," Emily hurried on, wondering who he thought she might be. "I'm a senior agent at the agency. I was with her when—"

"I'm afraid my sister's condition is private. I'm sure whatever needs to be done at the...business...can wait."

With that, he spun around and left her standing in the middle of the hallway with her hand outstretched. In another few seconds he'd rounded the corner and she heard the ding of an elevator. What a cold, unfeeling man. How could he be Henrietta's brother? As soon as she thought it, she reminded herself he was probably just stressed and preoccupied.

She knew all too well hospitals were horrible places. Impersonal, usually ugly, and filled with too many people who were too busy to stop and recognize the despair and anguish in the faces of so many. Lonely places where those left behind drowned in sorrow while others looked away. She shuddered and returned to the waiting area. She'd had years of practice waiting in places like this—waiting for word of her parents, waiting to hear from Pam's doctors. Martin Winfield, she knew his name as she'd been introduced to him on several occasions when she'd accompanied Henrietta to the corporate board meetings, reminded her of some of those bureaucrats who ran the very places where empathy and support should come first, but had been forgotten in the race to survive in an ever more competitive world. Even some of the health-care staff had forgotten their mission—to heal and comfort. Henrietta's brother reminded her of why it was so important that she keep Pam where she was now, in a warm, personal environment where she felt safe and everyone knew her name.

Emily sighed. She was tired and being unfair—she didn't know Martin Winfield, and he had no reason to acknowledge her. How could he remember her as he'd barely glanced in her direction the few times they'd been in the same space. She certainly wasn't being fair to the many dedicated doctors and nurses and other caring professionals who worked so hard to help.

Sitting out here for hours made her think too much of Pam, and she couldn't think about her right now. She couldn't think about her uncertain visa status or what might happen to her job if, heaven forbid, something serious kept Henrietta from returning to work. All she could do was send all her energy and thoughts to Henrietta and believe she would be fine. She leaned back and closed her eyes, willing the panic to recede. The nightmare gripped her, refusing to let her breathe. She couldn't imagine a day without Henrietta, whose strength was the guiding force at the agency and whose friendship the foundation on which Emily had built her future. She'd lost so much already—she couldn't bear to endure more.

"Here, take this," a deep voice said, and Emily's eyes snapped open.

A brunette about her age, her pale stark features undoubtedly beautiful when not smudged with fatigue, stood in front of her holding out a snowy white handkerchief. Startled, Emily jerked upright and only then recognized the tears wetting her face. Heat flooded her cheeks and she hastily brushed at the moisture on her skin. "Oh. I'm sorry."

"Why?" The woman took her hand and gently folded the soft linen into it. "Here. Go ahead. Use this."

Emily wiped her face, almost embarrassed to soil the pristine square. When her vision cleared, she focused on the stranger. Her breath caught. "Oh. It's you."

"We've met, haven't we. *I'm* the one who's sorry." She squeezed the bridge of her nose for an instant. Shadows pocketed her midnight blue eyes. Her coal-black hair, the same color as Henrietta's, was disheveled, her white shirt and dark suit hopelessly wrinkled. The topcoat she carried over one arm looked as sleek and soft as cashmere, which it probably was. "I'm Derian Winfield."

"Yes, of course." Emily stood up and swayed, tiny sparks of light dancing in the dark clouds dimming her vision.

Derian grasped her elbow. "Hey. Take it easy. Here."

"I'm sorry," Emily said again, weakly echoing herself and hating the way her voice quivered. Why wouldn't her head stop spinning? She never fainted, never. She couldn't now, not in front of her. "I'm sorr—"

"Stop saying that," Derian murmured in an oddly tender tone and drew her down onto one of the molded plastic chairs. Derian slid an arm around her shoulders. "Lean against me for a second until you catch your breath."

Emily had no intention of leaning against anyone, especially not Derian Winfield, Henrietta's niece. With effort, she stiffened her spine and forced her head to clear. She turned sideways so Derian's arm no longer encircled her. "I am so sorry, Ms. Winfield. I hope—"

Derian laughed, a deep full sound so rich Emily could almost taste the timbre. "Please. Anything but that. I'm Derian, or Dere, if you like."

"I—I'm Emily May. I work for Henrietta—Ms. Winfield."

"Of course. I remember now." Derian shook her head. How could she have not noticed this woman...*more* was the only word she could come up with, the first time they'd met? If she were introduced to her now, she'd certainly not forget. Emily was stunning, the kind of pure unadorned beauty the masters tried to capture on canvas and only managed to hint at: perfectly proportioned features, delicate but sure, green eyes the color of the sea kissing the white sands of some Mediterranean shore, glossy chestnut hair threaded with gleaming copper strands. Oh yes, Derian remembered meeting her now, and how little she'd noticed, too absorbed in her own anger. She'd been introduced to Henrietta's intern after an annual WE board meeting— the major one when all the Winfield Enterprise divisions came together to report. She'd probably only been thinking of how she could escape the formal after-affair she'd been roped into, and in her defense, Emily May had changed. Her heart-shaped face had lost some of the youthful softness but had gained the elegant contours of a woman, and she was all the more striking for the subtle maturity. She might have passed her over before, thinking her just a starry-eyed girl, but she wouldn't make that mistake again. "It's been a few years since we've met, but I have no excuse. Forgive my rudeness."

Emily stared. "Ms. Win—Derian, please. You have nothing to apologize for, under any circumstances, and certainly not these."

"I don't agree, but I won't argue with your absolution." Derian sighed. "I just tried to see my aunt and the attendants tell me I have to wait half an hour until she can have more visitors. Apparently my father just left."

"Yes. You must have missed him by only a minute or two."

"Believe me, that's not a hardship." Emily looked shocked but Derian didn't bother to explain the last person she wanted to see was Martin, and he probably reciprocated. She hadn't told anyone she was coming other than Aud, who wouldn't bring it up with Martin or his family unless she had to. "Do you have any word on Henrietta? How is she?"

Heat flared in Emily's eyes and was quickly extinguished. "No, I asked your father, but…"

Derian clenched her jaw. "I don't suppose he was very forthcoming."

Emily managed to look sympathetic. "No, but I'm sure he is very worried and has a lot on his mind."

"And you're very kind and diplomatic."

"I wish I knew more." Emily glanced down the hall toward the ICU. "I've been trying to get word, but I'm not family and this is the first time I've seen your father. Or…anyone."

"She's been in here for ten hours and he hasn't been by?" Fighting off a wave of fury, Derian closed her fist until her nails bit into her palm and washed away the red haze clouding her thoughts. "Still the same old bastard, I see."

"Oh, I didn't mean to imply—"

"Don't worry. I know how things work. I got here soon as I could." Derian rubbed the back of her neck and sighed. "I didn't know she was sick. We haven't talked in a while."

"I'm not sure she was aware either. I think she might have told me, had she known."

"You're close, then—I mean, friends?" Derian tried to pinpoint the last time she and Henrietta had done more than exchange a quick email. Last year before the race in Sochi? Time blurred, a repetitive loop of hotels, soirées, and meaningless conversations. Henrietta was the only person she ever really opened up to, and she hadn't done that in a very long time. If she had, she'd have to put words to things she didn't want to own.

"I think we are," Emily said softly. "She means the world to me—of course, we're not fami—"

Derian scoffed. "Family is an overrated concept. I'm glad you were with her. And I'm glad she has you."

"You must've broken some kind of record getting here—weren't you somewhere in Europe?"

Emily gripped her forearm, an unexpectedly comforting sensation. Derian regarded her curiously. "How did you know?"

Emily wasn't about to confess that she often followed celebrity news, mostly for entertainment and relaxation to break the rigors of the concentrated work of screening manuscripts and studying production layouts. Whenever Derian Winfield was mentioned, usually accompanied by a photo of her with a race car or some glamorous woman, she took note. She'd always thought Henrietta's niece was attractive, but the glossy photos hadn't captured the shadows that swirled in the depths of her eyes or the sadness that undercut the sharp edges of her words. "Perhaps Henrietta mentioned it. Somewhere in Europe, wasn't it?"

"That's right. Fortunately, I had access to a plane." Derian winced and took stock of her appearance. "Although I look somewhat like a street person at the moment."

"No," Emily said with a faint laugh. "You most certainly do not. You do look tired, though."

Derian touched a finger beneath Emily's chin and tilted her head up. "And you look beyond tired. How long have you been here?"

Emily stilled, the unfamiliar touch of Derian's hand streaking through her with the oddest blaze of heat and light. She'd never realized tactile sensations could be in Technicolor. "I've been here since Henrietta arrived. I rode in the ambulance. The EMTs were kind enough to let me."

Derian frowned. Realizing after an instant she still cradled Emily's face, she brushed her thumb gently over the tip of her chin before drawing away. "Then I'm in your debt. As soon as I've seen her, I'm taking you to get something to eat."

"Oh, that's not necessary. I'm sure you'll want to get together with your family."

"No, that would be the last thing I want to do." Derian glanced toward the hall in the direction of the intensive care unit. "The only member of my family I care about is in there." She glanced back at Emily. "You and I share that, I think."

"Henrietta is easy to care about."

"You see, I told you, you were diplomatic." Derian smiled. "Henrietta is a hard-ass, but she knows people. And when she cares about you, she's always on your side. If you've survived this long with her, you're tougher than you look."

Emily ought to have been insulted, but she laughed. She didn't hear criticism in Derian's voice and imagined there might actually have been a hint of respect there. "I'll have you know, I'm plenty tough."

"Then you'll be tough enough to wait until I've seen her. Agreed?"

"Of course. I'm not going anywhere."

"I'm glad Henrietta has you. She deserves someone like you at her side."

Emily found the statement odd and Derian's voice surprisingly wistful. All she knew of Henrietta's niece was that she was often referred to with raised eyebrows among the agency's staff and had never taken any interest in the business. The press made her out to be something of a reckless, privileged playgirl. But whatever the rumors and innuendo regarding Derian Winfield might be, she had dropped whatever she'd been doing and flown halfway around the world to be by Henrietta's side. And for that, she'd earned Emily's respect. Her curious urge to know what had put such pain in Derian's faraway gaze and the unexpected heat Derian's touch ignited were something altogether different.

CHAPTER FOUR

A youngish-looking man with skin the color of cinnamon, a broad jaw lightly dusted with what looked like a day's worth of beard, and a stethoscope slung around his neck appeared in the hall. The laminated badge clipped to the pocket of his maroon scrubs had a big *MD* in one corner. He glanced down at a piece of paper in his hand. "Is there anyone here with Henrietta Winfield?"

Derian shot to her feet. "We are."

The doctor came forward and held out his hand. "I'm Jim Burns, one of the ICU residents."

"Derian Winfield, Henrietta's niece." Derian gestured to Emily. "This is my…sister, Emily."

Burns gave a perfunctory nod. "This is the first chance I've had to speak with anyone from the family. I apologize that you've been waiting so long."

"I understand," Derian said tightly. So Martin hadn't bothered to ask about Henrietta's condition. Probably hadn't even visited her. She wondered why he'd come at all, but then, he'd want to see for himself she was incapacitated so he could plan his next campaign to force Henrietta out of the business. Tamping down the familiar surge of rage whenever Martin came to mind, she concentrated on what really mattered. "Can you tell us how she's doing?"

"She's stable and intermittently awake," Burns said, "although heavily sedated at the moment. Her CPK and troponin"—he paused, catching himself—"sorry, her blood tests measuring cardiac injury are pretty conclusive. She had a substantial MI…heart attack…and the thallium scan, which is a test to show heart function, indicates a serious area of damage."

A cold hand squeezed around Derian's insides. "What does all that mean?"

"We've already started her on a fibrolytic agent—an intravenous drug to help break up the clots in her coronary arteries. The cardiologists will repeat her noninvasive cardiac tests, but there's a very good possibility she's going to need open-heart surgery within the next day or two to reverse the damage."

"And then?" Emily asked, her voice steady and calm. "What's the prognosis?"

Burns regarded her directly for the first time. "Very good, luckily. She got here fast, and we started treatment right away. With adequate reperfusion, the cardiac muscle will likely recover, and once the blood starts flowing again, the heart will return to a near-normal state."

Emily's shoulders relaxed. "So we can expect her to make a full recovery?"

"Barring complications, of course, and assuming she follows a reasonable cardiac care plan."

Derian laughed shortly. "If that includes no stress and a slower pace, that's not likely to happen."

"Not uncommon in these patients," Burns said, "and that's exactly why surgery is the best approach. If everything goes well, your aunt won't need to curtail her lifestyle." He held up a cautionary finger. "However, she's still going to need significant time to recover from the surgery, rehab, and work back into her full daily schedule. I take it she's pretty active."

Emily huffed. "A locomotive headed down a steep incline would be an apt comparison."

He nodded. "Not surprising."

"Can we see her?" Derian asked.

Burns glanced at his watch. "For a minute or two. The nurses will be busy getting vitals and labs in ten minutes, but…come with me."

When Derian moved to follow him, Emily hesitated. Derian glanced back and held out her hand. "Come on, sis."

Emily's lips pressed together, the dancing light in her eyes saying she was suppressing laughter. She took Derian's hand, hers smaller, soft and warm and firm. Without thinking, Derian threaded her fingers through Emily's. The fit was so natural, she was momentarily disoriented. She wasn't a hand-holder, but the flow of heat from Emily's touch steadied her. Filing that disconcerting thought away as an anomaly due to the circumstances, she followed the medical resident down the hall to where he slapped a big red button the size of a dinner plate on the wall. The foreboding double metal doors with the tiny windows that blocked all view of what went on inside swung open with a hiss. She almost expected a warning sign above it: *Abandon All Hope…*

Derian shuddered. She was more tired than she'd thought.

Emily's fingers tightened on hers. She was pale, and her eyes had widened, as if she too sensed the despair radiating from the sterile surroundings.

Her own discomfort fading in the face of Emily's, Derian leaned close, her mouth near Emily's ear. She caught the fragrance of coconut and vanilla. "Are you okay?"

"Yes," Emily said, her voice tight. "I'm fine. Just a bad memory. Don't worry."

Derian wasn't convinced. Emily looked shaken, and her distress tugged at Derian, awakening a fierce desire to ease Emily's unhappiness that felt so right she didn't bother to question it. "I'm right here."

Emily turned away from the too-bright lights and righted herself in Derian's intense, sympathetic gaze. Derian's deep, sure voice—her comforting words—shut out the hum of machines and jumble of sounds that struck her like a tidal wave, threatening to pull her under. She wasn't used to being championed or protected by anyone and, for a few seconds, she basked in the comfort of Derian's unexpected chivalry. Feeling stronger, and slightly embarrassed, she squeezed Derian's hand and reluctantly loosened her grip. "Thanks."

Derian smiled, some of her tension easing away. "No problem."

The ICU was a long narrow room with a wide central aisle. Beds occupied one wall, separated from one another by heavy white curtains. Opposite them, a bustling nurses' station with a high counter that held beeping monitors, stacks of charts, and racks of test tubes bearing blood samples was staffed by a handful of men and women. Emily averted her gaze. Cold sweat trickled down between her shoulder blades, but she was steady again. Over a decade since she'd been in a place like this, but the memories were as fresh as yesterday. Her father and Pam in adjacent beds. Her mother gone. She released Derian's hand completely, afraid she would transmit too much in that touch, afraid to lean too much on the strength Derian so casually offered.

Burns pulled back the curtain at the end of a hospital bed situated in the middle of the long line of beds. A tall, narrow table stood at the end of it covered with printouts and more tubes of blood. Henrietta lay beneath white sheets folded down to midchest, her exposed arms punctured at intervals with intravenous catheters. Red blood flowed out of the snaking tubes, tinted yellow fluids flowed in. Her eyes were closed, her breathing almost imperceptible beneath the covers, her body dwarfed by the IV stands and monitors bolted to the walls on either side of the bed. Tracings revealed the steady blips of the EKG, the smooth rhythmic peaks and valleys of blood pressure, the steady line of oxygen levels. All so familiar and so foreign at the same time.

Emily forced herself to take it all in. She owed it to Henrietta to lessen the horror by sharing it. After she focused and let herself see, she whispered, "She's breathing on her own."

"Yes. We took the breathing tube out a couple hours ago. She's too alert to tolerate it," Burns said softly.

"That's so encouraging." Emily glanced at Derian, whose dark gaze was fixed on Henrietta's face. Of course the racing enthusiast, world-traveling adventurer would not be afraid to face down death, if that was at hand.

Derian must have felt her staring and smiled at her. "She'd probably pull it out if they left it in."

"Go ahead," Burns said. "You can talk to her. She'll know you're here."

Emily hesitated while Derian slipped along the right side of the bed in the narrow space between the rails and the curtain, leaned over, and gripped Henrietta's fingers below the tape and catheters. Emily eased up opposite her and grasped the rail.

"Hey, HW," Derian murmured. "I'm here. The doctors said you're too tough to die, and I told them I already knew that."

Emily really wasn't surprised at the words, not when she recognized the love in Derian's tone. Derian's tenderness shouldn't have been unexpected, and she chided herself inwardly for listening to too much office gossip and believing what she read in the tabloids. A reminder that others were rarely as they appeared on the surface.

"So I'm missing the first leg of the race for nothing," Derian continued, her thumb brushing back and forth over Henrietta's hand. "And who knows what kind of other action is going on over there without me."

Emily watched the rhythmic sweep of Derian's thumb, remembering the way Derian had stroked her cheek. Emily could still feel it, a strong warm wave moving through her, a gentle, nearly possessive caress that shouldn't have had the impact it did. It wasn't as if she wasn't used to being touched. She wasn't exactly virginal. Not exactly. She just hadn't found physical intimacy so earthshaking that she was pressed to repeat it, not when she had so many other things to be concerned about. And caresses and other unimportant things were foolish thoughts to be thinking about right now. Somehow, Derian had stirred feelings she rarely paid any attention to.

Derian glanced across Henrietta's still form and met her eyes. "I've got Emily here with me. I snuck her in. I told them she was my sister." Derian laughed, her gaze still on Emily. "So not true."

Emily flushed at the languorous drop in Derian's voice. Why did everything Derian Winfield said sound as if she was being touched by the words? She glanced down at Henrietta and finally reached over to touch her arm beneath the edge of the white and blue striped gown. Relief flooded through her, rinsing the taste of fear from her mouth. Henrietta's skin was supple and warm, alive. "Hi, Henrietta. You're going to be all right—no exaggeration. The doctors are on top of everything. All you need to do is rest and…"

Henrietta's lids fluttered and Emily caught her breath. She glanced at Derian, who was staring at Henrietta with such intensity Emily almost believed Derian was willing Henrietta to wake up.

"Nothing wrong…with my brain," Henrietta whispered, lids fluttering open. Her pupils were pinpoint, her gaze unfocused. Furrows creased her brow. "Fuzzy."

"That's because they doped you up." Derian brushed a strand of loose hair away from Henrietta's eyes. Her fingers trembled. "They probably didn't want you bossing everyone around."

"Ha," Henrietta muttered feebly. "What…happened?"

"You had a bit of a spell," Derian said, "but it's all fixable. Nothing to worry about just now."

"Don't...snow me."

Derian grinned. "Heart. Not too bad, but you're gonna need some engine work."

Henrietta's lids fluttered close. "You...decide..."

"You got it."

Emily started. She hadn't thought about Henrietta's next of kin. She suddenly hoped with all her being that it wasn't Martin Winfield.

"All out," Henrietta said with surprising strength.

"No problem." Derian's voice was gentle but her expression was fierce. "I know all about mechanics. I'll make sure you've got another hundred thousand miles under the chassis."

Henrietta's mouth twitched into a smile. After a long moment, she whispered, "Take care of...the rest...two of you."

Derian's eyebrows rose, and she glanced at Emily. "Don't worry. We'll have it all covered."

Emily wasn't sure what Henrietta intended by that, but nothing mattered now except Henrietta getting well. She wasn't sure she could bear too many more days or nights in the hospital. She'd do anything for Henrietta, except stand vigil while she slipped away. She squeezed Henrietta's arm. "It's going to be all right. Derian will see to it. I love you." She backed up, avoiding Derian's gaze. "I'll...be outside."

Silently, Derian watched her go, wondering at what old wounds put such pain in her eyes.

Burns appeared at the end of the bed. "I have to chase you out now or the nurses will skin me."

"Okay." Derian leaned down and kissed Henrietta's cheek. "I'll be back soon. Don't worry. I've got this. I love you."

Henrietta didn't respond, and Derian forced herself to step away. Henrietta would be okay, she had to be. Derian said quietly to Burns, "What now?"

"I don't expect we'll know much more until the CT guys have had a chance to review all the tests. I'll call you, or whoever takes over from me will, when we have a plan."

"I'm her legal next of kin," Derian said. "I want to be sure I get the call."

"I don't actually know anything about that. That would be in her records."

Derian nodded. "Who should I check with?"

"The nurses at the desk can pull up her admission forms."

"Okay, thanks." Derian held out her hand. "For everything."

"She's doing fine," Burns said as he shook her hand. "Someone will call."

Derian waited at the counter until an older woman with curly gray hair, in a pink scrub suit covered by a smock that looked like the kind of apron Derian's grandmother used to wear, turned and noticed her. "Can I help you, honey?"

"I just wanted to check that you had my contact information, and to be sure you had me listed as next of kin for Henrietta Winfield."

The woman's brows drew down as she looked Derian over. "That's you, isn't it?"

"Sorry?"

"Derian Winfield. You race cars in Europe or something?"

"Ah, yeah, something like that. That's me."

"Huh. Imagine that."

Derian didn't bother to ask how she was recognized. She made it a point not to look at the celebrity rags that graced just about every newsstand in the world. There was nothing she could do about paparazzi. Money attracted them like chum on the ocean drew sharks. She'd learned to pretty much ignore what was written or said about her, since it was 99.9 percent fabricated to begin with. If she'd had as many women as the tabloids made it out she did, she'd never get any sleep. Every time she escorted anyone anywhere, the papers had them involved in some kind of hot and steamy romance. Sure, she slept with some of them. But definitely not all. But why bother to try to set the record straight. Who would care? And secretly, if it pissed off Martin, she didn't half mind.

"Henrietta is my aunt."

The woman, whose name tag said she was Penelope, tapped in some information on a tablet and scrolled with her finger. "Yup, right here. Next of kin, Derian Winfield. No contact number, though." She glanced up. "You want to give me one?"

Derian read off her phone number.

"We've also got a copy of her living will and medical directives."

Derian frowned. "You do?"

"Yes, it looks like someone was very thorough."

Emily. Had to be her. She struck Derian as the organized, detail-oriented type. Surely it wasn't Martin. Derian was definitely in her debt.

"Thanks," Derian said, suddenly, now that she knew Henrietta was stable and being cared for, very much wanting to find Emily before she had a chance to slip away.

CHAPTER FIVE

Emily thought about leaving. She'd been at the hospital for twelve hours, and she was bone weary. The waiting, the worrying, the remembering had taken her back, and the old sorrow had surged anew. At first glance, this bustling, careworn city hospital seemed crude and unpolished compared to the luxury and near-grand-hotel opulence of Mount Elizabeth's, but as she'd discovered after a few days' vigil, hospitals were all the same beneath the veneer of civility—impersonal, often cold places. And wasn't she just getting morose, when she'd long ago set that all aside. She gave herself a mental shake. She'd be fine after she slept. Maybe had a cup of tea and a package of those cookies she kept for emergencies.

The idea of curling up under a blanket on the sofa by the big front window of her third-floor apartment filled her with longing, but Derian had asked her to wait. Or at least, implied that she wanted her to. Really, would it be so rude to leave? Surely Derian Winfield was just being polite. And when had she started thinking of her as Derian, as if they were actually friends? How could they be anything but strangers— they'd met exactly once before. She remembered the moment quite clearly, when obviously Derian hadn't.

To be fair, she *had* been so much younger then, not just in years, but in so many other ways. A newly minted master's degree, the first few months on the job as a real employee, pulling down a paycheck, and not just an intern on temporary assignment—she'd made it, realized the dream that had seemed so far away only a few years before. Here she was, in the land of opportunity where she actually had carved out the life she wanted for herself—researching, studying, making contacts, pushing to be noticed.

Emily smiled, remembering the first emails she'd sent to Henrietta Winfield, someone who had no idea who she was and probably wouldn't even be bothered to read the message. But Henrietta had read it, and had even emailed her back. Emily had been a college student then, an undergraduate at Harvard, double-majoring in English and creative writing, filling her résumé with everything she could think of that might make her more marketable in a world that could be viciously competitive behind the sedate and cultured façade. Positions in literary agencies were few and coveted, often passed along to those who had some kind of in—a friend or relation who knew someone who was part of the age-old world of New York publishing. She'd taken a chance and decided the only way to make an impression on someone who undoubtedly received hundreds of hopeful applications and queries every year was to demonstrate she understood what truly mattered. She hadn't written to Henrietta about her qualifications or her potential value as an employee or even her desires and aspirations. She'd written instead about one of her favorite books from an author Henrietta had shepherded from obscurity to *NY Times* best-seller status, and what the book had meant to her and why. How better to make a connection than to share the same passion?

She hadn't really expected a reply, but then it had come. Henrietta Winfield had actually emailed her. With the door open a tiny crack, she'd subtly, or so she'd thought, slipped her foot into it, and volunteered to do anything that would keep her in Henrietta's sight. And so it had begun, a relationship that eventually flowered into a job and most surprisingly, wonderfully of all, into friendship.

When she'd gone to work for Henrietta, she'd quickly become immersed in the other side of the literary agency, the politics of acquisition and promotion and selling. She'd been trained to recognize good writing, poignant themes, popular tropes, but she hadn't any experience negotiating the volatile waters of selling the manuscript to a publisher. Where were the best places to position a contemporary romance, a time-travel paranormal, a family saga? What was hot, and even more importantly, what would be hot next year? What were reasonable contract terms to expect for a first-time author, and what were the key items to be hammered out to the best advantage for her author clients? Those first few months she'd worked side by side with Henrietta and Ron, who'd been senior to her then and had graciously tutored her.

Part of her rapid-fire indoctrination had been in the art of networking, one of the things she'd liked the least at first. She preferred the quiet of her office and the solitude of her desk, immersed in manuscripts or making phone calls to authors—even contract review was better than face-to-face schmoozing with strangers. But she'd gone to the meetings and receptions, because Henrietta insisted she needed to. And there, at one of those very first too noisy, too crowded, and too false-friendly congregations, she'd first met Derian Winfield.

Even with dozens of people between them, Emily had recognized her right away. Derian was hard not to recognize. A few inches taller than most of the women, she'd stood out from the crowd precisely because she stood apart. She'd worn a suit, the dark jacket and pants well cut, not flashy, but superbly fit to her lanky form. Her hair had been fashionably layered to collar length, expertly setting off her chiseled features and accentuating the clean, crisp lines of her neck and shoulders. But it'd been her expression that had really defined her separateness. Unlike everyone else, she wasn't smiling, she didn't appear to be drinking the amber liquid in the short glass she held in her left hand, and she wasn't talking to anyone.

"Come," Henrietta had said, taking Emily's elbow. "I'd like you to meet my niece."

Henrietta had pulled her through the crowd, kissed Derian's cheek, and introduced them. Derian's expression had softened when she'd seen Henrietta coming, and after a few murmured words Emily couldn't hear, she'd glanced briefly in Emily's direction, nodded to her, and said something polite and totally impersonal.

After downing the rest of her drink with one swift tilt of her wrist, Derian had growled, "I think I've done my duty here tonight." She'd kissed Henrietta once again and disappeared into the crowd. Henrietta had looked after her with a faint smile and shake of her head before firmly pulling Emily off to the next group of people she wanted her to meet.

How young she'd been then, and how fiercely Henrietta had championed her. Emily struggled with the sadness welling inside. The doctors had said Henrietta would be well again, and that was what she must cling to. Despite everything, she hadn't given up on hope.

"I thought you might have left," Derian said from the doorway.

Emily started, feeling heat rise to her face. How did Derian sense so much, when others thought they knew her but rarely did? "Oh. How is she?"

"Sleeping. Probably conserving her strength to start ordering everyone around the next time she wakes up."

"I would never say I agree with you, but…" Emily laughed. "I thought about leaving, only I might be too tired to move."

Derian wanted to ask her what she'd been thinking about a moment before. She'd had the strangest expression on her face, half dreamlike, with a little smile that was sad in a way. But she didn't know Emily well enough to ask something quite that personal, and that constraint irritated her. She must be tired too. She'd never once in her life asked a woman what she'd been thinking. Had she never really cared enough to know? Aud had been the only one she'd cared about, and they'd always talked so much she'd never had to ask. The pain of their separation hit her out of nowhere, and she shrugged off the past. The past was history, the future merely chance. All that mattered was now, and she'd been determined to live it to the max since she'd walked out on what was left of her family. "Well, I'm sorry you're exhausted, but very glad you're still here. I owe you dinner, remember?"

Emily shook her head. "You definitely do not. And *you've* got to be even more exhausted than me. I've only been sitting here all day."

"Right. Sitting vigil when no one else did." Derian held out a hand. "I owe you for that. I owe you for more than that too. You took care of all the paperwork, didn't you?"

Emily stood, avoiding Derian's hand. She couldn't keep touching her. It wasn't appropriate, and besides that, it was upsetting. She wasn't used to all the feelings Derian kindled without the least bit of effort and, undoubtedly, unintentionally. "No, Vonnie helped. I don't deserve all the credit."

Derian nodded. "I'll call her and thank her too. But first, food."

"You're very stubborn, aren't you?" The words were out before she could pull them back. She was usually so much more cautious when she first met someone, and here she was saying everything that came into her head. "I didn't mean—"

Derian laughed. "That's a mild way of putting it. Most people might phrase it differently. But yes, once I set my mind on something, I'm kind of hard to dissuade. What's your favorite food?"

"Cookies," Emily said instantly.

Derian laughed again, a deep sound that rumbled in her chest and seemed to enclose Emily like a warm cloak wrapped around her shoulders. The image struck her as belonging to someone else. When had she ever been so frivolous? All the same, she couldn't help but smile.

"*Besides* dessert," Derian said.

"Who said it was dessert?" Emily said.

"All right, I'll admit to an occasional meal of ice cream myself, but not tonight. What would you like?"

"Almost anything—you choose."

Derian looked down at herself. "I could use a shower and a change of clothes. Would it be asking too much for you to stop by my apartment with me for a quick pit stop? I promise, it won't be more than fifteen minutes, and that will give me a chance to call and get reservations. I'll have you seated at a table in less than forty-five minutes."

"You can do that in New York City?"

"Trust me." Derian grinned and Emily suspected that grin took her a long way in the world—part charm, part devil, part sex.

And now she had the perfect opportunity to beg off dinner. She could simply say she was too tired to wait, and too disheveled herself. But she wasn't, really. She'd often gone all day at work and then out to an event in the same clothes, and she really had only been sitting most of the day. Derian wouldn't know that, though. Faced with the perfect opportunity to escape, she had to admit she didn't want to. She wanted to go to dinner with Derian Winfield. She wanted to hear her laugh again. She wanted to do something different, something out of her ordinary routine, and wasn't that odd. She could think about all of that later. "I don't mind a little wait at all. And you don't have to rush."

"I won't be rushing. I'm used to quick changes." Derian picked up Emily's coat from where she had laid it on the chair beside her and held it out for her. "Anyone you need to call? Change plans or anything?"

"No," Emily said casually as she let Derian help her on with her coat, something she couldn't ever remember anyone doing before. The gesture was unexpected and unexpectedly delightful. "They'll call us, right? If there's any…problem?"

Derian rested her hands for an instant on Emily's shoulders after the coat settled onto them. "They have my number. But it's going to be all right. It has to be, right?"

Emily leaned against her for the briefest of seconds. They shared the same affection for Henrietta, and Derian had to be even more worried. "Of course. Henrietta is probably even more stubborn than you."

"You're absolutely right." Derian slipped her hand down to Emily's elbow, leading her out into the hall. She liked the contact, the intimacy of that passing touch. "I'm sure I inherited all my bad traits from her."

"I actually think it might be catching—the stubbornness, at least. I've gotten a lot more persistent myself, since coming to work with her."

Derian reached out to press the button to the elevator, but the doors opened and she halted abruptly. "Aud!"

A willowy blonde with a stylish Tumi bag slung over one shoulder launched herself into Derian's arms. "Dere. I can't believe you got here first."

Emily hastily stepped back, but not before she registered the unbridled excitement in the blonde's eyes as she kissed Derian soundly on the lips.

"Why didn't you call me when you got in!" Aud scolded, one precisely etched brow arched in exasperation.

Derian slid an arm around the blonde's waist, her expression lighter than Emily had seen since she'd arrived at the hospital. "I tried. Did you check your voice mail?"

"Actually, no. I just got off a plane an hour ago and headed straight over here. I wasn't in the mood for business messages. Sorry."

"You never were very good at that anyhow. For a lawyer, you're really hard to get a hold of."

"Self-protection." The blonde glanced at Emily and held out her hand. "Sorry for being so rude. I'm Audrey Ames."

"Emily May, one of Henrietta's agents." She drew back farther. "I should probably go—"

"Aud, Emily is a friend," Derian said, tightening her grip on Emily's elbow so she didn't bolt the next time the elevator opened. "Henrietta is stable, and we were about to sneak out for some dinner."

"That's great news," Aud said. "Do they know what happened?"

"Looks like her heart. She might need surgery, but the verdict is open there," Derian said.

"Oh. I tried to reach your father, but he wasn't returning my calls."

"Not surprising. He's been here, but I think he just came by for a sit rep." Derian's expression darkened. "You know how that is."

Audrey sighed, her expression sympathetic. "Derian, you're going to have to make peace someday."

"I don't know why," Derian said lightly, although her tone held no humor.

"Your head's as hard as ever, I see." Audrey sighed. "I'm going to peek in on HW before I touch base with the family."

"Right. Have at it. We'll catch up tomorrow?"

Audrey leaned close and kissed Derian's cheek. "Absolutely. You'll be at the apartment?"

Derian nodded.

Aud sketched a wave and strode away.

"If you'd rather wait for her," Emily said, "I completely understand."

Derian regarded her quizzically. "You seem to think I'm going to let you break this date with me, but it's not going to happen. We're going to dinner."

Emily's lips parted. "I don't believe we mentioned anything about a date."

"All right, I stand corrected." Derian grinned. "But we're still having dinner."

"As long as we understand each other."

"For the moment, we're in agreement." Derian held the elevator door open for her. "Dinner. No date."

CHAPTER SIX

The dark sky surprised Emily when they stepped outside the front entrance of the hospital. She'd known, rationally, she'd lost the day to anxiety and memories and, most recently, a curiosity she couldn't shake about the woman beside her, but the black, cloudless night was still unexpected. She glanced at her watch to orient herself—almost seven p.m.—and started toward the line of cabs by the corner. Derian caught her arm, and she slowed.

"Hold on." Derian glanced at her phone. "Our ride will be here in nineteen seconds."

Emily laughed. "Uber?"

Derian grinned. "I never like standing in the road waving my arm and hoping a cab will take pity on me."

"No, I can't see you wanting to wait on anyone's pleasure." Emily stumbled. And hadn't that come out in just the worst possible way? "And please disregard that comment right now."

"I will, since it's totally inaccurate." Laughing, Derian slid her hand under Emily's elbow as a black Town Car slid to the curb. "Here we go."

To cover her embarrassment, Emily forged ahead. She'd never had so much trouble making casual conversation in her life. She didn't do it often, but she'd never tripped over her own words the way she seemed to do with Derian.

"Watch your step," Derian said, her hand tightening on Emily's arm. "He managed to park in a puddle the size of the Mediterranean."

"Thanks." Emily avoided the small lake as a tendril of heat snaked down her arm. She still found Derian's casual physicality a surprise, and her own sliver of pleasure mysterious. She certainly didn't need assistance walking across the sidewalk, but she liked the way Derian's body pressed against hers as they moved. The connection was entirely in her mind, of course. Derian *did* live in Europe, and everyone there touched more, completely casually, and it didn't mean anything. At least, so she understood.

She'd just have to learn to ignore the enjoyable pulse of electricity that accompanied Derian's touch. And just to be safe, she slipped her arm free of Derian's grasp as she slid into the backseat. Derian followed, and the driver pulled away. The vehicle was comfortably warm, but despite her fatigue, Emily wasn't the least bit tired. An unfamiliar energy suffused her, a sensation she eventually recognized as anticipation. She was doing something out of the ordinary for her—going to dinner with a stranger—even if Derian seemed far from that after the last few hours they'd shared. Beside her, Derian sat relaxed, one arm spread out along the top of the seat, her hand nearly touching Emily's shoulder. There was still space between them, but the inexplicable sense of somehow being connected persisted.

And she was being frivolous. Frivolous, something she had never been in her entire life. Even when she was much, much younger and life was much, much simpler, she'd never been frivolous. Pam had been the adventurer, the athlete, the daredevil. She'd been logical, studious, goal-directed, private, and driven. She enjoyed things, many things—loved books, films, long walks on the beach—and had some close friends she could be silly with. But she also cherished her private time, her private thoughts, and her private plans for the future. She'd never craved excitement or adventure or the busy social schedule that her parents loved and she tried to avoid. And here she was now, having a very out-of-character adventure with a very attractive woman who interested her in ways no one ever had.

"Where were you?" Emily asked. "Yesterday?"

Derian turned on the seat, studied Emily. The question, a simple one, didn't seem simple at all when Emily asked it. Emily was completely different than the women she usually spent time with. She was every bit as beautiful, more even, because she didn't try to be and didn't seem to notice that she was. Her beauty wasn't a tool, or in some cases, a weapon. Her beauty was simply what beauty should be, a thing unto itself to be enjoyed.

"I'm sorry, was that too personal?"

"Sorry, no," Derian murmured. She resisted the impulse to move her hand another four inches and clasp a strand of the silky, gold-laced hair that rested on Emily's shoulders. She was used to touching women, and being touched by them, in all manner of ways—casually, seductively, in invitation or challenge. She tried never to touch a woman unthinkingly, considering even the most innocent contact an honor, but just the slightest of contact with Emily set her system on high alert. Emily stirred her, a sensation she'd long thought she'd become immune to where women were concerned. With most things, really. "I'm afraid I was distracted. I was just thinking you were very beautiful."

Emily gave a little start, and in the hazy glow of reflected lights from marquees and streetlights, surprise flashed across her face.

"I can't possibly be the first person who's told you that," Derian said.

"Ah...maybe," Emily said, her tone pensive and thoughtful. "I think definitely, at least completely out of the blue."

The image of some woman murmuring compliments to Emily in an intimate setting jumped into Derian's head, and she smothered an irrational surge of annoyance that came dangerously close to feeling like jealousy. She had neither the right nor the desire to claim anyone's full attention, especially not a woman like Emily—who clearly did not play games.

"Well, if you haven't heard it before, you should have." Derian watched Emily register the idea, catalog it, tuck it away. She saw the small smile of pleasure flicker for an instant, and satisfaction heated her belly. She liked making her smile. "Monte Carlo."

"Oh," Emily said, "that's right. I read an article—" She broke off, catching her lower lip between her teeth.

"Really? One of those, huh?" Derian laughed. Even in the shadowy light she could tell Emily was blushing. And when was the last time she'd seen that response in a woman? She couldn't resist the urge to tease her again just to see her tug at her lip, a very sexy little movement. "I can categorically state that ninety percent of whatever it said was not true."

Far from looking embarrassed again, Emily's brows rose. "Is that so? So I shouldn't believe you're an avid patron of the arts, a major donor to several humanitarian aid missions, and, according to the interviewer, a passionate supporter of international human rights organizations?"

Uncomfortable now herself, Derian tried to shrug off the subtle praise. "Oh, that article. More charitable than most. I think the reporter might have been trying to score points with the Foundation."

"Maybe, although I recall that article in the *World Week* also mentioned your devotion to the race car circuit, your uncanny skill at the casinos, and your…hmm, penchant for attracting the attention of starlets and celebrities."

"The first part was true, the rest perhaps exaggerated."

Emily grinned, pleased at having turned the tables on Derian for a change, teasing back and watching Derian struggle with the mild praise. Obviously Derian preferred to keep her generosity a secret. Emily understood the desire for privacy. "If that's what you want everyone to think, I won't give away your secrets."

"Thanks," Derian said with unusual seriousness.

The driver pulled to the curb in front of an ornate, spired building Emily recognized—the Dakota, onetime home to John Lennon, Lauren Bacall, Bono, and many current celebrities. She glanced at Derian. "You live here? I thought the waiting list was years long."

"My mother had an apartment here from before her marriage, and I've inherited it. I keep it for when I'm in the city."

Emily remembered reading that Derian's mother, an heiress to an automotive family fortune, had died when Derian was a child, and much of Derian's wealth had been inherited from her. "I'm sorry."

Derian opened the door and paused. "About?"

"Your mother."

"Thanks," Derian said softly, not thinking it odd that Emily would offer condolences after almost twenty years. The loss never grew any less. She stepped out and waited for Emily to join her before guiding her toward the massive arched entryway to the inner courtyard.

A liveried doorman straightened when he saw them coming. "Ms. Winfield. How good to see you again."

"Hi, Ralph. Made it through another winter, I see."

The middle-aged man's face crinkled in a wide smile. "Never missed a day. It was a cold one too."

She squeezed his arm. "I wouldn't know. I spent it in Greece."

"Always somewhere sunny for you." He chuckled and escorted

them across the brick courtyard to the east entrance. "Do you have bags?"

"I sent them on ahead from the airport."

"Peter will have gotten them up by now, then."

He held the door for them and Emily stepped into the wide foyer first. She'd often imagined what it would look like, but she hadn't really come close to envisioning the grandeur of the sweeping staircases, the gleaming brass fixtures, the stories-high ceiling and ornate, old-world elegance. Beyond the breathtaking beauty, the quiet struck her first. The atmosphere was as hushed as a cathedral. In a way, it was, being one of the most exclusive residences in all of New York City.

"Thanks, Ralph." When the doorman tipped a finger to his cap and faded back, Derian led the way toward a bank of elevators with scrolled brass doors and inserted a key. Once inside she pushed one of the top floor buttons and the ride up progressed swiftly. As the doors opened, Derian said, "I'm not sure if I've anything stocked in the way of refreshments. They weren't expecting me."

"How long has it been since you've been here?" Emily couldn't imagine having an apartment in this magnificent building and not actually living in it.

"Almost three years, I think," Derian said, her expression remote.

"And the rest of the time you travel?"

Derian fit a key into the lock of a paneled wooden door, with a heavy cast-iron number four on it, and pushed it wide. "It depends on the season and the Grand Prix schedule. Sometimes I'll stay in one place for a few months, but not usually here."

"I'm being nosy, aren't I. I apologize." Emily followed Derian inside and caught her breath. Archways connected the spacious main rooms, with the windows in the living area facing Central Park. Streetlights on the labyrinth of the roads cutting through the park glowed, replacing the stars that rarely shone above the city haze. Twin high-back sofas, their fabric surfaces subtly patterned, faced one another with a huge coffee table larger than her dining table between them. Tiffany lamps, plush Oriental carpets, high sideboards in gleaming woods. She wasn't sure what she had expected, but the richness, not in money, but in detail and workmanship, astounded her.

"Did you expect glass and steel?"

Emily laughed. "You're reading my mind again."

"Am I?" Derian asked softly. "I didn't realize I was."

Emily colored. "It seems you hear what I'm saying when I'm talking in my head."

"I apologize if I'm intruding, then."

"No," Emily said quickly. "You're not. I…it's just unanticipated, that's all. Probably my imagination."

"And tell me," Derian said, still standing beside her, her topcoat open, her sleek frame somehow eclipsing the surrounding opulence, "what did you expect?"

Suddenly very warm, Emily shrugged out of her coat and folded it over her arm.

"Forgive me, I'm being a poor host," Derian said into the silence, taking the coat from her and hanging it in a spacious closet next to the door. She shrugged out of her topcoat and stored it next to Emily's. Her blazer she tossed carelessly over the arm of the sofa as she glanced back at Emily. "Well? What did you imagine?"

"I suppose I did expect something very modern and…" Emily, usually so good with words, always finding just the right one to shade any meaning, searched for a phrase that didn't sound shallow or deprecating.

Derian laughed. "Glitzy? Over-the-top? Flamboyant?"

"No," Emily protested, laughing. "I'm trying to think of how one would describe a race car. I guess that's what I expected—efficient, beautiful in a high-tech kind of way, but not so…personal. So intimate."

"Intimate." Derian glanced around the room as if she'd never seem it before. "You're right, about the cars. I do think they're beautiful, a perfect blend of form and function. But I wouldn't want to surround myself with them." She gestured to the marble fireplace, the carved wainscoting, the complex ceiling moldings. "I think this is probably Henrietta's influence. I spent a lot of time with her when I was younger, and she instilled an appreciation in me for the beauty of craftsmanship, the care of creating something that will last."

"I know," Emily said softly. "That's how I feel about the books we represent at the agency."

"Even today? Hasn't the art of publishing given way to the allure of big business? Haven't you all gone to a best-seller model? Here today, gone tomorrow?"

"You're not entirely wrong," Emily said, impressed that Derian even thought about what the world of publishing was like. She never appeared at the agency, never attended any of the business meetings, but she clearly knew the direction of change in recent years. "That's what I love about our agency. We don't just look for the kinds of works that will sell the most. We look for the kinds of works that will live on, that will add something to the understanding of our times or provoke thought, or simply be a beautiful example of the art."

Derian smiled. "I can see that Henrietta has had an influence on you too, or perhaps it's the other way around. Perhaps she chose you because you're a kindred soul."

"If that were true, I would be incredibly honored."

Derian walked to the far end of the big room, skirted behind a waist-high bar, and opened a tall mahogany cabinet to reveal a hidden refrigerator. She chuckled. "When I sent my luggage ahead, someone decided to stock in some supplies." She took out a platter of cheese and other appetizers and set a bottle of champagne next to it. "Help yourself while I shower. I did promise you dinner and no more than a fifteen-minute wait."

As she spoke, Derian opened the bottle of champagne, pulled two fluted glasses from a glass-fronted cabinet over the counter, and poured the frothing wine. She picked up hers and held the other out to Emily. "Do you drink?"

"On occasion." *And never anything with a label like that.* Emily took the glass and sipped. The bubbles played across her tongue like sunshine. "Oh. That's...nice."

Derian grinned. "I'll be right back."

"Take your time," Emily said, watching Derian move with smooth grace toward the hall. "I don't have anywhere to be tonight."

Derian glanced back over her shoulder, a dark glint in her eyes. "Good. Neither do I, and I'm enjoying the company."

CHAPTER SEVEN

Derian leaned on her outstretched arms, palms to the smooth tile wall, dropped her head, and closed her eyes as warm water sluiced over her shoulders and back. The long hours of the endless day and previous sleepless night settled into her bones with a soul-sapping weariness. Nothing new, really. Just another stopover on the merry-go-round of her life, aimlessly moving, never slowing, never stopping, not even when she was in one place. Some days, she had to concentrate to remember where she'd just been—the glaring casino lights, the roar of the crowds pressing close to the track, the urgent whispers in the dark of women she barely touched and remembered even less blurred and faded into indistinguishable links on a chain, tugging her along. And here she was, back at the beginning, like an ouroboros, a snake chasing its own tail while consuming itself in its never-ending rush to escape its fate.

"Man," she muttered, "I must be tired."

Straightening with an aggravated snort, she reached blindly for the shampoo, finding it where she'd left it who knew how long ago. She wondered idly as she soaped her body and washed her hair if the cleaning people replaced the products on a regular basis. She suspected they did. One of those little things she rarely gave any thought to. She was so used to living in hotels that her own home felt like one and was maintained in the same way as all the other elegant places she frequented. The Dakota, for all its history and charm, exuded the same careful attention to detail as a five-star hotel, and with the exception of the few employees like Ralph, was nearly as impersonal. Somehow she had stripped her life of all personal connections—valets delivered her car, bellmen picked up her laundry, porters and other attendants carried her luggage and delivered her food. Women almost as impersonal—charming and momentarily entertaining, but all the same, near strangers—satisfied her need for human contact where sex was a by-product, but not the goal. She was never one to foist responsibility for her situation onto others. She'd made her life what she wanted it to be, one of no attachments, no duties, and no obligations beyond the financial, the easiest of all for her to manage. She had no reason to complain in these odd moments when she found herself alone and the awareness registered, the isolation so intense the pain was palpable.

Vehemently, she twisted off the taps and stepped from the shower into the steamy room. She saw herself as only a wavy outline in the cloudy mirror. Even when the mirrors were crystal clear, she rarely glanced at herself. Maybe she was hoping to avoid seeing her reflection disappear along with the substance of her life.

"And aren't we just getting existential," she muttered, vigorously toweling her hair in an effort to restore a little sanity to the brain beneath. Wallowing in self-pity was not her style, and truthfully, she rarely even thought about herself or where she was headed. The only ones offended by her nomadic lifestyle were Martin and possibly Aud, although she'd never said so outright. Henrietta's sudden life-threatening illness had dragged her out of her complacency and shattered the lethal ennui, reminding her that life could still kick her in the gut, no matter how carefully she distanced herself from anything that might touch her. She hadn't counted on Henrietta disturbing the touchstone of her life by almost dying. Henrietta was just HW, like the Atlantic was always the Atlantic. Wherever Derian roamed, she knew where her center rested. Henrietta was the force that kept her connected to the world in any real way. Now she felt like a balloon on a fraying tether, in danger of floating off completely.

"HW is not going anywhere. You're going to make damn sure of it." Derian tossed the towel into the laundry chute, found the half-empty glass of champagne on the vanity, and downed it in a swift gulp. Enough already. What she needed was a meal to restore her strength, which Ralph could arrange with a quick phone call, and a woman to take her thoughts off her own pointless musings. And she certainly had that. Emily May was far more interesting than any woman she'd spent time with in recent memory. Everything she needed was only a few minutes away.

"Are you doing okay?" Derian called as she left the bathroom and headed toward her bedroom.

Emily materialized at the other end of the hall and stopped as abruptly as if she'd run into a stone wall. "Oh! Sorry."

"You know, you say that a lot." Derian stopped, cocked her head. "Is it just me that makes you uncomfortable, or everyone?"

"No, as a matter of fact, I don't. I'm not. Uncomfortable. Usually," Emily snapped, turning her head away.

"Then it's me. Why?"

"You have to ask?" Emily pointed one arm in Derian's direction. "Have you noticed that you're naked?"

Derian glanced down. "Oh, that. Should I apologize, then?"

"No. I'm fine. Apology not needed." Emily kept her gaze averted, but she hadn't blanked her vision fast enough to obliterate the impression of Derian's naked form, now firmly impregnated in her brain cells. Lean, toned, tanned, with enticing sleek lines sweeping from compact breasts down a long abdomen to the faint swell of hips and muscular thighs. Derian was as brutally elegant as the race cars she appeared to love, a perfect machine in human form, feminine in grace, masculine in power. Beautiful. Emily swallowed. "I'll be in the living room. Please, take your time."

She heard Derian laugh as she hurried away. A door closed behind her, and she breathed a sigh of relief at having a few moments to collect herself. She so needed to find her balance around Derian, a new and confounding experience. She appreciated beautiful women for the aesthetics, who didn't? The female form was such a fierce combination of delicacy and strength—the female face endlessly captivating. Why else would museums be filled with centuries of effort trying to capture the mystery of woman? Derian shouldn't have any more effect on her than an exquisite painting or a spectacular sculpture, but she kept losing her breath when she looked at her. And now she had the image of her nude emblazoned in her memory.

Totally her fault. If she'd been thinking instead of enjoying a second half-glass of champagne, she would've realized she was stepping into Derian's private space when she drifted into the hall. But she'd hardly expected her to be naked. The woman was so unbelievably casual about physical matters, touching effortlessly if respectfully, and treating her own body as if it was nothing special, and it certainly was. Special. Refreshing, exciting.

And best not to think about that too much. Perhaps she'd had a little too much of the very fine champagne after all. That must be it, although she didn't actually feel disinhibited in the least. After all, she didn't actually *plan* to go through with the mini-fantasy she'd had of running her palm over the gentle slope of Derian's chest and down...

Emily soundly set the unfinished flute of champagne down on an end table and dragged her mind away from dangerous territory. Determined to banish thoughts of Derian, naked or not, she scanned the living room again, finally pinpointing what she'd thought missing. Bookcases. Her much smaller apartment was crammed with bookshelves in every available inch of wall, nook, and cranny. And even then, she didn't have enough room for everything she wanted to keep and had piles of reads and to-be-reads secreted under tables, nightstands, even the bed. Sure, she was a child of the modern age and had plenty of digital books on several different electronic readers, but she still loved the feel of the physical form and had always been a collector. First editions, odd editions, little-known titles that represented something new and exciting at the time. She loved to keep those, each a piece of history that marked her own life, or milestones in publishing, or changes in the world around her.

Derian had no bookcases, at least none visible in the main part of the apartment, which was unusual given the traditional décor. Somehow, with her being Henrietta's niece, Emily would've expected Derian to be a book lover. She had no idea why she thought that, now. It wasn't as if a love of literature was genetically inherited. Her parents had certainly instilled in her a love of reading by example—her mother, more than her father, who restricted most of his reading to world news, finance, politics, and other areas that impacted his work. Her mother had been the fanciful one, reading everything from romances, mysteries, fantasy, biographies, to graphic novels. Emily smiled, remembering the first time her mother had shared a grown-up comic book with her. She could still feel the surge of excitement of holding her mother's copy of the bound book with the gleaming, colorful pages and how special the shared moment had been. So many moments in her life marked by the discovery of a beloved book.

"You can turn around now," Derian said softly. "I'm presentable."

Emily turned slowly, thinking Derian had been more than presentable just a few moments before. Finally, she managed to keep at least some embarrassing words to herself and said nothing.

Derian grinned as if she were still reading her mind, which was irksome and appealing all at once. A lot like the woman herself.

"If I didn't know better," Emily said, feigning annoyance, "I'd think you did that on purpose."

"I might have, if I'd known you would have enjoyed it."

"I didn't say that." Emily narrowed her eyes. "Do you actually enjoy shocking people?"

"Were you?" Derian asked quietly, suddenly very close. "Shocked?"

"No," Emily said, unable to hide the truth. "I was not."

"What then?"

"Surprised," Emily whispered, "that's all."

"So you don't really find me shocking?" Derian traced a finger over the top of Emily's hand.

"No," Emily said softly, feeling the weight of Derian's finger pulse in her center. "I find you unexpected."

Derian's gaze intensified. "Not like the rumors and gossip columns would have you believe?"

"I might be guilty of enjoying the glitz and glamour of your world," Emily said, letting Derian search her eyes, "but I can tell reality from fantasy in my own."

"Can you?" Derian murmured, catching Emily's fingers in her palm. "How about tonight?"

"What about tonight?" Emily had the oddest sensation she was falling into the undercurrents swirling in Derian's eyes and wondered if she cared.

"Are you sure you wouldn't like this to be a date?" Derian's fingers linked with Emily's. "Because I would."

"I can't think of a worse idea."

Derian didn't look offended. She looked curious. "Why?"

"Oh, a million reasons," Emily said lightly, resisting the urge to step back. She couldn't retreat. She never retreated. And if she did now, Derian would know in an instant she was attracted. She could hardly be blamed for an unconscious and purely automatic response. Derian Winfield was beautiful, intelligent, clever, and surprisingly tender. "You're Henrietta's niece, and it's probably not a good idea for us to have any kind of personal relationship under the best of circumstances, but definitely not these. You're likely to disappear at any moment, which is fine, really, but there's no point in pretending that we have anything in common. So I think any kind of relationship between us should be purely friendly and professional."

The corner of Derian's mouth worked as if she were trying not to laugh. Emily frowned. "What?"

"Friendly and professional. Right." Derian leaned forward, kissed Emily softly on the mouth. "Okay."

Emily's lips parted as Derian released her hand. Her heart thundered in her ears and a twisting sensation coiled inside her. She wasn't sure if it was the kiss or Derian's audacity that disoriented her, but for an instant, she forgot everything except the smooth heat of Derian Winfield's mouth. The kiss was barely a kiss, just a fleeting touch, silky soft. Just enough to make her lips tingle. She tugged at her lower lip for a second, willing the sensation to disappear. There. Much better. She stared at Derian, found her watching her with a dark, penetrating expression that made her shiver.

"Why did you do that?"

Derian shrugged, looking not the least bit perturbed by the annoyance in Emily's tone. "Because I've been thinking about it since I stepped into the shower. And because you have an incredibly attractive mouth."

"But I just said—"

"I know," Derian said easily. "I heard. But if it's all right with you, I'm going to disagree."

"With what?" Emily folded her arms, watching Derian light candles at each end of a dining table set into an alcove with floor-to-ceiling windows and a spectacular view of the park.

"The purely professional part. I'm good with friendly, though." Derian tapped a console on the wall and quiet strains of music filled the room.

Feeling began to return to Emily's hands and feet. She hadn't realized she couldn't feel them until then. She concentrated on keeping her voice steady. "I should go."

"We're having dinner, remember?" Derian smiled. "I'm sorry if I offended you. I didn't mean to make you uncomfortable."

Emily sighed. "You didn't. I'm not offended by a beautiful woman kissing me."

Derian's smile turned to surprise. "Thank you."

"Surely you've heard that before," Emily said, echoing Derian earlier.

"Not when I actually believed it." Derian shook her head, as if chasing away an unwanted thought. "I called the hospital while I was getting dressed. No change."

"I guess that's good." Emily was glad for the abrupt shift in subject. Jousting with Derian over the subject of kisses and dates was far too dangerous.

"I think so." Derian gestured to the table. "I also called Ralph. Dinner should be here momentarily. I did promise you no more than a forty-five-minute wait."

"I thought we were going out."

"I don't know about you, but I'm beat." Derian pulled out a chair, held it as she watched Emily. "I thought this might be quieter and more relaxing. Do you mind?"

"It's really not necessary. I can grab a cab—"

A knock sounded at the door.

"Stay, Emily," Derian said softly. "Please."

Emily sat.

CHAPTER EIGHT

Thanks, Peter," Derian said to the porter who delivered the large food trolley covered with gleaming stainless-steel chafing dishes. "I'll take it from here."

His face registered the slightest surprise before he quickly nodded. "I'm happy to serve you and your guest, Ms. Winfield."

"I can handle it, but thanks." Derian stepped aside so Peter could slide the cart into the room and closed the door behind him. She didn't want company. She wanted to be alone with Emily May, and setting up the table would give her a few moments to get her game in order. She hadn't intended to kiss her. The thought had crossed her mind, that was true. She'd wanted to kiss her from the moment she'd found her nearly asleep, waiting for her outside the intensive care unit. Emily had looked vulnerable and delicate, but Derian'd known better than to think she needed rescuing. She'd seen Emily's strength as well as the shadows of some past pain when she'd stood by Henrietta's bedside and declared her certainty that Henrietta would be all right. Daring the Fates to disagree. Emily was anything but fragile, which made her all the more desirable.

But an inexplicable urge to shield her from whatever plagued her and a primitive instinct to claim her attention were no excuse for kissing her. She knew better than to toy with women who weren't open to being toyed with, and Emily was one of those. She didn't give off a single player vibe, nor had she given any indication she wanted to be kissed. Derian was good at ferreting out signals, at reading seduction in apparent disinterest that merely invited her to the chase, and she never pressed where she wasn't wanted. She hadn't been thinking about sex when she'd given in to the impulse to taste, she'd only been thinking about another touch—another incendiary instant of contact that shook her more than the most abandoned encounter. This time, she'd been the one pressed by desire, driven to break her own rules by an unfamiliar need to stir in Emily the same kind of yearning that stirred in her.

Emily had said she wasn't offended by the kiss, but taking liberties wasn't like her. Derian didn't want to stray into those waters again. A woman, especially Henrietta's protégé, who could so easily make her forget all the reasons why she only played with players, had danger written all over her. No—Emily was too close to home, too dangerous in her appeal, too altogether beyond the safety zone.

"I can't say I've ever done this before," Emily said, glancing over her shoulder to watch Derian approach with the cart.

"What's that?" Derian asked, promptly forgetting her resolution to stay away. Emily had a way of looking at her with such absolute clarity, as if the screen Derian placed between herself and the rest of the world was completely invisible. Her skin heated as if Emily touched her simply by looking. Most women couldn't touch her even when they were naked together.

"Had dinner in such a beautiful place, with a view like this." Emily swept her hand toward the window and the glittering night.

"I'm glad you like it."

"I do," Emily said softly. "Thank you."

The quiet thrum of pleasure in her voice made Derian's blood pound. She cleared her throat. "I hope you don't mind, I ordered for us. You're not allergic to anything or averse to particular foods?"

"Actually, I'm gluten, dairy, meat, carb, and acidic free."

"Well, I ordered sparkling water. That should be safe."

Emily laughed. "I'm mostly vegetarian, but I confess to succumbing to a good steak now and then. I live for pasta and never met a seafood dish I didn't like. I'm sure whatever you ordered is fine."

Derian began to uncover the chafing dishes. "That was unkind."

"I suspect you can handle it." Emily grinned. "Can I help you?"

"No, stay right there." Derian folded a snowy white napkin over her forearm and rested a dish on it. "I shall serve Madame tonight."

Faint color rose to Emily's cheeks. "Very well, then. Thank you."

"My pleasure," Derian murmured.

Emily settled back in her chair and prepared to be waited on.

She remembered being waited on at formal functions her parents had held at their home for visiting dignitaries when the party was small and the embassy would've been too cold and impersonal. She'd never liked being seated at the big table at the far end, away from the adults, always feeling as if she was there more for show than for her presence. Every now and then her mother would glance her way and smile as if to tell her she knew she was still there, but her father rarely gave her a look, too lost in conversation with whomever they were feting. Her memories of the impersonal formal dining faded as Derian silently moved around behind her, sliding dishes in front of her with a whispered description, filling her wineglass with a calculated cascade of blood-red liquid, slipping other dishes to the center of the table with sterling silver serving utensils positioned within.

"You do this very well," Emily murmured.

Derian sat down beside her, close enough for Emily to catch her spicy scent. "My father always insisted on a formal table when the family dined together. I learned from watching the maids. Sometimes I even helped them, just to annoy him."

"Teenage rebellion?"

Derian sipped her wine. "More than that, I guess. Maybe lifelong rebellion."

"Do you have siblings?" Emily asked.

"I do now, a half brother. He's..." She paused as if counting in her head. "He must be six. I haven't seen him in quite a while."

Emily took a bite of the very delicious food. "It must be odd, having such a younger sibling."

"Truthfully, I don't think of my father's second family as having anything to do with me. I have nothing against the boy, of course. But I don't know his mother or him, and my father and Marguerite—that's his wife's name—took up well after I left home."

"What's his name?"

"Daniel." Derian poured a little more wine in Emily's glass.

"No more," Emily said, laughing lightly. "I'm not used to it."

"Of course." Derian replenished her glass and put the bottle aside. "How about you? Big family, small family?"

Emily carefully set her fork down. She usually managed to avoid talking about family, which wasn't all that difficult since her associates were business ones and the topic didn't often come up. Henrietta knew, but she'd never shared the story with anyone else, not even Ron. Not the whole story. "Small, I guess. One older sister. Pam."

"She here in the city too?" Derian asked conversationally.

"No. She isn't."

"That's hard, when you're close." As if picking up on the tension in Emily's voice, Derian regarded her steadily. "Sounds like you are."

"Yes," Emily said around the lump in her throat. "I miss her."

"Where is she?"

"At home—in Singapore."

"Ah, I didn't realize." Derian smiled. "You sound very American."

Emily laughed. "English-speaking schools, and I've been here almost a decade."

"Do you get back often, then, to Singapore?"

"A couple times a year." Emily shook her head when Derian offered another helping of one of the entrées.

Derian covered the dish. "Are the rest of your family still there?"

"Pam and I are the only ones left."

"Ah. I'm sorry too, then. It must have been a challenge, coming over here alone."

"I was determined, so I didn't think of it much at the time." Emily let out a breath, forced a smile. "And I've been lucky. The agency is a great place to work, and I've made some good friends."

"So tell me about you and Henrietta," Derian said. "How did you end up here? Winfield's isn't the biggest literary agency in New York, and you strike me as going for the top."

"Winfield's is smaller than some, true," Emily said, knowing she sounded protective, "but it is also one of the most respected."

"Ah," Derian said softly, "so you value substance over show."

"I like to think so."

Derian leaned back, cradled her wineglass. "How did you and Henrietta meet?"

"Well," Emily said, "I guess you could say I chased her."

Derian laughed. "Now there's a story I really want to hear."

"All right." Emily recounted for Derian how she had first contacted Henrietta, and the gradual development of their long-distance working relationship that culminated in her move to the agency, and finally their very deep friendship.

When she'd finished, Derian nodded. "I can see where Henrietta would've been intrigued by someone who cut through all the bullshit. You're good at that, aren't you?"

"I suppose that's true." Emily shrugged. "I've always been the pragmatic type. For me, most things are black and white. I say what I think, and I prefer others do the same. I like life to be straightforward."

"That would put you in the minority." Derian finished her wine and slid her glass away. "In my experience, people rarely say what they think, and oftentimes don't mean what they say. Everything is a little bit of a game."

"For you too?" Emily asked.

"Oh," Derian said, laughing. "Most definitely."

"And how do you know when something is real?"

"Well everything is real in the moment, isn't it, even when it's a game? You just have to know you're playing."

"You're not just talking about cards and cars, are you."

Derian's expression flattened. "No."

Emily frowned. "I'm quite certain I would be terrible at pretending other than what I felt."

"I think you would be too. Don't gamble."

"Actually, I'm very good at cards. I've been told I have an excellent poker face."

"Do you bluff?" Derian asked.

"Yes, insomuch as I am quite capable of keeping my thoughts and feelings to myself."

"I suppose that could be considered a bluff." Derian tapped a finger to Emily's hand. "We'll have to play sometime."

Emily flushed. "I don't think so. I'm afraid you're far too experienced for me."

"I don't know," Derian said musingly. "I might've met my match. But I was thinking more of playing together, not against each other."

Emily sensed the conversation veering once again away from the topic and into some realm she couldn't quite comprehend. She was never entirely sure they were talking about what they were actually saying. Subtext was everything in fiction, but she preferred plainer language in real life. "You would not find me a very good partner. I'm afraid I don't know any of the rules."

"Oh, not to worry. I'd be happy to demonstrate."

"I doubt we'll ever have the chance," Emily said a little frostily.

Derian's grin was infuriatingly arrogant and just a little too compelling to contemplate.

"So what do you do to occupy your time," Derian asked, seemingly unfazed by Emily's tone, "if you don't enjoy games?"

"I read, of course," Emily said.

"No, no, that's work."

"Not at all. Well, of course it is sometimes, but even though it's work, it's still one of my greatest pleasures. Don't you feel that way about your work?"

"I don't work. You must've read that. I spend my time searching for new ways to avoid it."

"Ah," Emily said, not believing her for a minute. Derian might not have a conventional job, but nothing about her suggested she was lazy. If anything, she vibrated with dynamism and restless vitality. "Isn't winning a job? I mean, coming in first or beating the odds requires effort and thought and probably stamina. Certainly, a professional gambler works."

"Very true," Derian said. "But I'm not a professional gambler in the sense that I make my living doing it. I like to win, no doubt about that, but if I lose, no one suffers for it."

"Semantics."

"I won't argue language with a literary type," Derian said lightly. "What besides books?"

Emily noticed how deftly Derian diverted the conversation away from herself, but she appreciated the desire for privacy, valuing it herself. "Films—"

"They're just another form of books, right? Scripts translated into visual form?"

Emily smiled appreciatively. "There are definite similarities, of course, in terms of story structure and characterizations, but with the ability to inject narrative, as authors do in fiction, for example, books aren't obligated to the kind of rapid characterization and plot development that scriptwriters are."

"Nor dependent on actors who must communicate subtext through body motion and speech," Derian added.

"Yes," Emily said. "Which do you prefer? Films or books?"

Derian was silent a long moment. "I like films but prefer listening to books when I have the time."

"Ah, you're an audiophile. I like them too, but I miss the slower pace of reading," Emily said. "I wondered where you kept your books, but of course you'd want them to be portable since you travel so much."

Derian glanced around the room as if it was a strange new place. "I don't have any books because I'm not a very good reader."

Emily stilled. Derian's voice had faded, as if she'd drifted someplace beyond their conversation.

"When I was small I couldn't read at all," Derian said matter-of-factly, as if relating a story about someone else. "They labeled it dyslexia, but I didn't demonstrate all the signs. I don't mix up the words, I have mostly directionality confusion. It was quite an embarrassment to my family."

"Surely not to Henrietta," Emily said vehemently.

Derian smiled thinly. "No, not to Henrietta. But my father was embarrassed by what they initially thought was some kind of mental disability."

"I'm so sorry," Emily murmured.

"Once I was old enough to verbalize what was happening, they figured it out and I got the right kind of therapy—all on the QT, of course." She grimaced. "I can interpret most maps with a little effort, but it put an end to my desire to drive race cars."

"So you sponsor them." Emily knew Derian wouldn't appreciate sympathy for something she'd obviously conquered, but she couldn't help being saddened. Such a hard burden when her family had been so unsupportive. The idea of Derian suffering alone incensed her.

"I'm okay with it all now," Derian whispered, taking Emily's hand as if she were the one in need of comfort.

"I'm glad that we have audiobooks, then. And that you enjoy them."

"Fortunately, it turns out I have an eidetic memory for numbers." Derian grinned. "I can remember an entire spreadsheet of values after a quick glance. It gives me a very good edge in anything that requires probability."

"Such as cards?" Emily said, trying for a lighter note.

"Exactly. Probability, statistics, anything requiring numbers is easy for me. It took a while for that to show up, but once it did, the rest—" She shrugged. "Let's say my luck at the tables comes naturally."

"Is that why you're not interested in the agency?"

"I wouldn't be any good at it, and as much as Henrietta has wanted me to join her on the fourth floor, I think she knows I'm not suited for it." Derian rose and began clearing the table. "Besides, the board would never stand for it. I'm the black sheep, remember."

Emily rose to help her. "Let me help. You've waited on me all night."

"I enjoy waiting on you," Derian murmured.

"And I've taken up quite enough of your time this evening," Emily said as Derian pushed the food cart aside. "I really should be getting home."

"Of course. I'll call you a car."

"Oh, that's not necessary. I can easily get a cab—"

Derian cupped Emily's cheek and brushed her fingers through Emily's hair. "No, you won't. I'll see you downstairs and into a car."

"You're very kind," Emily murmured, leaned into Derian's hand without thinking, and watched heat flicker through Derian's eyes. She thought for a heartbeat she was about to be kissed again. She didn't move.

"No," Derian whispered, "I'm not."

And she stepped away, leaving Emily unkissed and unexpectedly disappointed.

CHAPTER NINE

Derian slid her hands into her pockets and watched the cab pull away, following its course along the park until it turned and disappeared. She'd escorted more women than she'd ever thought to count to a cab or car in the middle of the night, seeing them off to their other lives, their other lovers. Fortunately, few of her liaisons cared to spend the night, like-having-recognized-like before the assignations had begun. Even when the night gave way to dawn, she couldn't recall a single instance when she and her bedmate had shared breakfast. Sitting opposite someone over a meal required a level of intimate conversation she usually avoided. Not so with Emily, though. Somehow they had effortlessly traveled into regions Derian rarely traversed, even in her mind. Thoughts of family, lost to time or tragedy, were not landscapes she cared to view, but she'd touched on all of that with Emily. And Emily had ventured there with her too, for a moment, before pulling back from whatever sorrows populated that part of her past. Derian wanted to know, wanted to help ease that grief, but she'd wait until invited, even though waiting was not her usual stance.

The evening with Emily had been a departure in more ways than one. Spending time with Emily was not like spending time with other women. She hadn't been eager for her to leave—just the opposite. Even now, a hollow ache percolated in her chest, as if Emily had taken some of the energy and excitement of the night with her. Derian wasn't inured to the company of other women—she appreciated the intimacies they shared, but she'd always been satisfied with the physical. Oh, she was aware of Emily physically, all right. She could envision making love with her. Sitting across from her at the small table, she'd imagined it more than once. Even now, the vibrant images were so clear and insistent, desire surged like a heavy hand squeezing deep inside.

She grimaced, caught off guard and not at all pleased. She'd already mentally cataloged all the reasons why even thinking of Emily in that way was a bad idea, and being reminded that her head did not rule her body only made the unruly physical urges more aggravating. She wasn't going to be able to sleep until she banished the persistent craving for a woman she didn't want to want. A walk in the brisk dark and a diversion of a more familiar type might refocus her interest in a safer direction.

Hunching her shoulders inside the light wool blazer she'd tossed on to accompany Emily downstairs, she headed toward Midtown and the metrosexual club she remembered from her last visit. If Cosmos wasn't there any longer, she could surely find another without any difficulty. New York never slept, after all, and New Yorkers were notoriously adventurous and nonjudgmental, at least where sex was concerned.

As she strode quickly through the still busy streets, dodging puddles and the occasional slush pile left over from the late snow, she contemplated calling the hospital to check on Henrietta. After eleven. Surely if there was some change, some problem, someone would've contacted her by now. What the hell. The time didn't really matter— hospitals ran twenty-four seven. Skirting between cabs crowding across the intersection, she pulled out her cell phone and scrolled to the number she'd saved earlier. After half a dozen rings, the hospital operator answered and sent her through to the intensive care unit.

"ICU, Higgins," a man said.

"This is Derian Winfield. I was wondering if you could give me an update on my aunt's condition. Henrietta?"

"Hold on for a second."

A little more than a second later, a woman came on the line. "Hi, this is Sally, Henrietta's nurse. Who is this, please?"

"Derian Winfield. Henrietta's my aunt."

"Oh, right, Penny mentioned you earlier. She's fine. All her vital signs are stable, her lab results look good, and she's resting comfortably."

Derian wondered how they knew if Henrietta was resting, comfortably or otherwise. If Henrietta had any say in things, she'd be half-awake at all times, just to be sure everyone was keeping on track. "Has she been alert, talking?"

"Every now and then she surfaces for a few seconds—a minute, maybe—and she knows where she is. But it's not unusual for patients who've sustained this kind of physical insult to kind of draw back inside. It's part of the healing process. It's perfectly normal."

"Uh-huh." Derian would have preferred hearing HW was haranguing the staff and causing a fuss, but she knew it was too soon. Her desire to make the whole damn nightmare go away wasn't going to be enough to make it so. "Thanks. You'll be sure someone will call me if there's any change?"

"I'll be here all night. If there's any problem, I'll call you, and I'll let her know you were asking for her if she wakes up."

"That'd be great. Thanks." Derian disconnected and slid the phone back into her pants pocket. The uneasy sensation of her world being slightly atilt persisted. Trying to set aside her worry over Henrietta, she let her thoughts drift back to Emily. She should be home by now. A phone call would be out of line, but the need to hear her voice made her fingers clench around her phone.

"Goddamn it," she muttered. Somehow, she'd let Emily escape without getting her phone number. For the best. Maybe her head was in the game after all—only this time it was a game she wasn't used to playing.

She rarely took a woman's number or exchanged hers, unless she met someone she'd like to see again—someone whose sense of humor, sharp intelligence, and love for the game matched her own. Then she gave her number and took theirs after they agreed to the ground rules. No promises, no strings, and above all, discretion. But she'd never been driven by some urge deep inside to reconnect, to hold on.

Cosmos was where she remembered it, its sign shimmering in reds and blues. She headed for it, shaking off the uncomfortable sensations and unanswerable questions. A mix of traditional wine bar and dance club, the long rectangular space was jammed from the entrance to the far back reaches. People congregated six deep around the bar, shouting, drinking, laughing. Everyone was young or wanted to be, beautiful and reckless and seeking the next adventure. Music accosted her, a fast, frenetic beat that matched the sexual frenzy of the crowd. Ignoring the glances of women and men, she edged her way to the bar and flagged down one of the two bartenders who shimmied and slipped around each other in the narrow aisle in a mad pantomime of the dancers out on the floor.

"What'll you have?" A sloe-eyed redhead in a white open-collared shirt and tight black pants slid a cardboard coaster toward her.

"Whatever dark brew you've got on tap," Derian said.

The pretty bartender nodded, pulled a draft, and passed it across the bar. Derian pushed a twenty back, waved off the change, and turned to survey the bacchanal. Bodies writhed on the dance floor, heads bent close over small tables, and figures shifted stealthily in the shadows, surreptitiously initiating the dance they would play out before the evening ended.

Derian pointedly did not encourage the appraising glances that came her way, avoiding eye contact, a slight nod, or a tilt of her glass that would signal she was ready to play. She wasn't interested in a hookup. The impersonalness of casual sex with a stranger never held much appeal—especially when sex was just a desperate attempt to ward off loneliness. She'd rather replay the evening with Emily than settle for a poor substitute. And she wouldn't even be thinking about Emily if she hadn't been so damn tired and worried over Henrietta. She needed some sleep, not a few hours of physical forgetfulness, and she'd be herself again.

She stayed long enough for a second beer and when the alcohol finally seeped into her muscles and she knew she'd be able to sleep, she headed out into the night alone. Fifteen minutes later she was back in her apartment, stripping off her clothes by the side of the bed she hadn't slept in in three years. As she pulled back the covers and slipped nude beneath, she thought back to the fleeting kiss she'd stolen from Emily.

She smiled to herself. Stolen kisses. Something she hadn't done since she was a teenager. She hadn't had to steal kisses after that. Willing women were always quite willing to give them. The unanticipated desire for Emily's was as fresh and innocent as anything she'd experienced during those first youthful couplings, and that realization was as troubling as it was impossible to forget.

❖

"How much is that?" Emily asked when the cabbie double-parked in front of her apartment building.

"The other miss took care of it," the driver said, turning in his seat with a wide smile. "Very generous."

"Oh, thank you, then." Of course Derian had taken care of it. Derian was obviously very used to looking after women. Her confidence and easy way of taking control did not strike Emily as overbearing, but merely customary. And, she had to admit as she fit her key into the foyer door and made her way up to her apartment, she'd enjoyed being pampered.

She'd grown up wanting for nothing—she'd gone to good schools, had all the clothes she'd needed, had the advantages of her father's station and her family's position, and never given much thought to her wants. As a child and young teen, her needs had always been met. Life had changed after the accident, but then she'd been too focused on what she must do to be concerned about luxuries, physical or otherwise. All she'd wanted was to succeed. She was doing that. She wasn't there yet—she still had goals, things she wanted to accomplish at the agency. And she was still far from securing Pam's future.

She was so used to every day being another step toward achieving all that, the evening with Derian had unexpectedly awakened her appreciation for things she had put aside. Simple things like enjoying a woman's attention—and Derian was a master at that. She had friends she talked with, socialized with, but none of them gazed at her with the intense focus that Derian had all evening. Derian's attention was so absolute, Emily could easily have believed she was the only thing in Derian's world that mattered. For a few hours, she'd let herself enjoy the feeling, knowing all the while it couldn't be true.

She laughed at her silliness as she put her coat away and headed straight for the bathroom and a shower. As enjoyable as the evening with Derian had been, it wasn't likely to be repeated. Once Henrietta was on the mend, Derian would disappear, returning to a life so far from Emily's as to be unimaginable. Constantly traveling, searching for the next excitement—the next exciting woman. Emily was definitely not one of those. The most excitement she usually ran into during the course of a day was a fascinating new manuscript culled from the slush pile.

When she closed her eyes to lather her hair, an image of Derian's face formed beneath her eyelids. Deep gaze boring into hers, drawing closer and closer until soft heat glided across her mouth. The kiss. Eyes still closed, steam rising around her, enclosing her in a warm cloud, she let herself drift on the memory for just a few more minutes. Fingertips to her lips, she could still feel the electricity. She'd never in her life been kissed when she hadn't expected it, when she hadn't somehow known it was coming. When she'd spent an evening with someone whose company she enjoyed, who she found attractive and knew was attracted to her, a kiss had been the next logical step, or the last. Usually the last. Some had gone further than that. She wasn't a nun, after all. But truthfully, the few pleasant hours in bed hadn't been enough to drive her to repeat the encounters. She knew herself too well to think she could have a sexual relationship with someone merely for the sake of the physical, and she hadn't felt anything deep enough to offer anything else. She would never misrepresent herself to anyone. To her, lies were about far more than spoken words. Actions were truth.

She stepped out into the small mist-filled room, leaving only the light in the shower on. She wrapped a towel around her hair and dried off with another, deciding the evening was a moment out of time for both her and Derian. They both loved Henrietta, and her illness had shaken them. Their shared affection was a bond that had drawn them together in a moment of fear and uncertainty. Derian was fascinating, but *she* was anything but. She couldn't imagine a single reason why Derian would seek her out again.

As she slipped into bed, she accepted the evening for what it had been, a fleeting intersection of very different lives, not to be repeated. As she turned on her side and drew the covers around her, she pressed her fingers to her lips again. The memory of the kiss remained.

CHAPTER TEN

Heart pounding, Derian grabbed her phone off the nightstand before the second ring. "Winfield."

"Still up before the sun, I see," Aud said. "Or have you not been to bed?"

Derian's breath shot out on a curse. "I thought it was the hospital."

"Oh my God." Aud sounded crushed. "Derian, I am so sorry. I didn't think—"

"No, that's okay." Derian rubbed her face, glanced at the time. 5:30 a.m. "I was lying here awake. You're right about that."

"I just thought I'd try to catch you before the day got away from us. Really, I'm an idiot."

"No comment, Counselor."

"Can I make it up to you over breakfast? That's actually why I was calling. It's been a long time."

"There was Rio," Derian pointed out.

"Yes, and that was nine months ago. And I think we had about as much time together then as we had last night. I seem to remember your attention was on a redhead, or was it the brunette with the tattoo on her—"

"Breakfast would be good." Aud had a way of making her affairs with women seem like they were dalliances with *other* women, when there was no *us* to consider in the first place. She couldn't cheat on a best friend, could she? She didn't think so, but Aud appeared to disagree. Ordinarily she didn't mind, but today she was too beat to find the implied criticism just friendly teasing. They were both responsible for the distance between them, and her involvement with other women was not the cause. Hell, Aud hadn't likely been sitting alone in her Madison Avenue penthouse pining for company these last five years. "I'll meet you. Half an hour?"

"Good. Lindy's?"

Derian smiled wryly. Aud was determined to keep the past alive. She couldn't count the number of breakfasts they'd shared in the late hours of the night at Lindy's, when they were young and still best of friends. "Sure. Why not."

"I'll get us a booth."

Aud disconnected and Derian headed for another shower. Her head was muzzy and her stomach queasy. Four hours' sleep was usually enough to recharge her batteries, but the transatlantic flight, the stress, and too little real sleep punctuated with restless dreams had her running on empty. She didn't often dream, and never dreams like these. Dreams filled with amorphous faces and a seething sexual unrest that left her agitated and unsatisfied. She flipped the shower dial to hot, waited for the steam to rise, and left the lights off in the bathroom, preferring a few more minutes of dark solitude before the day intruded. The heat brought blood rushing to the surface of her skin, and as her flesh awakened, the persistent tension between her thighs accelerated. The drumbeat of insistent desire was not to be denied. She slid one hand down the slick surface of her abdomen, caught the taut pulsing heat between her fingers, and squeezed. Her breath caught, her vision swam, and a spring coiled deep inside. A low moan escaped.

She stroked and tugged, her pulse pounding loud in her ears, her abdomen hard and tight. A fist of pressure clenched and spread.

Yes. The soft pull of a warm mouth enclosed her. She shuddered. *Just like that.* She rocked, clasped the neck of the woman kneeling between her thighs, slid her fingers into long silky strands of dark wet hair, drawing the pale face closer, the relentless mouth nearer. Muscles flexing, hips lifting, pushing, thrusting, moaning, she strained for the connection, for the ultimate union.

Yes. Close. Pleasure spiked, pierced her center. Eyes squeezed shut, she clawed toward the peak. Breathless, lungs burning, loins aching. She had to, had to, had to… *Don't stop. Don't stop.*

Behind closed lids, she saw herself looking down, met the eyes of the woman looking back, watched the glint of triumph when the soft circle of lips drew her in, pushed her over. *Yes. Yes! You'll make me come.*

The orgasm jolted her. Her hips jerked, once, twice, three times, and she shot out an arm to catch her balance. She moaned, a long sigh of relief. God. When had she last come so hard? Thighs loose, heart hammering against her ribs, she quickly finished showering, dried off, and dressed, all the while aware she'd just imagined Emily May making her come.

Just a trick of the unconscious. Nothing more.

She walked through the park, a glint of early a.m. sun snaking down through the trees, most of which were just beginning to leaf out. The air, not yet fouled by exhaust, hinted at spring. Aud was already ensconced in a booth with a steaming cup of coffee in front of her and another across from her. Derian slid in. "Morning."

"Hi. I ordered for us."

Derian added cream and sipped the strong brew. "What did you get me?"

"Please," Aud teased. "It hasn't been that long. Like I could forget what you've ordered for the last ten years? Fried egg and bacon on English."

"Thanks."

Aud looked ready for a day at the office, sharp and fashionable in a gray pinstripe jacket, a textured linen shirt in a paler shade of gray, and a diamond pendent set in dusky gold glinting in the hollow of her throat. A matching bracelet circled her right wrist and a gold Rolex adorned her left. One ring—an engraved signet—gleamed on her right hand. Not showy, but everything about her spoke of power and privilege. The look suited her well. Derian doubted she actually spent much time in court. Corporate lawyers with wealthy clients like Winfield Enterprises usually settled issues with money. Long drawn-out court battles just interfered with business as usual, and that's what really mattered. That the money kept flowing.

"Any word on HW?" Aud's shoulder-length blond hair framed her face in loose layers, and her clear green eyes regarded Derian with questions. For an instant, she looked like the tender, supportive confidant she'd once been.

"I haven't heard anything from the hospital, so I hope that's a good sign." Derian's chest tightened and she pulled herself out of the past.

She and Aud were strangers now, their bond one of shared memories, memories of different times, when they'd been different people. "I'm going to run by there when we're done."

"Have you talked to Martin?"

"Why would I?"

Aud sighed. "Because he's your father?"

"Come on, Aud. You know better than that."

"Life would be a lot easier if the two of you would actually communicate now and then."

"Easier for who? For you, probably. Definitely not for me."

"You know he wants you in the business."

"No, he doesn't. Not unless I undergo a personality transplant and change my internal wiring at the same time."

"You are a voting member of the company, and—"

"Right. That's what matters to him, that we present a solid front. I'm not going down that road. Maybe I got lucky and nature did me a favor." Derian rubbed the faint headache between her eyes. "You know I'm not cut out for business, even if I was capable."

"Oh, come on." Aud sighed in exasperation. "You're perfectly capable. You've got a mind like a calculator and we both know it. So does Martin."

"Maybe so." Derian took a bite of the sandwich the waitress slid onto the table in a quick wordless pass. Funny, the old favorite had lost its appeal, like so many things that shone in hindsight and paled in the present. "But the last time I attended a board meeting—"

"Uh, excuse me? When was that—three, four years ago?" Aud speared a section of omelet and shook her head. "The board members might be inclined to take you more seriously if you actually showed up now and then."

"They made it perfectly clear I would never sit in the big seat." Derian sipped her rapidly cooling coffee. "I think I heard the words *image* and *irresponsible* tossed around quite a lot."

"You could change that, Dere. All you'd have to do is come home, show some interest."

"Sure, if I *had* any interest, which I don't."

"God, you're stubborn."

"And you're not?" Derian pushed her plate away. "Have you ever thought you're starting to sound an awful lot like Martin?"

Aud's eyes cooled. "I'm your friend, Derian. And I also happen to be looking out for your interests, even if you like to pretend they don't matter."

Derian blew out a breath. "You're right. I'm sorry."

"Apology accepted." Aud smiled faintly. "I'm just trying to get you to look further ahead than your next race. You're in line to inherit, and it might be good if you and Martin were on speaking terms so you'd have some idea—"

"You mean he hasn't changed his will yet and made Daniel his heir?"

"You know I can't talk about that."

But there was something in her eyes. "He has. But he can't cut me out all altogether, can he? Because of the terms of my trust fund."

"I can't comment on that."

"But you know, and you still push me to return to the fold. Why?"

"Because you're wasting your life, Dere," Aud snapped.

Derian laughed. "Really? This from someone who copped out? Whatever happened to family law and serving the public sector?"

"It's not a cop-out to follow family tradition," Aud said stiffly.

"It is when it's not what you wanted."

"Maybe when I was eighteen I didn't know what I wanted."

"Maybe when you were eighteen you did, and now you've forgotten."

"I'm happy with what I'm doing, proud of my work."

"And I'm happy with my life."

Aud's shoulders sagged and she slumped back in the booth. "Do we always have to fight when we see each other?"

"Maybe we wouldn't if you'd stop trying to talk me into a suit and an office."

"Maybe I just miss you? Maybe I'd like to see you more than every year or so. Dammit, Derian. I love you."

Derian let out a slow breath. "Come on, Aud. We've been down that road too."

"You know what I mean."

"Yeah, I do." Next to HW, Aud was the person who knew her best, who she trusted the most, even after all they'd been through. They'd grown up together, dreamed together, been best friends, and briefly, sweetly, young lovers. They'd managed to stay friends even after their romantic stage had waned, at least until the halcyon days of college ended and they'd had to move on. They'd both made choices that had taken them in opposite directions, but she still remembered the dreams, and the sweetness. "I miss you too."

"Enough of this." Aud reached across the table and took her hand. "I'm sorry about Henrietta. She's going to be all right."

Derian squeezed Aud's hand, and for a moment, she remembered when the two of them stood against the world. "She damn well has to be."

❖

Emily woke before her alarm, switched it off, and padded into the kitchen to make a cup of tea. At just after six, she cradled the mug in front of the window, wrapped in her favorite pink fuzzy robe, thinking about the day ahead. And purposefully not thinking about the night before. When snippets of conversation floated into her head, or some tactile memory of Derian's hand on her arm flooded through her, she firmly set the images aside.

Mentally, she constructed her to-do list. She needed to get to the office to confer with Vonnie about covering Henrietta's appointments. More importantly, she wanted to assure everyone that business as usual would continue. She was familiar with the day-to-day workload after six years at Henrietta's side. She'd already taken on most of the manuscript review and contract negotiations, and she'd just have to make room in her day for the ones Henrietta still handled. She'd find a way. As soon as everyone was in, she'd schedule a meeting with the division managers and get updates on all the current projects. Thankfully, Winfield's staff were experienced and loyal—they'd all pull together until Henrietta returned.

Emily's throat tightened. Of course she would return. Resolutely, she washed her cup, set it on the drainboard, and dressed. As much as she wanted to go directly to the hospital, she'd be doing more for Henrietta to take care of the agency Henrietta had nurtured and grown for thirty years than to sit outside her hospital room worrying. Besides, Derian was there, Henrietta's family, to take care of her. So she would take care of the agency, her family.

Taking care of family was what mattered more than anything else, and she had to put that first, as she always had.

She checked her watch. Seven p.m. in Singapore. Pam would probably be in bed, but that didn't matter. She just needed to reach out to the rest of her family. Her call was picked up after half a dozen rings.

"Alexandra Residential Care Center. How may I direct your call?"

"Floor three, please."

"Hold on."

Another moment passed. "This is Adlina."

"Adlina, hi. It's Emily May. I just wanted to check on Pam."

"Hello!" Adlina's smile came through the line. "Let me get Yi Ling."

"Thanks." Emily smiled. No amount of money could be too much for this kind of personal care, from men and women she trusted with the person she loved most in all the world.

"Hi, Emily," Yi Ling said brightly. "She had a good day. A heron mating pair built a nest by the little pond at the far edge of the back lawn. She sat outside most of the day, and you know how much she loves to watch the birds."

"I do, thanks."

"When will you be coming by again?"

"Not for a few months, I'm afraid. But will you tell her that I called?"

"Wait, wait." After a pause. "Go ahead. Here she is."

"Pam? Hi, Pam." Emily pressed the phone harder to her ear, willing her sister to hear her voice in the silent world where she dwelled. Every time she called, she waited, breathless and frozen in place, for the sound of Pam's voice, once so full of life and wild adventure. "It's Emily. I've been thinking about you. I love you, Pam."

Seconds ticked by. The sadness never eased.

"She knows, Miss Emily. I know she does."

"I know, Yi Ling. Thank you." Emily hung up, the memory of Pam's voice undiminished after a decade.

Fifteen minutes later she was headed to the office, a sense of relief driving out the lingering sorrow. Strange, how work had become her safe place. She let herself in on the ground floor with her key and took the stairs to the top floor, looking forward to a free hour or so to review the month's calendar and organize her agenda. No one should be in until at least seven thirty.

Vonnie's desk was empty, but a light shone behind Henrietta's partially open office door. Vonnie must have come in early, like her. She pushed the door open and stopped abruptly.

"Oh!"

A woman she didn't know sat behind Henrietta's desk. Midfifties, short jet-black hair cut in a sharp edge at jaw level, attractive in a thin, knifelike kind of way. Dark suit, white shirt, unsmiling eyes.

"Can I help you?" Emily said when the woman stared at her as if she were the one intruding.

"I don't think so."

"Might I ask what you're doing in Ms. Winfield's office?"

The woman smiled thinly. "I am Donatella Agnelli. I'll be in charge from now on."

CHAPTER ELEVEN

Emily sat behind her desk, a cup of tea she couldn't remember making cooling in front of her, an untouched pile of manuscripts on one side and her laptop open and waiting for her by her right hand. She didn't drink the tea, scan her emails, make a list of the manuscripts she intended to review that afternoon, or schedule the author calls she wanted to make before lunch. She didn't pull up the latest marketing plans for the fall release schedule from their biggest publishing clients. She didn't get to the proposals from the rights department on what titles to present at the International Rights Conference.

She didn't do anything at all except gather her scattered wits and struggle for some kind of perspective. The panic ballooning in her chest, making her breath short and her head light, was totally unwarranted. The last twenty-four hours had shaken her world, but she could fix that—she'd been through far worse. She just needed to be rational and ignore the fear clutching at her throat. She'd survived the phone call that had destroyed life as she'd known it when she was eighteen years old. Of course she could handle a passing disruption now. She had to.

Emily sipped her cooling tea, pleased that her hand was not shaking. There. Better. The constriction in her chest eased and she mentally ticked off what she knew, and what she needed to know. First and most importantly, Donatella Agnelli's reign would only be temporary. Henrietta would be back soon and everything would return to normal. Even as she thought it, wished it, she knew it wouldn't be true. Henrietta would be fine, everyone knew that, but she wouldn't be able to run the agency as she always had, with a finger in everything, working fifteen-, sometimes eighteen-hour days, regularly outpacing many of the younger staff. She'd want to, Emily didn't doubt that, and any changes in her schedule would have to be subtle ones. Emily and Vonnie would have to wage a stealth campaign to shift some of Henrietta's workload to senior people without her knowing it, but as long as Henrietta was at the helm, behind that enormous desk that could probably float Manhattan if a second flood of biblical proportions suddenly arrived, business would return to normal.

Until then, where exactly Donatella Agnelli had come from and what her agenda might be were the critical questions. Vonnie might know who she was, and if she didn't they had to find out. Perhaps she didn't have the power she seemed to claim. Her proprietary occupation of Henrietta's private space rankled. So disrespectful, so unfeelingly arrogant. Emily drew a breath. Perspective, she needed perspective, especially now when her emotions were riding roughshod over her reason. She didn't know the woman, and she was probably being unfair. Usually she was far more methodical and clearheaded when faced with a challenge.

Now she was tired and frightened and a little bit angry. More than a little. Fury simmered so close to the surface her skin itched. Henrietta should *not* be ill. Some stranger should *not* be sitting at her desk. Her sister, the one she'd always looked up to, admired, envied for her bravery and reckless joie de vivre, should *not* be locked inside her own broken body, forever sentenced by a quirk of nature to silence. Emily's eyes stung.

For the first time in many years, her safe haven no longer felt safe and she wanted—needed—someone to blame. Derian Winfield's rakish face flashed through her mind and her swirling anger pointed at her. Derian was Henrietta's niece, one of the Winfield heirs, and where was she in all of this? Betting on cars and cards and, in all likelihood, women. Why wasn't she here to hold back the storm, to make everything solid and safe again?

Emily drew up short.

Oh. My.

She was not thinking straight. Derian was no more responsible for what happened here at the agency than a hot dog vendor on the corner. She'd chosen not to be part of Henrietta's world, Emily's world, and she had every right to do that. Derian and Henrietta obviously had an understanding, and it was none of Emily's concern. Expecting someone else, especially a woman she didn't even know, to solve her problems was not her way. She damn well solved her own problems, and she would solve this one. Straightening her shoulders, she reached for her tea, only to discover the cup was empty.

As she started to rise, Ron rushed in, his normally perfectly coiffed brown hair windblown, his cheeks flushed, and his eyes wide and unblinking.

"Who is that?" he stage-whispered, tilting his head almost imperceptibly in the direction of Henrietta's office two doors down.

Emily motioned him in. "Shut the door."

He pushed the door closed with one loafered foot, shrugging off the quilted down parka he would wear until daytime temperatures stayed above sixty. His Florida blood, according to him, was too thin to accommodate the Arctic temperatures of New York City.

"She said her name is Donatella Agnelli. I don't know who she is."

"Never heard of her, and I would have remembered if I'd seen her." He mock shivered. "She looks like Maleficent in Versace. Why is she in Henrietta's office, and she's going through Henrietta's papers."

"I don't know that either, except she said that she's in charge now."

He stopped midway across the room, his mouth agape. "What? In charge as in...WTF?"

Emily shook her ahead, as frustrated as Ron at being in the dark. "I don't know what that means or what she intends to do, but I suspect we'll find out soon. Is Vonnie here yet?"

"I didn't see her." Ron dispiritedly dragged his coat behind him and slumped into one of the leather-backed guest chairs facing her desk. "How's Henrietta, really?"

"I don't know." Emily closed her eyes and sighed. "God, I don't seem to know anything."

When Emily opened them again, she read anxiety and compassion in Ron's gaze and regretted making him worry. Time to leave the pity party behind. "All the tests weren't in last night, but the ICU doctors seemed to think her condition is very treatable. The last word I had, she was doing well." She looked at her watch, even though she knew what time it was. Past time she should have been working. "That was last night about seven. I'm sure if anything had happened since then, Derian—"

Ron pounced. "Derian? The Derian? Derian Winfield?"

"Is there more than one?" Emily asked calmly.

He crossed one leg over his knee and rested his elbow on his bent leg, eyeing her with speculative interest. "Derian. First names already. How did that happen?"

"I met her at the hospital," Emily said, not at all sure why she felt like she needed to explain. "She and Henrietta are obviously really close. She was very kind and I'm sure she would let me...us...know if there were any worrisome changes."

"What's she really like?" Ron asked. "I've only met her a couple of times, brief introductions, and she wasn't exactly friendly."

"She's very gracious and very...polite."

"Polite? What does that mean, polite?"

Emily could feel her cheeks heating. That was a stupid thing to say. Of course, what she'd wanted to say was chivalrous, which would've sounded even more inane. "Never mind. I just meant that she was very kind, and very helpful. She was clearly worried about Henrietta and nice enough to recognize that I was too."

"So you met her at the hospital."

"I said that."

"And talked with her."

"Yes, Ron, I talked with her."

"And..."

"And nothing." Emily tried not to bristle. "We were both there because of Henrietta. It was only natural that we talk, and it was a long day and we were both hungry, so we had dinner."

He straightened, his eyes narrowing. "Dinner. And when were you going to tell me about that?"

Never, and as soon as she thought it, Emily recognized how odd that was for her. She and Ron were good friends. Beyond just their professional bond, they socialized as often as Ron could convince her to. She'd even told him a little bit about Pam, and that was something she never shared. But she hadn't planned on telling him about Derian. What could she say? Nothing she wanted to put into words, not only because words might not do justice to exactly how unique the evening had been, but perhaps—like the fear of reducing the brilliance of a sunrise to the ordinary in a photograph—she didn't want to put words to the experience lest she fail in her description and tarnish the memory.

"It must've been a very interesting dinner," Ron said at length.

Emily blinked. "It was pleasant, and like I said, she was very gracious."

"If you say so. I just hope she's not too gracious when she comes in and boots Ms. Interloper Agnelli out from behind Henrietta's desk."

Emily's heart plummeted. "I don't think that's anything we should wait for."

❖

At eight thirty a.m. Vonnie appeared in Emily's doorway, arms folded over her chest and thunder in her eyes. "Ms. Agnelli wants all of the senior staff in the conference room now, please."

She spoke so stiffly her face barely moved with her words.

Emily recognized rage and hurried to her side. Keeping her voice low, she said, "Don't worry. Whatever's going on, we'll handle it until Henrietta returns."

"I'm not taking orders from her," Vonnie said through clenched teeth. "I swear, I'll quit first."

Emily grasped her arm. "You most certainly will not. None of us can get along without you, and I need you to help me sit on Henrietta when she comes back to work. It's going to take both of us to get her to slow down without realizing she is."

Vonnie's lips curved for an instant and she let out a long breath. "If I didn't love this place and most everybody in it, I swear…"

"I know, I know. It's horrible right now, but we'll get through it."

"We sure don't need any help from some outsider to handle things." Vonnie glanced over her shoulder and huffed. "She's asking for all sorts of confidential papers."

"Do you know her?"

Vonnie shook her head. "No, but she got a call from Mr. Winfield. I couldn't hear what she was saying before she shut the door, but they sounded chummy."

Emily hadn't expected Henrietta's brother to take an active role in the agency, certainly not so soon. She wasn't at all sure that was a good sign. "I'm sure someone will fill us in soon."

"Well, you'd best be going. The way she shoots out orders, if you're late you might not get through the day."

"As soon as this is done, I'm going over to the hospital. No matter what she has to say."

"Good enough. I was planning to go by on my lunch hour."

"We should probably take turns or something."

"That will work," Vonnie said. "In the meantime, I'll do a little more digging on our guest."

"Don't worry. Maybe this won't be as bad as we think."

She heard Vonnie's snort of disbelief as she hurried down the hall to the meeting. Like the library, this room retained its classic features, with tall, narrow windows framed with glossy dark woodwork, ornate ceiling moldings and antique light fixtures, and a long narrow oak table with a dozen chairs around it. Donatella Agnelli stood at one end, her back straight, her dark eyes sliding from one individual to the next, assessing in an unsmiling way. Ron and the other acquiring agents sat on one side, with a seat for her open next to Donatella, while Mark Ramsey from business, Brian Rood from marketing, and several interns occupied the other side of the table.

Donatella's gaze landed on one of the interns. "Who are you?"

The thin young man in the open-collared plaid shirt and khaki Dockers jumped to attention in his seat. "Aloysius Benson. I'm an intern in—"

"Out." She pointed toward the door with one long finger, the manicured nail sculpted in bloody red. "Is there anyone else in here not of managerial level?"

The other intern shot up and hastened to catch up to Aloysius.

Mark cleared his throat. "We like to have the interns present for these discussions. It helps them learn the workings of—"

"You can save that for the ad in *PW*. Their role is to get coffee, pull files, and pick up laundry if necessary. Let's not pretend otherwise."

Mark's neck turned purple, and Emily could actually hear his teeth grinding.

"As of today," Donatella said briskly, "I will be assuming the duties of the CEO. Division heads will report directly to me on all projects. I would like a summary of all ongoing by the end of the day. Who handles contract negotiations?"

Emily glanced at the other agents. "Each acquiring agent handles their own, after discussion with—"

"That accounts for the backlog." Donatella's full, scarlet-hued lips thinned. "From this point forward, all contracts in process will be referred to me for review. I will decide which ones are offered and the terms."

"I'm sorry," Emily said calmly, "but do you also intend to discuss terms with the authors? Or just—"

"If you have a manuscript you think might have value, bring it to me. I'll decide who we sign and take over from there." She waved a hand. "If you want to be the one making the happy phone call, be my guest."

"Excuse me," Emily said, proud that her fury didn't result in a scream. "I'm afraid I don't understand how you're going to determine terms when the agents are the ones making the recommendations based on our knowledge of—"

"As we're all getting to know each other," Donna said icily, her smile as sharp as a razor blade, "I'll explain myself. This time. Winfield's bottom line is barely acceptable, and it's not difficult to discern why. My cursory review reveals an alarming percentage of titles with slim to no profit margin. The only way to turn this poor performance record around is to be more selective in the works that we take on. While I appreciate that the acquiring agents may have a certain fondness for some works that won't, shall we say, pay for themselves, we are not a charitable organization. We want books that are guaranteed to sell. I can assure you, I'm quite capable of determining what those might be."

Ron raised his hand.

Donatella eyed him with an arrowed brow. "Yes, Mister—?"

"Elliott. Ron." He gave her his best guileless, I-never-make-trouble look. "So what I'm hearing is our expertise as acquisition agents is not going to play a role in deciding which authors we sign. What do you expect us to do, then?"

"I'm sure you're quite adept at wallowing through the slush pile. Get rid of the flotsam and jetsam. We only want the pearls." She lasered in on Mark. "I'd like to see the budget projections for the rest of the year in my inbox by eight tomorrow morning. That will be all for now."

She swiveled on a needle-thin, six-inch heel and shot out the door, sucking most of the air in the room out with her.

Finally Mark sputtered to life. "Who the hell—can she do this?"

Every head swiveled in Emily's direction, some faces outraged, some shocked.

"I don't know," she said for at least the hundredth time that morning, "but I'm going to find out."

CHAPTER TWELVE

Derian's phone rang as she was reaching for her wallet to pay the Lindy's bill. They'd managed to work their way through multiple refills of coffee and a second round of toast while staying away from the incendiary topics of Winfield Enterprises, Derian's relationships or lack thereof, and Aud's career. Derian checked the readout and her breath caught. "It's the hospital."

"I've got this," Aud said, grabbing the bill from Dere's other hand. "Go ahead—get that."

"Winfield," Derian said.

"This is Dr. Carter Armstrong. I'm one of the cardiothoracic surgeons consulting on Henrietta Winfield. I understand you're her medical surrogate."

"That's right. I'm her niece." Derian tamped down the suffocating swell of anxiety. "Is something wrong?"

"Your aunt's coronary arteries are extremely fragile, with substantial blockages in all three major tributaries. Unfortunately, the obstructions occur at multiple levels, making stenting impractical."

"What does that mean in terms of treatment?" Derian wondered why it took doctors and lawyers so many words to say the simplest things. Did they want to make communications difficult or was it just safer to be incomprehensible?

"She needs surgery, and my recommendation is to proceed immediately."

"Has something changed?"

"No, she's medically stable, but another insult could irrevocably damage substantial portions of the cardiac muscle, endangering her long-term prognosis."

Derian rose and started for the door, vaguely aware that Aud was following her. "I'm on my way. Is she awake?"

"Enough that she appears to understand what I've told her, but I don't believe she's capable of signing a surgical consent form."

Derian stepped into the street and waved for a cab. "When do you plan on operating?"

"As soon as you say I can."

"I want to see her first."

"The OR will be ready in forty minutes. I'd prefer not to wait."

Derian lunged in front of a cab and it screeched to a stop, spraying her trousers with the melt from yesterday's snow. "Don't worry, I'll be there." She yanked open the back door and jumped in. Aud, close on her heels, yanked the door shut.

"You crazy, lady?" the cabbie shouted, scowling at her in the rearview mirror. "I almost hit you."

"I knew you wouldn't. Get me to St. Luke's in fifteen minutes, and I don't care how you do it."

"I couldn't get you there in fifteen minutes if the streets were empty, and that isn't going to happen."

Aud leaned forward. "There's a hundred-dollar tip for you if you make it happen."

He shoved the car into gear and shot into traffic, squeezing into line in front of a bus. When he slammed on his brakes to narrowly miss hitting a black stretch limo, Derian and Aud were thrown back against the seat. Brakes screeched and horns blared.

"Maybe you should've offered him fifty," Derian muttered, as Aud, pressed to Derian's side, struggled to right herself. "We might actually get there alive."

"We'll get there. What did they say?"

Derian recounted the doctor's recommendations.

"Emergency surgery. God, Dere. Everything is happening so quickly."

"You know Henrietta. She'd want to go all out. And that's what we're gonna do."

"I'm really glad you're here." Aud gripped Derian's hand.

"So am I." Derian rested their joined hands on her knee. She'd forgotten what it was like to face uncertainty and fear with someone by her side. She thought back to the night before and Emily waiting so patiently for her, despite her exhaustion, despite that they'd been strangers. The memory warmed her. She needed to call Emily. As soon as she saw Henrietta, she'd call Emily.

The cab driver earned his tip even though it took him twenty-two minutes instead of fifteen. After handing the driver his cash, Derian jumped out and held the door for Aud. They hurried across the sidewalk, through the lobby, and to the elevators. Outside the ICU, Derian said, "I'll be out as soon as I know what's going on. I don't think I'll be long."

"That's all right, do whatever you have to do."

"You don't have to wait—you must have a busy day ahead."

Aud smiled, stood on her tiptoes, and kissed Derian's cheek. "Dere, don't be an idiot."

"Okay. Right. I'll work on that." Derian turned away.

"Dere," Aud said quietly behind her, "I'll have to call Martin."

Derian looked back over her shoulder. "Why?"

"Because he's her brother, because it's my job, and because it's the right thing to do."

"Do what you have to do." She slammed her palm into the red button and it thunked satisfyingly into the wall. The doors whooshed open and she strode in. Martin wouldn't care, and he wouldn't come. She put him out of her mind.

Immediately, a young woman with short red hair and maroon scrubs moved to intercept her. "I'm sorry, visiting hours aren't for—"

"I'm Derian Winfield. My aunt is going to have surgery soon. A Dr. Armstrong—"

"Oh, of course." She held out her hand. "I'm Dr. Carolyn Wayne, the intensive care fellow. I've been looking after your aunt during the night."

"Is she all right?"

"Yes. Come on, I'll take you down. She may or may not wake up while you're there, but she has been lucid for short periods."

"And the surgery is still scheduled?"

"The OR just called. They're sending for her now."

Derian's stomach tightened. She didn't know much about surgery, but she knew this was major. And Henrietta, always bigger than life, seemed smaller, diminished, lying so still beneath the light white sheets. Acid burned its way up her chest.

The resident disappeared as Derian leaned over the bed and took Henrietta's hand. Like yesterday, the metronomic beep of machines, the rhythmic scroll of the digital readouts, the tubes and vials and bags all heightened the surreal sensation of having been catapulted into an alien universe. "Hey, HW. It's Dere."

Henrietta lay motionless and Derian rubbed her hand between both of hers. Absolutely certain Henrietta was cataloging every word and action, even if she didn't show it, Derian reported in the no-nonsense, get-to-the-point way HW had drilled into her when she was young.

"So the doctors think the best way to get your heart tuned up and running optimally is to take you into the chop shop for an overhaul. Something about redirecting the fuel lines. The mechanic—a guy by the name of Armstrong—sounds like he knows what he's doing, so I told him to go ahead."

She cleared her scratchy throat. "I really need you back behind the wheel, HW. I think a lot of people do. This is no time to be sitting out the race."

A furrow formed between Henrietta's brows and her lids slowly opened. Her eyes wandered for an instant and then found Derian's. The haze gave way to sharp clarity. "Who's sitting out?"

Derian laughed, a great weight lifting from her heart. "Just making the most of a rest stop, were you?"

"How bad?"

"Fixable." Derian kissed her hand. "You're gonna have surgery in a few minutes."

"Huh. The agency—"

"Will be there when you get out of here," Derian said vehemently. "Don't worry about it."

"Emily—"

"Emily can take care of everything." Derian pushed a hand through her hair. "Hell, she's like a miniature of you."

"Not true. Softer." Henrietta's voice was a weak imitation of her usual full-bodied trumpet.

"That's what you want everybody to think," Derian scoffed, "but I know better."

"She'll…need…help. Martin—"

"To hell with Martin." Derian leaned closer. "Listen, stop worrying about the agency. It's been there a hundred years, and it'll be there a hundred more. But I'll do whatever I can, I swear."

"Good…always counted on you…"

Her eyes drifted close and Derian's heart twisted. She'd never wanted anyone to count on her, especially when she was afraid she'd disappoint. But she couldn't say no to Henrietta. "I swear."

❖

Emily didn't go back to her office but walked directly out of the conference room, down the stairs, and out into morning rush hour, pausing just long enough to grab her coat and purse from her office. She was too angry to think, and if she stayed she was likely to say something she'd regret to one of the staff. No matter how infuriating she found Donatella's unnecessary presence, she was one of the senior staff members and, as Henrietta's de facto second, she had to maintain order and keep the office running. If that meant putting up with Donatella Agnelli for the time being, that's what they'd all have to do until Emily could figure out some other plan. She was a planner. That's what she did. No matter what challenge confronted her, she didn't back down. She took her time, sorted out the options, made a plan, and made it happen.

If only she could talk to Henrietta. For the last half dozen years, Henrietta had been her sounding board, professionally and personally, and she hadn't realized until now just how much she counted on her. If Winfield was her family, Henrietta was the heart. No wonder they all felt so lost.

She cut through the crowd as if guided by radar, reflexively avoiding the slowly ambling groups of early-morning tourists, the commuters as focused as she on getting to their destinations, the throngs of street vendors setting up stands, and delivery people pushing handcarts across the sidewalk laden with cases of beer and boxes of food and all the other commodities that kept New York running twenty-four hours a day. When she finally reached St. Luke's, slightly out of breath but no longer on the verge of raging, she put Donatella from her mind. Time for all of that later. Now was only about Henrietta. As she pushed through the double doors into the bustling lobby, she wished as she hadn't in a long time that she could call her mother, just to hear the comforting welcome in her voice and know there was one place in the world everything would be all right. A wish as foolish as wanting to undo the past.

She closed her eyes in the elevator, waiting for the pain to settle into a dull ache in the recesses of her soul, as it always did. Composed again, she followed the crowd into the hall and turned right toward the intensive care unit. Out of nowhere, she thought of Derian. Did her directional dyslexia make something as simple as remembering which way to turn a challenge? What kind of effort did it take to navigate an increasingly complex physical world when faced with an inherent block to one's place in it? Derian would not want her sympathy, nor did she have any—only respect for a challenge met and conquered. She had never heard or seen one word about Derian's condition, which only spoke to how well she handled it, since nothing else about her life seemed free from public scrutiny. Emily flushed with unexpected pleasure, realizing Derian had shared something so private with her.

She glanced at her watch, not exactly sure when visiting hours started, but it didn't really matter. She'd wait.

"Emily?"

Emily peered into the waiting room. "Aud! Good morning." Even as she spoke, fear flashed through her. "God, is it Henrietta? Has something happened?"

Aud, looking stylish and composed, rose quickly and hurried toward her. "No, no, at least no emergency. But Dere got a call this morning at breakfast, and the surgeons want to operate right away. She's inside. I haven't heard anything more than that."

Emily struggled to decipher the barrage of words. Henrietta. Surgeons. Dere. Breakfast. This morning. Aud and Derian, together. And of course, why not. Grabbing on to her runaway thoughts, she edited the extraneous, what was none of her concern, what didn't— couldn't—matter.

"Is she worse? Is that why they want to operate so quickly?"

Aud shook her head. "I don't think there've been any new developments—but from what I could gather, when they reviewed all of the tests, they felt they couldn't wait."

"God," Emily whispered.

"Come on, sit down. Would you like some coffee? Tea?"

"What? No, I—"

"You're looking just a little shaky," Aud murmured.

"No, I'm all right. Just a shock." Emily pulled her fraying nerves together. "But I could certainly use some tea."

Aud said, "I'll get it. I need more coffee too."

"No, I'm really all right now. I just rushed over here, and I wasn't ready."

"Who is?" Aud muttered. "How do you take your tea," she went on, pouring hot water from a large carafe.

"I don't suppose there's milk?"

"Mini Moo."

"That'll do."

Aud returned with a simmering tea and a cup of coffee of her own and sat down next to Emily. "We've met before, at one of the Winfield meetings. It was brief, I think right after you started interning for Henrietta."

"I'm sorry," Emily said, "I don't remember, but it was very overwhelming at first—so many people I only met for a few seconds. I'm sure I've forgotten ninety percent of them."

Aud smiled wryly. "After a while you get the hang of facial imprinting. But you probably don't need that skill at the agency. It's kind of its own little universe—cloistered."

Emily laughed. "Well, it's hardly a monastery, but we are pretty close-knit. Everyone is very concerned about Henrietta."

"She inspires that kind of loyalty." Aud glanced in the direction of the ICU as if she were trying to see inside the barred doors. "I don't think there's anything else that could've gotten Dere back here that quickly."

"I imagine if you'd called her, she would have come."

Aud, in that moment every inch an attorney, riveted her with a piercing stare. "How so?"

"I could see last night that you're good friends," Emily said. "I think she would be very loyal to her friends."

A shadow stirred in Aud's eyes, a swirl of gray passing through the startling aquamarine.

"Loyal. She is. In fact, I don't think there's a single thing that means more to her than that."

"That rather says it all, doesn't it," Emily said. "Trust, truth, everything that matters."

"Exactly what Derian would say, if she ever really talked about those things," Aud said in a distant tone. Her attention refocused on Emily. "You have a pretty good read on her. I thought you just met?"

"We did, but"—Emily gestured to the room, the empty hall, the low hum of distant voices—"this place tends to strip away the surface very quickly, doesn't it. We spent quite a long time waiting yesterday with nothing to do but talk."

"I've known Derian all my life," Aud said. "She's not usually a sharer."

Emily smiled. "That doesn't surprise me. You grew up together?"

"Our *fathers* grew up together—prep school, college, even studied law together. Our families were like one big extended family. We're almost the same age, so we literally knew each other from the beginning."

"I didn't realize Mr. Winfield was also an attorney."

"Martin never practiced. My father, like my grandfather, is the Winfield attorney."

"And now you."

"And now me," Aud said softly.

"Did you always know you'd work with your father?"

"No," Aud said. "I had visions of a different path, but somewhere along the way, I gave in. Or maybe I just changed my mind."

"Would you happen to know Donatella Agnelli?" Emily asked.

"Donatella? Oh," Aud said, "did she show up at the agency already?" She gave a short laugh. "That sounds like Donatella. She doesn't waste time."

Emily stiffened. "Yes, she's there. We weren't expecting her."

"Martin instructed her to review the agency, since of course, Henrietta won't be available for an indefinite period of time."

"Review?"

"Keep things going," Aud said, probably being deliberately vague, the way lawyers often were.

"I see," Emily said, hoping she was wrong about Donatella's true agenda.

CHAPTER THIRTEEN

Emily got up to deposit her cardboard cup in the trash just as Derian walked in. She stopped abruptly, ambushed by a shock wave of sensation. She'd hoped to see her, but hadn't anticipated the impact. She actually shivered, and she wasn't the least bit cold. If anything, she felt feverish—everywhere. All her mental rationalizations as to why she shouldn't be captivated by Derian Winfield promptly disappeared with the first glance. Derian's face was set in tight lines, faint shadows bruising the skin beneath her eyes, but she was still every bit as arresting as she had been the night before. When she saw Emily, a spark ignited in her dark gaze and that intense laser-like focus fixed on her. Emily's instant desire to comfort her warred with her faltering sense of self-preservation. Caring for someone was safe enough, as long as one kept a firm grip on reality—wasn't it?

"Hello, Derian." Emily couldn't keep the pleasure at seeing her from her voice. So much for the firm grip on reality. She ought to move out of the way, let Derian go to Aud, who'd accompanied her, after all, but she couldn't escape the hold of Derian's gaze. Despite the clouds roiling in Derian's eyes, Emily grew even warmer, as if she'd stepped into a pool of sunshine on an overcast day. She couldn't give up that heat, even if she risked being burned. Not yet.

"Emily, you're here," Derian said, struck by a wave of relief that left her light-headed. She hadn't realized how much she'd wanted to see her until Emily's steady, compassionate voice enfolded her. She ought to be wary of such an atypical reaction, but she didn't have the energy to fight what she needed just then. Emily was here, and just seeing her helped ease some of the fear clawing at her insides. "I was going to call you."

Emily reached for her hand and stopped, as if an invisible wall stood between them. "How is she?"

"She was awake a bit. She sounded like herself, just really weak." Emily sighed. "Oh, that's great news."

Aud stepped beside them, running a hand down Derian's arm. "Is surgery still scheduled?"

Derian glanced at Aud, all her senses still attuned to Emily, as if a giant magnet aimed at the center of her chest drew her in that direction. "Yes, momentarily. They were preparing to take her to the OR just now."

Behind them, the ICU doors opened with a hydraulic rush. Two men and three women pushed a stretcher half the size of a hospital bed laden with monitors, bags of IV fluid, an oxygen tank, charts and papers, and mounds of other equipment. Henrietta was lost in the midst of that chaos, and the fear simmering in Derian's middle flashed into an outpouring of choking dread. She hurried to catch up to the rocketing stretcher, searching beneath the sheets and apparatus for Henrietta's hand.

"HW," she murmured urgently, "it's Derian. I'll see you in a while, okay?"

Henrietta didn't answer, but her fingers tightened on Derian's.

"You'll be fine." Derian's back brushed the wall as the team halted in front of the elevator. The doors opened and Derian searched desperately for a way to stop the madness.

"I'm afraid you can't come any farther. I'll keep you updated," the ICU fellow said.

"I love you," Derian said as Henrietta's hand slipped from hers and the team maneuvered the bed into the elevator. Derian stood in the doorway. "Where—"

The doors slid shut and she was left staring at nothing, more helpless than she had ever been in her life. She clenched her hands, a breath away from beating on the shiny metal surface. "Dammit."

Emily was suddenly at her side, grasping her arm. "Come on. They'll look for you in the waiting area."

Derian glanced at her, momentarily torn. She hated waiting, hated being helpless. She sucked in a breath. "Right. Right. You're right. Thanks."

Emily smiled. "No thanks required."

Aud had halted a way down the hall and fumbled in her shoulder bag. She pulled out her phone, looked at it, and frowned. "Oh, for God's sake."

"Problem?" Derian asked as she walked up.

Aud dropped the phone into her bag and stared at Derian, clearly weighing her options. She let out a long breath. "I'm going to have to go. I'm so sorry."

Derian grimaced, a chill rippling through her. "Let me guess. Martin has summoned you to the office. Did you tell him where you were?"

"Yes, of course."

"With me?"

"Dere," Aud said, an unusual pleading note in her voice. "He's my client and Henrietta's family. I had—"

"Never mind. You should go. You don't want to keep him waiting. He might have a company to buy or something equally important."

Aud glanced from Emily to Derian, her cheeks flushing. "Really, I'm sorry."

"Don't worry about it."

"You'll call me?" Aud pushed the down button on the elevator bank.

"Sure," Derian said wearily.

"I wouldn't go if I didn't have to, Dere. You know that."

Derian squeezed the bridge of her nose and nodded. "I know. It's okay."

Emily spoke into the sudden silence as the elevator doors closed. "I was going to stay, if you don't mind the company."

"I wouldn't mind at all." Derian smiled ruefully. "Sorry about the family drama. Martin knows how to push all my buttons."

"No need to explain," Emily said softly.

"I'm glad you're here. I hate waiting."

"I'd say you get used to it, but that's not true." Emily remembered well the barely tolerable panic when everything in the world spun out of control and one crisis piled on top of another. Time became a blur of adrenaline-fueled anxiety and stretches of soul-sapping waiting. She rested her hand lightly in the center of Derian's back. "Come on. Do you want some coffee?"

Derian grimaced and dropped into a dull orange fabric sofa against the wall. Two matching chairs flanked it, along with a faux-leather sofa on the opposite wall. The carpet was industrial-grade dark brown fabric. "No. I've had more than enough."

Emily sat next to Derian. "Have you had anything to eat?"

"Breakfast. I'm good."

Emily remembered. Breakfast with Audrey. She'd conveniently forgotten that. And she conveniently wasn't going to think about how they came to be together first thing in the morning, or what might've happened before breakfast, or last night, more accurately. She had, after all, turned down Derian's fairly subtle but unmistakable invitation to stay the evening before. An invitation that could only have meant time in bed. Of course she'd said no, and why wouldn't Derian look for other company? Especially with someone like Aud, an incredibly attractive woman with whom she shared a history and obvious deep affection. They were probably part-time lovers.

"What about you?" Derian asked.

Emily jumped. "Sorry? What about me?"

Derian gave her a curious glance. "Have you eaten?"

"Tea and a cookie about..." She shrugged and grinned sheepishly. "What feels like a million years ago, but I don't want to go anywhere."

"I bet I can find someplace to deliver."

Emily grasped Derian's arm when she reached for her phone. "No, really. I mean, I'm certain that you can. But I don't want you to. I'm too nervous to eat anyway. I'll be hungry later when we have good news."

Derian turned her hand over and Emily's palm slid easily over hers. Emily stared at their hands together. She couldn't. She didn't even know her. Even as she thought the words, she slid her fingers between Derian's and squeezed gently. "It really is going to be all right."

"Thanks."

"You're welcome." Emily reluctantly extracted her hand from Derian's. "Just sit and close your eyes for a while, then. It will help."

Derian glanced at her. "You sound like you've had some experience."

"I have," Emily said quietly.

Derian waited, watching her, and her silence, the unspoken

compassion in her gaze, brought the past rushing back before Emily
could throw up the barriers.

❖

"I was seventeen, just a few weeks before I was set to travel to
America for college."

As always happened every time Emily thought about it, or, rarely,
spoke of it, the present faded and she was back in her old bedroom
again, staring into her closet, trying to decide what to leave behind.
Living where it snowed would be fun—she hoped. At least it was a
good reason to shop, although she planned to do most of that once she
arrived. For the last month she'd scoured the university website, not
just for the classes she wanted to take—which was the most exciting
part—but also for activities of interest on campus and off, wondering
how well she'd fit in when she didn't know anyone. As intimidating as
the idea of being alone in a new place was at times, she still couldn't
wait to go. What an adventure, especially for her, the least adventurous
member of the family. The phone rang and she ignored it, taking out
three shirts, holding them up and then putting one back. She simply
couldn't take everything, and she *had* to take her books. She couldn't
live for four years without them.

Footsteps in the hall were followed by a brisk knock on her
partially open door. She glanced over at the butler. She started to speak,
but the look on his face strangled the words in her throat.

"A call for you, Miss May," Joseph said in an oddly tight, formal
tone. He held out the phone. His hand trembled. "It's the police."

Frowning, she took the phone. Shouldn't they be speaking to her
father, if something was wrong? He'd be home soon. An hour, if traffic
from the airport wasn't heavy. "Hello? This is Emily May. I'm afraid
my father—"

She remembered a man's voice, words that made no sense, her brain
suddenly slow and sluggish, trying desperately to discern the meaning
behind phrases that couldn't possibly apply to her or her life. Accident.
Injuries. Airlift. Hospital. Emergency. Emergency. Emergency.

She'd been so cold, frozen, for days and days.

Emily shivered and a warm hand closed over hers. She blinked,
and Derian was there, solid and real and warm. "My father had a

short meeting in Jakarta, and he and my mother tacked on a few days' vacation. My sister wanted to scuba dive and went with them. I begged off, I had too much to do getting ready for my trip to the States." She took a breath, the pain in her chest cutting her breath short. "They were in a small plane—it went down just short of the airfield. No one was ever able to determine why. The pilot and my..." She swallowed. "My mother was killed instantly."

"Emily," Derian murmured gently. "I'm so terribly sorry."

Emily blinked the searing pain of memory away. "A car came for me, from the embassy. My father worked for the foreign office. My father and my sister Pam were taken to the trauma center. I didn't know about my mother until I got to the hospital. Even then it took hours for anyone to tell me anything."

"I can't begin to imagine how horrifying that must've been."

"I don't have any other close family, and all my friends—" She shrugged. "Well, they were teenagers, and this was something no one knew how to deal with."

"So you were alone." Derian bit off the words, angry at something she couldn't change but wished desperately she had been able to. That she could have somehow been there, to share some of the pain, to shield her somehow from the horror.

"Of course, people came from my father's post to help me with the details, and looked after the bills and insurance, things like that. I don't remember. I didn't really even pay any attention. I stayed with my best friend's family at first."

She hadn't realized she was cold, hadn't realized Derian had moved, until Derian handed her a hot cup of tea. Her fingers were numb on the cup. "Thank you."

"You don't have to tell me the rest."

Emily smiled weakly. "I want to, if you don't mind."

"Of course not."

"My father never woke up. About ten days after the accident, he developed severe pulmonary complications. He died without ever knowing what happened, and part of me is almost glad. He would've so hated to be without Mother." She grimaced. "I don't know if that's selfish of me or not."

"There isn't a selfish cell in your body." Pain speared Derian's heart. She couldn't think of a single word that would be adequate solace, but Emily seemed to welcome her touch, and she needed to touch her just then. She clasped Emily's hand again, cradled it in hers.

"Pam was in a coma for six weeks," Emily said, her voice stronger now. "Severe brain contusion and, of course, many broken bones that eventually healed. But she..." She rubbed her eyes, brushed at the moisture there. "She suffered a severe brain injury and has never fully recovered. She's not communicative and requires twenty-four-hour care."

"In Singapore," Derian said.

"Yes. I delayed coming to the States until she was released from the hospital and settled. Everyone—the doctors and social workers— felt she would do better if she remained in familiar surroundings."

"And the long term?" Derian asked gently.

"Miracles happen, of course, and physically she's still young and strong, but..." Emily sighed. "She's likely to need a lifetime of round-the-clock care."

"Moving her here is out of the question?"

"The immigration issues aside, I believe she knows and responds to the staff who have taken care of her since the beginning," Emily said. "Plus, health care in Singapore is very good, if you can afford to pay for it. There was insurance money from my father, but, well, that doesn't last forever. I'm lucky I have a wonderful job that I love, and that allows me to earn enough to take care of her."

"So you help pay for her care," Derian said. "You're very remarkable."

"No, not at all. She's my sister." Emily flushed. "I can't tell you how many times I've wished that my life was less complicated. I was angry for a very long time, at everyone. But I had no one really to blame. That's the worst of it, having no one to blame."

"Say what you will," Derian murmured, "but I find you amazing."

As warmth spread through her, Emily marveled at how special Derian could make her feel. For the moment, she'd let herself believe it.

CHAPTER FOURTEEN

A woman in a blue scrub suit with a wrinkled paper mask hanging around her neck turned the corner into the waiting room and stopped midway, glancing from Emily to Derian. "Ms. Winfield?"

Derian shot to her feet. "Yes?"

"I'm Louella Vix, the head cardiac OR nurse. Dr. Armstrong wanted me to give you an update."

"Is everything all right?"

The nurse nodded. "Yes, the case is going perfectly. The doctor is just starting the last anastomosis. It will be at least another hour and a half before your aunt is headed to the recovery room, and midafternoon at the earliest before you'll be able to see her." She smiled. "I thought you might want to take a break. Go get something to eat. We have your number, don't we?"

"Yes," Derian said.

"Then if you're not here when the doctor finishes, we'll be sure someone calls you."

"We'll be here." Derian wasn't leaving anything to chance, and if positive energy played any role in fate, she intended to give it all she had.

"All right then. We'll be out as soon as we're finished."

She left as quickly as she had come and Derian turned to Emily. "Are you hungry?"

"Not really," Emily said. "These places always seem to take my appetite away."

Derian grimaced. "I know what you mean." She glanced around at the bare-bones décor in the bland, somewhat dingy room that seemed to have absorbed all the tragedies played out within its walls. "They try, I get that, but this place is two parts desolation, one part desperation, and the last part despair."

Emily regarded her with concern. "I think it might be a good idea if we take a walk."

"I'm sorry, you're right." Derian rubbed the headache between her eyes. "The waiting is getting to me. I hate being helpless."

"Believe me, I know."

Derian heard the pain creeping into Emily's voice and cursed herself inwardly. She wasn't the only one suffering. "And this has to be terrible for you. I'm sorry, it's not very sensitive of me to want to keep you here."

"I want to be here for Henrietta," Emily said, adding softly, "and if it's helping you, I'm glad."

"It helps more than you know," Derian murmured, "but I'm feeling pretty damn selfish right now. This has to be bringing back some terrible memories for you."

"I'm all right, really. Please don't worry about me."

"I know you're all right. You've convinced me you're tough," she teased gently and felt rewarded when Emily laughed, "but I believe I'll worry about you all the same."

"Just not too much," Emily chided, touched by Derian's tender tone and surprised by how readily she could accept comfort from Derian when she rarely could from anyone else. Derian's sympathy and understanding strengthened her, rather than making her feel small and diminished. She'd worked so hard to be neither. She rose, and in an impulsive reversal, took Derian's arm and tugged her toward the hall. "Come on, let's get outside for a little while."

Gratefully, Derian let herself be guided to the elevators. Giving up control didn't come naturally, but with Emily it was easy. The tightrope she'd been teetering on since she'd gotten the phone call from the surgeon gave way to solid ground for the first time all day. "Thanks."

"You're welcome," Emily said. "If you need anything, anytime, just let me know."

Derian regarded her so seriously, for so long, Emily blushed. She wished she could read Derian's mind at that moment and was happy Derian couldn't read hers, especially since she'd suddenly started thinking about the kiss. Derian couldn't imagine she meant that kind of help, could she?

The elevator doors opened onto the bustling lobby and saved her from worrying about how Derian might have interpreted her offer. Once outside, in the sunlight, away from the scent of antiseptic, disease, and death, they strode toward Central Park, dodging through the crowds while managing to stay close together. When the throngs got too heavy and threatened to separate them, Derian curled Emily's hand through the crook of her arm as naturally as if they'd walked together a hundred times.

When they passed a street vendor roasting nuts, Derian slowed. "You know, I think I probably need to put something in my stomach. Cashews?"

"I confess," Emily said, "I'm a little bit addicted to the honey-roasted ones."

Derian grinned. "Done."

She purchased two bags, handed one to Emily, and they walked on.

"When my mother died," Derian said after a few moments of silence, "I was lucky. I had Henrietta to help me make sense of it all."

"I envy you that," Emily said softly. "Neither of my parents had siblings, so our family was a pretty small unit. My father was often away on business, or when he wasn't, he was preoccupied with it. He loved us, I know that, but he wasn't always present for us. My mother and my sister were my world."

"Then we're even—I envy you that." Derian shrugged. "Of my parents, I was closest to my mother. I loved both of my parents as children do, looking to them for support and protection and praise." She laughed, with no humor in her voice. "Although there was precious little in the praise department."

"Parents sometimes have an odd way of showing their affection," Emily ventured. "And some just don't see their children, or see the worth of them. There's certainly no excuse for holding something against you that wasn't your fault."

Derian cut her a glance, a wry smile softening the tight line of her jaw. "You're very kind and very perceptive, and I appreciate you taking my side. I suppose the fault lies on both sides—I wasn't a particularly appreciative child, at least not of the things that my parents could provide." She lifted a shoulder. "Security, and good schools, and not wanting for any of the physical things. I realize I'm very lucky, and it's totally undeserved. I was born into safety and wealth." She laughed again and shook her head. "And complaining about my childhood now makes me sound like something of an ass."

"Not at all. I don't think any child appreciates the circumstances of their birth, whether it's difficult or not, privileged or not, and every child has the right to feel loved."

"Yes, well, I have no complaints. My mother didn't exactly have a great time of things either. She'd been groomed her whole life to be a man's wife, and she was that first. My father's disappointment at not having a son, but a daughter who didn't even measure up, made their relationship pretty rocky."

They stopped when they reached the entrance to Central Park. The weather was still cold enough to dissuade all but the most stalwart to stay still for very long, and Derian pointed to an unoccupied bench. "Are you too cold to sit? I promise to stop moaning about my horrible past. I've survived quite well and Martin must be much happier now, with a son and a young wife to give him what he always wanted."

Emily caught back a protest. Derian's experiences seemed terribly unfair to her, but she appreciated Derian wanting to make light of them. "I have to confess, I'm not quite ready to go back to that room. But I just want to say I think your father is the one who's lost the most by not seeing what an accomplished, successful woman you've become."

Derian stared. "Thank you. Not many people would agree with you."

"What other people think doesn't matter, though, does it?" Emily said as they sat side by side, finishing their cashews. "What about you?"

Derian raised a brow. "What do you mean?"

"Are you satisfied?"

"With what I've made of my life? Sure," Derian said instantly, wondering as she did about the truth of her words. "I'm successful as far as making the right choices and backing the right teams, and I'm damn good at the tables."

Emily laughed. "So I understand."

"As I said, I have no complaints."

Something about their shared waiting, and their shared worry, made for disclosures Emily never would've made otherwise. Knowing

Derian loved Henrietta in the same way she did made her bold. "What about the other things in life? Do you want a family?"

"God, no. What would I do with a wife and children? What would I do *for* them," she said, voicing thoughts she rarely entertained. "I'd probably be no better at child rearing than my parents, and I have no desire to saddle some poor kid with the Winfield legacy."

"What makes you think that you would parent the way your parents did? I think you're incredibly perceptive and you obviously love Henrietta, and what is more important to raising children than understanding and caring?"

"Nothing," Derian said, fearing Emily gave her far too much credit and damn certain she could never measure up to the kind of unselfish loyalty Emily displayed toward her sister. Wanting to deflect the conversation, Derian countered, "And how about you? What are your long-term goals besides ruling the literary world?"

Emily laughed. "Really, I can't see myself settling down for quite a long time. I work—well, I work when Henrietta works, and you know how that is."

Derian frowned. "I do know, and we're going to have to do something about that when she recovers."

"I agree with you totally. Vonnie and I will do our best, but it wouldn't hurt if you put in a word for her to slow down too."

Derian winced. "I think that might result in shooting the messenger, but I'll try." She tapped a fingertip against Emily's chin. "And you are pretty good at deflecting questions. What do you want besides work in your life?"

Emily's face flushed from the brief touch and a thrill of excitement raced through her. She could never remember being so sensitized to another's physical presence. She'd held hands with women, kissed women, been in bed with several, and she couldn't remember her heart beating so fast or the electricity shooting beneath the surface of her skin from the most casual of touches. Concentrating on the conversation was difficult, but she grasped on to the question to avoid thinking about Derian's hands on her. "When and if I'm in a position to provide for a family, or at least substantially contribute, I'd like to get married and have kids. I don't see that anytime soon."

"Because of Pam?" Derian asked gently.

"That's partly it, since I know I would be bringing substantial financial responsibilities to any kind of long-term relationship," Emily said, "but most of it is because right now my goals are career oriented."

"Well, I imagine any woman who loved you would understand about Pam, and no one worthy of you would want you to do anything differently."

Emily's throat tightened. "Thank you."

"How often do you get home to Singapore?"

"Two or three times a year," Emily said, "when I take my vacation time."

"I'm sure Henrietta would give you all the time you need, vacation time or not."

"Oh, she would," Emily said slowly, "but as much as I want to see Pam, it's always difficult."

"When's your next trip?"

"Well," Emily sighed, "I was planning to go at the beginning of July, right after we get the summer releases all tucked away. Now, though—"

"Listen," Derian said, "Henrietta won't be back to work by then, but I'm sure the agency will run without you for—what—two or three weeks?"

Emily laughed. "I'm quite sure it can. Vonnie could probably run everything, or most of it, by herself at this point."

Derian chuckled. "You're absolutely right."

"Although now, until my visa situation is straightened out, I don't want to leave the country."

"Sorry?" Derian frowned. "What do you mean?"

"Oh, it's just some kind of snafu," Emily said quickly. She hadn't intended to bring her problems to Derian. "It'll get sorted out as soon as things settle down a bit."

"What kind of snafu?" Derian said insistently.

"Henrietta was just telling me, right before it happened," Emily said, "there may be difficulty renewing my visa. Immigration policies have gotten a lot more restrictive, and unless…*until* the labor application is approved, I'm a little bit in limbo."

"Who's handling it?"

"The agency's attorneys, but I confess, I don't actually know who." Emily gasped. "Oh God, I hope it's not Donatella."

"Donatella?" Derian frowned. "What has she got to do with anything?"

"Oh, do you know her?"

Derian snorted. "Donatella has been around as long as I have, I think. She's something of a hatchet man for my father—she takes care of trimming the fat, in his words—weeding out personnel and retooling acquisitions that aren't producing." She made a wry face. "I used to think there was something personal between my father and her, and maybe there is, but that's not something I really want to think about. So what about her?"

Emily had a hard time imagining Donatella Agnelli intimate with anyone, but then, her idea of intimacy was a lot more than just sex. "It's really not something you need to be worried about right now."

Derian studied her for a long moment. "Why is that?"

"You're here for Henrietta, and once she's well, your job is over. The agency isn't your problem."

"How do you know Donatella?" Derian said, ignoring Emily's attempts to change the subject.

"She showed up this morning at the agency and says she's in charge."

"Martin's idea, I'm sure," Derian said.

"I didn't think to ask exactly where she came from. She was already ensconced in Henrietta's office when I arrived, and it didn't occur to me that she might not belong there."

"The lines of command in Winfield Enterprises are pretty tangled, but Martin and Henrietta are siblings, as you know, and inherited all of the family's holdings when my grandparents passed on. Henrietta didn't care to be involved, so I understand, in anything other than the agency. She'd already been there from the time she got out of college. In order to keep the peace, my father went along with it, and they basically separated the business interests between the two of them."

"Formally?" Emily asked.

"I don't know. I never had any reason to ask. What's she been doing so far?"

Emily grimaced. "She's settled into Henrietta's office, and as of this morning, plans to take over all the major decisions."

"Dammit," Derian said. "The last thing Henrietta's going to need while she's recovering is some kind of fight over who's in charge at the agency."

"Maybe it won't come to that."

"Nothing Martin and Donatella might do could be good." Derian balled up her cashew wrapper and stuffed it in her pocket. "Aud might know what's going on, if she'll tell me. She doesn't handle the agency's legal business, since Henrietta was smart enough to see that as a conflict of interest, but all the Enterprises attorneys know one another."

"I'm sorry to drag you into this."

"Henrietta would want you to run things in her place."

"I don't know—"

"I do," Derian said with conviction. "And we'll need to see that that happens. I'll call Aud later today."

"You've got more than enough to worry about. At least let it wait until—"

Derian touched a finger to Emily's lips. "Let me do this for you. It's nothing compared to what your being here means to me."

Emily's heart raced as her eyes met Derian's. "Would it do me any good to argue?"

Derian's thumb whispered over her lips.

"None at all."

CHAPTER FIFTEEN

D r. Carter Armstrong sauntered into the waiting room a little before noon, looking as polished and superior in a set of rumpled scrubs as he would have in a ten-thousand-dollar suit. His coal-black hair with just the slightest hint of white at the temples was perfectly in place, showing no signs of the surgical cap he'd been wearing when Derian had talked to him right before Henrietta had been taken to the operating room. He zeroed in on her and flashed a practiced smile. "We're done. She's fine."

Derian impulsively wrapped an arm around Emily and pulled her close. After a second of head-spinning relief, she met the surgeon in the middle of the room. "Where is she?"

"In a recovery room, right now. We like to keep the patients close to the OR for a few minutes after we close, just in case—although I don't expect any problems."

"Can you tell me what you did?"

He gave her a look as if she might not understand what his greatness had accomplished, but he lifted a shoulder and acquiesced. "As I explained earlier, her coronaries showed multiple levels of blockage, probably as a result of some long-term hyperlipidemia—abnormal fat metabolism—and hypertension. We jumped four grafts to reperfuse the cardiac muscle. Her signs all look great right now."

"And long-term?"

"Anything can happen, of course, but barring complications and if she sticks to her rehab program, watches her diet, and accepts some reasonable modification in her lifestyle, she should do fine."

"Define reasonable modification," Derian said.

"Well, her hypertension appears to have been poorly controlled up until this time, and she'll need to adhere to whatever program the medical management team institutes. We always suggest cardiac patients moderate their work schedule and reduce stress." He must have read the disbelief in Derian's face as he shrugged. "Honestly, the future is up to your aunt—we can only make recommendations. But the surgery was a success."

"All right, thanks," Derian said.

"Not at all. The nurses will let you know when she's been moved to the cardiac care unit." He turned and walked away.

Derian had a feeling that was the last she would see of him, but if he'd done his job, she was fine with that. She turned to Emily, who'd come to stand beside her. "I didn't know she had any health problems, and I should have."

Emily smiled softly. "You don't really think she would've told anyone, do you?"

Derian blew out a breath. "If I'd been around she might have."

"Derian," Emily said, "none of this is your fault. You couldn't have changed this even if you'd been here. Henrietta is Henrietta. You know that."

A muscle jumped in Derian's jaw, and she nodded perfunctorily. "You might be right, but I still feel like I let her down."

Emily grasped her arm. "You didn't. You're here, and that's what she needs."

"I think you're a lot more of what she needs than me," Derian said almost to herself. "When I'm not here, you're the one she'll be counting on."

Emily flinched inwardly, Derian's words a cold dose of reality. Of course Derian wouldn't be staying. She might be leaving at any time. Emily squared her shoulders. "Once Henrietta recovers, she is going to get on with her life, and she'll expect you to get on with yours."

"Expect me to disappear again, you mean."

Emily jammed her hands on her hips and gave Derian a look. "You don't strike me as the kind of woman who beats herself up over things that can't be helped. Since you seem to be determined to kick yourself, I think you need to take a break. Get something to eat and probably some sleep."

Derian grinned wryly. "Diagnosis and treatment plan appreciated,

Doctor, but I'm going to stay here until I've seen Henrietta. And I promise to stop whining."

Emily softened. "You can whine all you want, but you still need to take care of yourself." She glanced at her watch. "I'd like to stay to see her, but I should get back to the agency. Vonnie probably needs some help, and she wanted to come over here on her lunch hour."

Fleeting panic coursed through Derian's chest, a sensation she could never recall having before. She didn't want Emily to go. "When will I see you again?"

Emily's brows drew down. "I'm sorry?"

"Look," Derian said, raking a hand through her hair, never having been so off balance in her life. "This is crazy. Every time I see you, we're in the middle of some kind of crisis. You've been keeping me company, hell, keeping me steady, and I want—" Derian broke off. Emily was staring at her like she was a little crazy, and she was. She didn't know what she was trying to say, what she wanted, but she couldn't shake the feeling if she let Emily walk away, she'd regret it forever. "I don't know how well I would've done through all of this without you being here."

"You would've done just fine," Emily said gently. "But I'm glad I was here, and you've helped me a lot too." She paused, felt a tremendous wave of gratitude swell within. "I've talked to you about things I've never talked to anyone about. It helps. I didn't realize how much I needed that."

"Have dinner with me," Derian said.

Emily laughed, surprise and disbelief in her voice. "What?"

"Tonight. When everything has quieted down, and we're not both scared and anxious. To celebrate Henrietta's successful surgery." Derian took Emily's hand. "To get to know each other. Please."

The idea was mad—mad and wonderful, and Emily broke ranks with her habitual caution, refusing to second-guess the excitement pulsing through her. "All right, under one condition."

Derian's eyebrow winged up. "Oh?"

"This time, I'll make dinner."

"You mean, actually cook it?"

Delighted at the consternation on Derian's face, Emily laughed. "Yes. You have heard of that?"

"Rumors, but I've never actually witnessed it."

"Then you're in for a treat. Seven o'clock."

"I can't wait." Derian grinned, and the worry and fear in her expression gave way to the rakish charm Emily had glimpsed when they'd been alone in Derian's apartment—when Derian had been unabashedly naked, and unabashedly seductive.

Emily swallowed. What was she doing? Why did she have to ask? Emily gave her the address and her phone number. "But if you're too tired, or if something comes up—"

Derian stroked her finger along the edge of Emily's jaw, stilling her. "Nothing will come up. I'll be there. Red wine or white?"

"Red," Emily said softly, looking into Derian's eyes. For an instant, nothing else in the world mattered, only the pull of Derian's gaze. Warning bells rang, and she ignored them. All her life she'd been careful and cautious and responsible. She regretted none of it, and she would not regret this moment, when she chose something because her heart urged her to.

"Then tonight."

"Tonight," Derian whispered.

❖

"Any news?" Ron asked the instant Emily entered his office and plopped onto the sofa across from his desk.

She leaned her head back, closed her eyes, and let out a long breath. "Surgery is over, successful, and she's in recovery."

Ignoring the nearby chair, he sat on the coffee table across from her, his elbows on his knees, and his chin resting in his hands. Leaning even closer, he muttered, "Thank God. At least something around here is going right."

She opened her eyes, suddenly more tired than she could remember being in days. She gazed at him. "How bad is it?"

"I can't imagine it could get any worse. Well, I can, but I don't want to." Shuddering, he glanced toward the door as if checking that no one was listening. "Donatella has been cloistered behind closed doors all morning, but every now and then edicts emerge via email. She's already terminated four pending approvals and cut Jeremy's marketing budget by thirty percent."

"That will gut our summer title promotions," Emily said. "We've got co-op agreements with publishers for author tours. We have to have the funds to cover those."

"Who's going to tell her that?"

"I guess that would be me." Emily rubbed her eyes. "God, this is terrible. How's everybody holding up?"

"Everybody's still pretty much in shock. But if this goes on—"

"It won't," Emily said emphatically. She needed to stem the decline in morale right now. "Henrietta will be well enough to delegate responsibility in a few days, and whomever she puts in charge—"

"What are you talking about? That will be you, of course."

Emily wasn't so sure, especially with Donatella already in residence. If her visa status remained uncertain, she might even be seen as expendable. The thought was paralyzing, and she forced it into a dark corner of her mind. She had to deal with what was actually happening, not what might happen. Still, with the exact timing of Henrietta's return uncertain, she had to consider the long term. "Bill might be a better choice."

"No way," Ron said. "I like Bill, you know that, but he's terrible at delegating, plus he's—" He paused as if searching for a diplomatic term. "He's got tunnel vision in terms of the marketplace. If it were up to him, the only thing we'd ever represent would be best-seller potentials, and that's not us!"

Emily couldn't argue. Bill would probably be one of the few agents who agreed with Donatella's assessment as to what kind of titles they should carry. "Right now, none of that matters. We're going to have to deal with Donatella."

He made a face. "What about Henrietta's niece?"

"Derian?" Emily's heart actually raced just saying her name. Another thought she pushed aside.

"Is she likely to step in?"

"No," Emily said. "She's made it very clear she has no interest in the business."

"Maybe she'll change her mind," he said hopefully.

"I wouldn't count on that," she said as much to herself as to him. One thing she knew for certain, Derian's stay was only temporary.

❖

Restless and agitated after Emily's departure, Derian walked outside for some air. She bought a hot dog from a vendor on the corner and ate it standing out of the way of the crowds. When she finished, she called Aud.

"Dere?" Aud said. "Everything all right?"

"Surgery is done. She's doing okay. I haven't had a chance to see her yet."

"That's great news. Are you still at the hospital?"

"Yeah, I'm gonna stay here for a couple of hours still."

"I can't get away, but I should be free by dinnertime. I could meet you—"

"Ah, I'll be tied up later." Derian smiled to herself, thinking about dinner with Emily. The anticipation kindled the kind of excitement she usually only experienced before a big race or a high-stakes gamble at the tables.

"Oh," Aud said with a hint of surprise. "Okay, then."

"What's going on at the agency, Aud?" She expected the silence, but that didn't prevent the quick flare of annoyance. "Look, I know Donatella is there, and that's Martin's doing. Don't tell me you don't know."

"That's not my territory," Aud said evasively.

"Bullshit. You're your father's right-hand man, and *he's* Martin's personal attorney. Don't pretend you don't know what the long-range plans are."

"I swear, Derian," Aud said, "I don't know exactly what Martin has planned. Someone has to take over at the agency in Henrietta's absence. It's perfectly reasonable that Martin wants someone he knows to have decision-making power."

"You mean someone who will institute his agenda. There are qualified people at the agency who can run things in Henrietta's stead. We both know that."

"We don't actually." Aud made an exasperated sound. "Look, as much as I love Henrietta, she and Martin aren't all that different. She keeps a lot of information about the agency to herself. As to how qualified anyone else is to take her place, that remains to be seen."

"Emily May is Henrietta's choice."

"Another thing we don't know, and even if that's the case, Emily is—"

"Experienced, and personally trained by Henrietta. Come on, Aud. The agency is a tiny part of Winfield Enterprises, and the only reason Martin even cares about it is because he and Henrietta have been feuding their whole lives."

"As I said," Aud said coolly, "I don't presume to know Mr. Winfield's plans."

"Oh, for God's sake," Derian muttered. "Look, just get Donatella out of there for now. Let Emily run things until Henrietta is through the postoperative period, and then—"

"That's not going to happen."

Derian stiffened. "Why not?"

"Derian, you haven't cared to be involved in any of the business matters your entire life. I'm glad that you're here, and I know that Henrietta needs you, but this is not your concern."

Anger welled in Derian's chest, even as she knew Aud had a point. She had no right to make demands. And she had no one to blame for that except herself.

"Look," Aud said, sounding tired, "I understand your concerns. Emily May might not even be at the agency in a few more months, and until we get a reasonable transition team in place, Donatella is your father's choice."

"Wait a minute, back up. What do you mean, Emily might not be there?"

"Martin wants to downsize, and Emily isn't even a permanent resident. Even if her visa is renewed, and right now, that's up in the air, the board is not going to approve her taking over as head of the agency. Besides, she's not family, and you know how things work."

"And Donatella is?"

"Donatella at least has your father's blessing."

"And we all know how much that counts for."

"Derian—"

"Never mind, Aud. I don't know why I forgot whose side you're on. I seem to keep making that mistake."

"Dammit! If you'd bothered to be here once in a while—"

"You're right," Derian said. "But I'm here now."

She disconnected, dropped the phone into her pocket, and walked back into the hospital. Maybe the smartest thing to do was stay out of the way, let Martin do what he wanted to do for years—turn the agency into a moneymaking enterprise or kill it altogether. She'd opted out of that battlefront years ago. Ran from it, if she was being honest. Once Henrietta was on the road to recovery, she could get back to her life. She slowly climbed the stairs, her footsteps echoing in the silence of the stairwell. Back to her life. She couldn't think of a single thing about it that she missed.

CHAPTER SIXTEEN

At 6:59, Derian rang the buzzer next to the small white rectangular tab with the name *E. May* typed in bold and tugged down the sleeves of her navy blazer. She'd paired it with dark jeans, a pale gray shirt, and black boots, hoping casual was a good choice for dinner in. She had an instant of uncertainty and laughed in wry amusement. Since when did she worry about impressing? A moment later, the intercom crackled to life. "Yes?"

"It's Derian."

"3C. Come on up—my door is unlocked."

The small vestibule grew quiet until a few seconds later a long, low buzz sounded from the double interior doors and Derian let herself in to a narrow foyer leading to a set of stairs at the far end. The mosaic tile floor was mud-free despite the recent storms, the waist-high dark wood wainscoting and curved banister glowing with polish with only the occasional scuff mark, and the stairs free of trash and dirt. A nice apartment building, one of maybe five or six stone edifices in a row on a narrow side street. She climbed to the third floor, found apartment C, turned the brass knob, and she let herself into a softly lit living room in a high-ceilinged, open-plan apartment. Across the room, Emily worked at an island flanked by several tall bar stools that separated the small galley kitchen from the main seating area just to Derian's right. Beyond the living area, floor-to-ceiling windows opened onto a view of a small pocket park she'd passed when the Uber driver let her off at the corner. At the opposite end of the room, other doors presumably led to the bedroom and bath. Focused spots illuminated the kitchen workspaces, leaving the rest of the large apartment in muted shadows cast by floor lamps with tasseled ivory shades. The mix of old-world elegance and modern efficiency seemed a perfect reflection of Emily.

"Hi," Derian said, her heart beating rapidly for some reason.

"You're right on time." Emily greeted her with a bright, easy smile, looking sexy and relaxed in a black shirt with small iridescent flowers scattered over the front, body-hugging jeans, and strappy black shoes with low heels. Her hair was caught back with a plain tie, leaving a thick tail at her nape.

The heavy feeling Derian'd been carrying all afternoon since leaving the hospital fled her chest. "You sound as if you thought I wouldn't be here."

Emily laughed. "I did no such thing. If I'd been the slightest bit worried, I wouldn't have done all this prep." She gestured to the counter and an array of vegetables and other foods in a line of small, hand-painted ceramic bowls. She resumed expertly slicing vegetables on one of several cutting boards. "Is that the red I see?"

Derian hefted the Château Mouton in its unassuming paper bag. "As promised."

"Would you open it, and we can have a little while I cook."

"Excellent idea." Derian carried the bottle to the counter, removed it from the bag, and opened it with a corkscrew Emily handed her.

Emily raised an eyebrow. "Where did you find that?"

"Ah, I had the wine steward at the Dakota procure it for me. Will it work?"

"Oh, I should think so." Emily shook her head at the extravagance, secretly flattered by Derian's efforts toward making the evening special, and went back to chopping.

Derian set the red aside to breathe and settled onto the high-backed stool to watch Emily work. Her hands flashed, the gleaming knife blade a blur, and small piles of colorful vegetables appeared as if by magic. Although the area was small, it was easy to see it had been laid out with care by someone who actually intended to use it. The range was a new compact high-end commercial model. Gleaming pots and pans sat on several burners and hung from a copper rack affixed to the ceiling. She watched as Emily efficiently assembled items into a roasting pan and slid it into the oven. "Looks like you have a calling. Ever considered being a chef?"

"I've always loved to cook. But the books captured me first." Emily nodded toward the wine. "Would it be a sin to try that prematurely?"

"I'd say it's breathed enough. Besides, there can be no sin in shared indulgence."

Emily regarded her silently, and Derian held her gaze. She couldn't be anywhere near Emily without that stirring of excitement, and tonight she didn't want to avoid it. The last days had been hell. Meeting Emily was the only good thing to come out of the whole nightmare, and for a few hours, she intended to bask in the pleasure. Derian poured wine into the two glasses Emily set on the counter, then lifted hers and held it out. "To Henrietta."

"To Henrietta." Emily lightly touched her glass to Derian's. A high, clear chime of crystal rang out. "Thank you for calling me this afternoon."

"Not at all." After Derian had visited Henrietta in the recovery room, she'd called Emily at the agency with an update. Henrietta was stable, but not yet awake. She wouldn't remember Derian visiting, holding her hand, informing her that all was well. That didn't matter. She'd been there, as she'd needed to be—for herself as much as Henrietta. "Tomorrow she'll be more aware and you can visit."

"I hope so."

"So," Derian said as the warm, sharp taste of the wine teased all her senses, "who taught you to cook?"

Emily made a wry face. "I always wanted to spend time in the kitchen when I was young, but my parents thought trailing after the cook was unseemly. They didn't mind, however, when I took cooking lessons as soon as I was old enough." She shrugged, her expression distant. "I stole off to the kitchen at the embassy as often as I could when they were entertaining foreign dignitaries, trying to master as many national dishes as I could."

"You must have quite an eclectic repertoire, then."

"I don't get much chance to use it these days." Emily shook off whatever memory had momentarily clouded her expression. "I hope you like Asian fusion."

"I enjoy food, but I must admit, after hundreds of meals served in restaurants and hotels, the allure fades."

"Well, perhaps we can reinvigorate that."

"Perhaps." Derian sipped her red. "That and other diminishing pleasures."

Emily flushed and quickly looked away. Derian smiled inwardly, recognizing she wasn't the only one feeling the pull of attraction. Ordinarily she wouldn't resist the draw, especially not when the woman in question obviously shared her desire. This time, though, she needed to proceed a great deal more carefully. Emily was no innocent and certainly not a child, but despite her apparent openness to mild flirtation, she *had* already weighed in on the subject—and her answer had been no. Still, people were known to change their minds, and Derian enjoyed the gentle chase. And she liked that nothing beyond dinner had been suggested. She didn't want any of her time with Emily to resemble the empty, and ultimately forgettable, evenings she'd spent with other women. She didn't want to play games, she didn't want to forget the night as soon as it had passed. She simply wanted to enjoy the company of a bright, beautiful, exciting woman.

"Is something wrong?" Emily asked quietly.

"No," Derian said quietly. "In fact, everything is surprisingly all right."

❖

They ate at a small round table covered by a snowy white linen cloth in a shallow alcove off the living area. Three tall narrow windows gave a view down onto the park. Emily had opened one of the windows and surprisingly warm evening air wafted in, carrying the sounds of the city.

"It's nice," Derian said, "seeing a bit of green."

"Not exactly the kind of view you're used to," Emily commented.

"No," Derian said, her eyes on Emily. "Actually, far better."

Emily blushed. "Where were you staying in Monte Carlo?"

Derian grinned briefly at the deft deflection. Emily's shy blush just made her want to tease her more. "Hôtel de Paris."

"Ah, yes. That overlooks the racecourse on the plaza."

"You've been there?"

"Only vicariously."

"You're very well informed, then."

Emily laughed. "I don't travel frequently, but I enjoy reading pretty much everything. And I already confessed to being a celebrity addict."

"I would imagine for a woman like you, that would not be satisfying for very long."

Emily poured tea from an ornamental pot into small glazed cups. "Why is that?"

Derian tried the tea. It was surprisingly fragrant but not the least bit cloying. Full and aromatic. "I've never been a tea drinker, but I think this might persuade me differently."

"It's practically the national drink where I grew up. High tea is one of the customs left over from colonialism that is still embraced in Singapore. I enjoy coffee, but I find it's only good when taken sparingly. Like so many things."

"Not necessarily a popular sentiment."

"And you're dissembling again." Emily pointed a finger. "What do you mean, a woman like me?" Emily wasn't fishing for compliments. She was genuinely curious. Oh, she wanted Derian to be interested. She wasn't so self-deluding as to deny that. Having the interest of a beautiful woman was not something she could ignore or pretend she didn't want. But she so rarely wondered how others thought of her, she couldn't fathom what clues—or what secrets—she'd exposed.

"A woman of substance."

"Oh," Emily said with mock horror. "That sounds ghastly. Stodgy and boring and—you make me sound like a stereotypical librarian."

Grinning, Derian looked around and tilted her chin in the direction of an entire wall of floor-to-ceiling bookcases, every shelf filled and many overfilled with books. "Observe."

"Of course I love books," Emily said. "Why on earth would I do what I do if I didn't?"

Derian took Emily's hand and gave it a playful shake. "I've never in my life known a librarian who looks like you."

"Nice try, but you obviously haven't met many librarians. Contrary to the stereotype, many of them are far more attractive and interesting than me."

"I doubt that," Derian murmured.

Emily's playful protests flew from her mind. She'd never known she was so susceptible to flattery, but every time Derian looked at her as if she were seeing someone beautiful and intriguing, Emily was

test

transported into a world of possibility she'd never imagined. She felt sexy and desirable and desirous. She swallowed. "You have a way of making me forget myself."

Derian played her thumb over Emily's knuckles. "Is that a bad thing?"

"I really don't know. It's unique."

"Good. I'd hate to be ordinary where you're concerned."

"Oh, believe me. You're anything but that."

"And to answer your question," Derian said with unusual seriousness, "I already know you're strong and independent and determined. I also know you're kind and loyal and generous. All of those things to me equal substance. You wouldn't find a steady diet of parties, cocktail conversation, and the constant striving for greater and greater thrills very interesting."

"And is that what your life is like?"

Derian sighed, glancing out the window as twilight crept across the park, blurring the shadows of pedestrians into formless shapes. "My life passes by so quickly, I don't really notice."

"I imagine a steady diet of excitement and adventure would be like that," Emily mused, not sounding critical but more contemplative. "I think it must be tiring, never to have a moment to reflect."

"I think that's exactly the point."

"And yet you're here," Emily said. "You left all that behind without hesitation. I can tell you're not happy to be here, but you came despite that. Out of loyalty and love. To me, that's substance."

Derian released Emily's hand and lifted the teacup, cradling the small beautiful object of art in her palm. "Staying in the first place might have been more impressive."

"I don't see anything wrong with searching out the life you want," Emily said. "I take it you left because that wasn't here."

"I don't know," Derian said. "I'm afraid I was too angry to ask myself if there was anything here I wanted."

"Well," Emily said softly, "you're here now."

"Yes," Derian said, savoring the delicate beauty of the woman across from her. "I am here now."

Suddenly self-conscious and afraid her enjoyment of Derian's attention would be far too obvious, Emily rose to clear the table. "Why don't you pour the rest of the wine, and I'll meet you in the living room in just a minute."

Derian rose with her. "Let me help you."

"Absolutely not." Emily gave Derian's shoulder a playful shove, appreciating the play of muscles beneath her fingers. "Guest, remember?"

"If you insist." Derian filled the glasses, set them on a coffee table opposite an ornate white marble fireplace with a broad mantel bearing filigreed candlesticks at either end, and settled into a comfortable floral-patterned overstuffed sofa.

Less than a minute later when Emily sat down, her scent, light and spicy as a fragrant tea, teased at Derian's senses. A different kind of hunger emerged, sharp and demanding. "Thank you for dinner. It was one of the most enjoyable meals I've had in a very long time."

"I'm glad you liked it."

"The food was delicious," Derian said, placing her wineglass carefully back on the table. She slid closer until the outside of her thigh touched Emily's. When Emily didn't draw away, but just looked at her with the question in her eyes, Derian framed her face with both hands. "But it was the company that made it so special."

This time when she kissed her, it wasn't fleeting, and she didn't ask permission. She didn't wait to be invited. She'd wanted to kiss her since she'd walked in the door, and pretending otherwise was fruitless and self-deluding. Emily's mouth was soft and sweet and delectable as the finest wine. When Emily made a small surprised sound of pleasure, Derian's heart leapt into her throat. A surge of want so powerful her thighs tightened shot through her. She slid her hand around to Emily's nape, soft hair gliding over the top of her hand, and drew her closer until their bodies touched. Emily's breasts pressed into her, firm and compelling.

Emily nibbled at her lip and Derian groaned, fingers tightening. She slid deeper, exploring the heat and soft secrets of Emily's mouth. Emily slid both arms around her shoulders, stroked her back, explored in a way Derian hadn't expected. Hands probed her muscles, traced the ridge of her spine, caressing and delighting her, inflaming her. Derian pressed closer and Emily leaned back against the pillows, half reclining. Derian braced herself on an arm over Emily, wanting to cover her, wanting to consume her with such urgency she had to struggle to be gentle. She kissed the corner of Emily's full, yielding mouth, the angle of her jaw, her long graceful neck, the hollow of her throat. Unable to stop, she unbuttoned the uppermost button of Emily's shirt and kissed the soft triangle between her breasts.

"God, I want you." Her voice was hoarse, an unfamiliar desperation cutting through it.

"Derian," Emily murmured, her voice low and foreign. Her fist tightened in Derian's hair. "Wait—"

Derian gripped Emily's shoulders, angled a leg between hers. The touch of Emily's body sent heat sweeping through her. She searched for another button, her mouth on the curve of Emily's breast. "Emily. I want to make love to you."

Emily tugged Derian's head up and kissed her, catching Derian's hand before Derian could clasp her breast. "I'm not—I can't—"

Derian shuddered and gritted her teeth. Taking deep, gasping breaths, she forced her head to clear. As soon as she could manage, she pushed herself up and stared down. "Are you all right?"

Emily didn't hesitate. "Yes. Of course."

"You're very beautiful." She smiled wryly. "I can't help wanting you."

Emily smiled, color flooding her face. "Thank you."

"I should go." Summoning all her will, Derian stood, extending her hand to help Emily up. "Thank you for tonight."

Emily grasped her hand. "Derian, I—"

"No," Derian said quickly. "You needn't explain. I won't apologize this time, though, especially since I very much want to do that again "

"I enjoyed tonight too," Emily said. "*All* of the night."

"I'm not a patient person," Derian warned.

"I'm not worried." Emily walked her to the door. "Good night, Derian."

Emily didn't say any of the things Derian expected. She didn't say she didn't want to be kissed again. She didn't say they should keep their relationship professional. She didn't say no.

For tonight, that was enough.

"Good night, Emily."

CHAPTER SEVENTEEN

Still grinning as she reached the street, Derian strode to the corner, double-checked the street signs, and texted Uber for a pickup. She typed in her destination and waited. The new service made getting around so much easier. She didn't have to think about which direction she needed to walk to get a cab or explain to a driver where she needed to go, a sometimes challenging feat when so many cabbies needed help with directions. When she traveled and didn't have a driver of her own, she'd found getting around even in the cities she knew difficult, despite all the tricks she'd learned over the years to defeat her directional dyslexia. She leaned against a lamppost, feeling the smile fill her. Emily had definitely kissed her back. There'd be another time, another kiss. She wanted it, and she wasn't going to waste time asking herself why. The answer was simple. Kissing Emily was exceedingly pleasant.

When their lips touched, her body came to life, her senses pulsing with forgotten hunger. Emily's hands moving over her, the soft sounds she made in her throat, the invitation in her body when they pressed close was nothing she hadn't felt before, and absolutely unlike anything she'd ever experienced. Oh yeah, there would be another kiss.

A black SUV emerged from traffic and pulled over in front of her. She climbed in and gave her address. When she got back to the apartment, she poured a glass of port and carried it into the bedroom. It wasn't that late, but she was tired and knew she'd sleep. After undressing, she slipped into bed in the dark. Her mind was at last blessedly quiet and oddly content. She set the glass aside, pulled up Emily's number, and hit send.

"Hello?" Emily said softly on the second ring.

"Did I wake you?"

"No, I was just…"

"Just?"

Emily laughed, a bright, self-conscious laugh. "I was just thinking about you."

"Funny," Derian said, "I was just doing the same thing."

"Were you."

"I was thinking about kissing you again."

Emily was silent.

"Were you thinking about that too?"

"Derian? What are we do—"

"It's safe enough. You're there and I'm here, right?" Derian laughed. "And really, as much as I feel like I'm in high school right now, I'm not trying to talk you into phone sex."

"Really? High school and phone sex?" Emily exploded with laughter.

"Come on, don't tell me you've never—"

"Absolutely not. I'm not telling you my deep, darkest secrets."

Derian smiled. "All right, then I'll go first. Janie Mankiewicz."

"Your first girlfriend?"

"Tennis instructor," Derian said. "Ten years my senior, making her the older woman. Also married, and very bored."

"How old were you?"

"Sixteen when we had the sexy phone conversations. We never did get much beyond that."

"All right," Emily said, "you've got my attention. Who started it?"

Derian laughed. "Well, in hindsight, I think she might've flirted a little bit at first, but I was too busy thinking about how good her breas—"

"I think I get it," Emily said archly, a laugh undercutting her mock criticism.

"Let's say it was mutual."

"Fair enough. So which one of you mutually instigated this scintillating conversation?"

"Hmm…Yeah, that would be a good word for it."

"Derian," Emily said warningly, "you're stalling."

"Not at all! I'm building suspense."

"Consider me suspended."

"You have an interesting way with words," Derian teased. "What are you wearing?"

"None of your business."

"Okay, I'll just make it up—let's see, a black lacy—"

"A peach tank top and...plain, boring...underthings."

"Underthings? Somehow I thought you were in bed."

"I am."

"Then why—"

"The tennis instructor?"

"Oh, right, Janie." Picturing Emily in a flimsy tank and panties was a lot more interesting. Her throat was suddenly dry and she wished for some more port. "So, after one particularly hot, sweaty afternoon, I came up with some excuse to call her after I'd gotten home and showered. Somehow, I managed to mention I'd just done that."

"And?"

"She said something about it being too hot to wear clothes and maybe I mentioned that I wasn't, and you know...descriptions were involved."

Emily's voice caught. "I can imagine that might have been... interesting."

Derian skimmed her fingertips down her stomach. The memory of Janie and what had been so exciting at the time was now merely an amusing memory. Emily's voice, though, filled her with slow, simmering pleasure. "If you'd like, I could fill you in on what I'm—"

"I've seen you, remember?"

"Oh." Derian chuckled. "In the hall. I'd forgotten."

"I haven't."

The breath punched from Derian's chest and the heat ratcheted up a couple hundred degrees. "Emily. This could get serious."

"We're not going to have phone sex," Emily murmured.

"Why not?" Derian enjoyed playing, and Emily was a great partner. The low, speculative note in Emily's voice intrigued her. But she intended to be touching her, watching her, devouring her, the first time Emily came with her.

"As much as I find the idea interesting," Emily said, "I'm afraid I might miss too much."

"We wouldn't want that." Derian pressed her hand more firmly against her stomach, enjoying the low steep of arousal in her belly. Emily kept her on edge, every cell incredibly alive. "I promise to be sure you don't miss…anything."

"Oh, I'm not worrying."

Derian sighed. "I should let you get some sleep."

"You must be tired too."

"I am, and I think I'm going to be able to sleep tonight."

"Good. Thanks for calling."

"I'm glad you didn't mind. I wasn't ready to let you go."

"I didn't mind. Good night, Derian."

"Good night, Emily." Derian set the phone aside and closed her eyes. The lingering arousal, along with the memory of Emily's voice, shadowed her into sleep.

❖

Derian emerged from the ICU after her ten thirty visit the next morning to find Emily waiting in the hall. She was dressed for work, in dark green pants, brown boots, and a slightly lighter brown soft wool sweater. Derian couldn't help conjure an image of pale peach panties, lacy in all the right places. "Hi, I was…ah…about to call you."

"I knew you'd be here," Emily said. "Did you get any sleep at all?"

"I slept fine." Derian grinned, her mood lightening by centuries as it always did whenever she saw Emily. The change was like stepping into sunlight after emerging from a long walk through a cave filled with winding tunnels, blind ends, and no sense of direction. She shook off the disconcerting sensation. "Better than fine. How about you?"

Emily grinned. "I had the most interesting dreams…"

When her voice trailed off and her brows lifted, Derian laughed. "You know, there's really a bad girl hiding under that very good girl exterior."

"You mean there's a sexy librarian somewhere?"

Derian leaned a shoulder against the wall, moving out of the way of two attendants pushing a hospital bed carrying a patient with all the usual equipment toward the ICU. When they'd passed, she nodded. "I think the shy librarian is just a ruse."

"Really? And what exactly do you think I'm hiding?"

"Dark, wild passions, hopefully."

Huffing, Emily shook her head. "I'm afraid you would be very disappointed."

"I don't think so. But I hope to find out." Derian couldn't help but inject an invitation into her voice. God, when was the last time just being near a woman made her tremble?

Almost as if Emily realized their flirtations had crossed the border into seduction, she colored and looked away. "The nurses told me she's better."

Derian accepted Emily's silent request for a time-out. "She had a good night. She's a little bit more alert, but I'm not entirely certain she'll remember we've been here. They've got her pretty doped up."

"Probably just as well. Who would want to remember this part of it?" Her tone was tinged with uncharacteristic bitterness.

"Hey." Derian slipped her palm around Emily's elbow and drew her closer. "How are you doing?"

Emily lightly rested her fingertips on Derian's arm, the brief contact electric. "I'm okay. Really."

"I should let you go in."

"I know." Emily sighed. "I don't want to stay away from the agency too long, but I needed to see her."

"I'll keep you updated during the day."

"Thanks."

"How are things going over there?"

"I'm afraid rebellion might be fomenting. No one feels comfortable or particularly secure without Henrietta or someone else they trust in charge. And then with all the changes—" She grimaced. "Somehow, in less than twenty-four hours, Donatella has redirected the entire focus of the agency, at least in theory. How well everyone is going to accept her mandates is another question."

"I talked to Aud about it," Derian said.

"Oh, Derian." Emily was grateful, relieved, but concerned too. She hadn't wanted to draw Derian into a situation she'd clearly wanted to avoid. "I'm so sorry all of this has spilled over onto you."

Derian lifted a shoulder. "Maybe it's time."

"You ought to be able to pick the timing of your battles yourself."

"I'm not sure life works that way. Sometimes the battles come to us, and until they do, we don't know where we stand."

"Well I don't expect you to go to battle for us."

"So far I can't say I have. I don't know much more today than I did yesterday. Donatella is my father's choice, and exactly what his agenda might be, Aud probably knows, but, well—"

Emily doubted Derian wanted to create difficulties with Aud over something she'd never wanted to get involved in. Especially if they were in the process of reconnecting. "I'll do my best to keep everyone calm. I'm sure this will all be straightened out before long."

"I promised Henrietta I'd do my best to help, and so far I haven't done much."

Emily took Derian's hand. "That is so very untrue. Just your being here means everything."

"Your faith in me is a little scary."

Emily smiled. "Don't worry, I don't expect miracles."

"What do you expect?"

"Only that you do what feels right."

At the moment, kissing Emily again was the only thing on Derian's mind, and she was pretty sure, under the circumstances, that probably wasn't the right move. All the same, she savored the heat of Emily's hand in hers. "I'll do my best."

Emily's gaze held hers, as warm as an embrace. "That's more than enough."

Derian's chest filled with a sensation she couldn't immediately place. Finally she recognized it. Emily's certainty filled her with pride, and she'd do anything not to disappoint her. All she had to do was figure out where to start.

❖

"You're awake." Derian grinned broadly and leaned down to kiss Henrietta's cheek. The light tentative touch of Henrietta's answering caress on her cheek lifted her heart almost as much as the clear recognition and familiar sharpness in Henrietta's eyes.

"You look better than the last time I saw you," Henrietta said slowly, her raspy voice fainter than usual but clear.

Derian chuckled. "As a matter of fact, so do you."

"What is this place?"

"Intermediate care." Derian pulled a chair close to the bed. "They tell me you made it out of the ICU in record time."

"Too long for me."

"I think a day and a half, most of which you were sleeping, is a record."

"Who can sleep with all that constant noise, perpetual lights, and interruptions every five seconds."

Derian folded her arms on the low rail encircling Henrietta's bed and leaned her chin on her arms. The nurses had said the first twenty-four hours were the most crucial, and she'd spent most of the past day prowling the halls outside the ICU, visiting as often as they would let her in. Emily had been there twice, and each time she'd seen her, the acid in her belly had calmed. Aud had called. Martin had not come. "I bet the nurses in the ICU miss you."

"Ha. How long have I been here?" Henrietta sounded irritated and a lot like her old self, even if the volume of her voice was considerably reduced. "I can't seem to keep track of time."

"You've been in the hospital about three days. Your surgery was a little over two days ago."

"What day is it?"

"It's Thursday."

Henrietta's brows drew down. "Thursday. I have a very full calendar today. Who's taking care of that?"

"I wondered when that was coming," Derian mused.

"Don't get smart."

Derian grinned. "Vonnie and Emily have things totally under control."

Since that was the truth as far as Henrietta's calendar, she didn't mind obfuscating just a little bit. Telling Henrietta that Donatella had moved into her office was the last thing she was going to do.

"They won't give me a phone," Henrietta fussed. "So I need you to give Vonnie a few messages."

"No deal. HW," Derian said, "you're just going to have to let them take care of the agency for a while. You're not ready to start working."

"I'm hardly working, lying here," Henrietta said, but her voice was flagging and she looked tired.

"Trust me," Derian said, vowing again to keep her word,

"everything at the agency is under control. Emily, Vonnie, and I will make sure of it."

Henrietta's eyes closed for an instant, then slowly opened. "Sorry, I know you never wanted…"

"It's okay," Derian murmured. "I'm not sure I ever really knew what I wanted."

Henrietta drifted off to sleep and Derian leaned back in the chair, listening to her breathe. HW wasn't out of the woods by a long shot, and the staff had made it pretty clear she wouldn't be ready to take on any kind of work-related activity for an indefinite period of time. The longer Donatella was at the helm of the agency, the harder it would be to reverse whatever destructive mandates she put in place. Emily needed to be in charge, just as HW had directed. Martin would oppose that on principle. Aud had said without Henrietta's backing, and considering Emily's nonresident status, the chances of Emily taking charge were slim.

The first order of business, then, was to do something about that. She needed to think like HW—what was the goal, and what was the most direct route to success. She'd need to spend more time at the agency, and with Emily, to find out. She closed her eyes and smiled. Not a bad plan at all.

CHAPTER EIGHTEEN

At eight o'clock in the morning, the streets were teeming with taxis, people, delivery trucks, and the occasional unwary traveler who hadn't any idea that driving in New York City would be like navigating in an unknown universe at warp speed. The temperature was much more springlike, the sky was an unusually clear blue, and Derian opted to walk to Midtown, enjoying the bright sky and keeping her mind a careful blank. Anticipating what was to come would only sour a perfectly good morning that had started with memories of an even better evening. When she thought of Emily, she had a completely irrational urge to whistle. Next thing she knew, she'd be skipping. She laughed softly, wondering if she looked as crazy to the passersby as she felt. This was a crazy she liked, and seeing Martin, however unpleasant, would be no worse this time than it ever had been before. Funny, how coming face-to-face with his disdain never got easier, despite how much time had passed. Ridiculous, really, to be bothered by it after all this time.

She strolled into the lobby of the Winfield Building, an ultra-sleek glass and steel structure that took up half of one block and had absolutely no redeeming architectural features. Martin probably thought the gleam and polish and imposing façade bespoke power, which she suspected was the only thing that really mattered to him. When she thought of all the incredibly beautiful buildings she had seen throughout the world, unforgettable testaments to human creativity and art, she was reminded again how shallow his vision really was.

She didn't know the guard at the desk commanding the center of the foyer, placed there to disrupt the flow toward the elevators on either side of the marble-floored lobby beyond and facilitate more intense surveillance. He watched her with bored disregard as employees with badges prominently displayed passed by. He was probably forty, well on his way to middle-aged seed from too many hours sitting behind that desk, his thick, ruddy neck bulging slightly over his buttoned collar. His tie appeared on the verge of strangling him. He wore a faux-military type uniform as would befit Martin's vision of his company having the importance of a small country, making him the king.

"Help you?"

"I'm on my way to see Mr. Winfield. I know the way."

"Just a minute." The guard turned to a computer, pulled up a screen she couldn't see, and said, "Name?"

"Derian Winfield."

He typed, scanned the monitor for a long moment, and slowly turned back to look at her. "You're not on the list," he said, a little uncertainty in his flat voice now.

"No, I'm not. Martin's offices still on sixty-five?"

"Look, I'm not supposed to let anyone up who's not on the admit list or daily appointment schedule."

"I'm his daughter," Derian said, the words sounding foreign and ill-fitting.

"Uh, I better call up."

"I'll just go up and speak directly to his secretary. If anyone mentions it, you can just tell them I didn't give you a choice."

"Right, well, I'm sure there won't be any problem."

She smiled. "Absolutely not."

He pointed to the left. "Last elevator."

"Have a nice day."

As she turned away, she heard him mutter, "Yeah, you too."

Maybe she would. Nothing like starting the day with unpleasantries. At least then it could only get better.

The elevator opened onto an expansive maroon-carpeted foyer as big as some hotel lobbies, filled with comfortable seating areas and an unobstructed view of midtown Manhattan through the floor-to-ceiling windows on the opposite wall. She wondered how many buildings Martin had had to buy and demolish in order to maintain that view. A thirtysomething blonde sat behind a black U-shaped desk, her hair drawn back in a sleek French braid, her dove-gray suit jacket doing nothing to conceal her voluptuous figure. She smiled at Derian in a practiced, wholly impersonal way.

"Good morning. How may I help you?"

"I'm here to see Martin."

Her expression never changed. "I'm afraid Mr. Winfield has no meetings scheduled this morning. You must have mistaken the date of your appointment. If you give me your name, I'll check to see the correct date."

"I don't have an appointment, but he'll see me." Derian held out her hand. "I'm Derian Winfield."

Color rushed to the blonde's face and she rose hastily, leaning across the wide desk to extend her hand. Derian was right, she had a killer body underneath her expensive, professionally stylish suit. "Oh, I'm so sorry. I'm Victoria, let me get Mr. Winfield's admin. I didn't...I don't believe we've ever met."

"No," Derian said, returning the handshake, "we haven't." There was a time she might have added she would've remembered meeting such a beautiful woman, because she certainly would have. Flirting with women was second nature, but as attractive as the woman was, Derian hadn't any interest in playing. She released her hand. "The admin?"

"Oh! Of course." Victoria reached for a phone, punched in an extension, and a second later said, "Anthony, Derian Winfield is here to see Martin." Her flush deepened and she partially turned away. "What? No, why would I..." She glanced at Derian, her expression mortified. "I'm terribly sorry. Do you have identification?"

Derian laughed. "It's okay." She reached inside her coat pocket, brought out her passport, and showed Victoria her photo.

"Yes, of course," she said into the phone. A second later she hung up, looking relieved and chagrined. "He will be out shortly."

"That's fine, thank you."

Derian walked to the bank of windows and thought about how much she detested these little displays of dominance. Everyone jockeying for their small bit of power. Her name had been all she needed growing up to give her that power, and as soon as she'd recognized that everyone she knew was subtly trying to maneuver for even more, she hadn't wanted any of it. Henrietta had been the only one who didn't care about appearances or the standing on the social register or the best seat in the banquet hall. Even though Derian had done everything possible to escape the Winfield net, no matter how far she traveled, how vigorously she worked to dissociate herself from her family mystique, she hadn't been able to shake the celebrity that had nothing to do with her. As she learned very early in life, people were attracted to her for her money and her family name, and the presumed influence and prestige that came with both, making every relationship suspect. And sadly, she was rarely wrong. Keeping people at a distance became a self-protective habit, until Emily. She smiled to herself. Emily was completely unimpressed by her status, despite admitting her penchant for following celebrity news with some dedication. What for Emily provided entertainment, for others provided a foundation for a relationship—exactly what Derian rigorously avoided.

Emily effortlessly changed everything. From the very first meeting, Emily had seen a part of her no one except Henrietta had ever perceived—her vulnerabilities and her fears—and none of that made her feel diminished or discounted. She didn't always have to pretend she didn't hurt, didn't need comfort, didn't need someone else to be strong, if just for a few moments. Emily allowed her to be human and didn't reject her for it. Suddenly she wanted nothing more than to be out of Martin's domain, beyond his circle of malicious power, and somewhere, anywhere, with Emily.

"Ms. Winfield," a cool male voice said from behind her.

Steeling herself for the next round, Derian turned and saw a man she didn't know, but whom she recognized from his perfectly cut hair, dark gray Armani suit, monochromatic shirt and tie, and diamonds glinting in the square gold cufflinks, as one of the sleek corporate sharks regularly following in Martin's wake.

"Yes."

"I'm Anthony Marconi, Mr. Winfield's executive assistant. I'm afraid Mr. Winfield wasn't expecting you. He's presently involved in back-to-back Internet conferences."

"I won't be long. I'll wait until he's in between." She grinned. "Bathroom break or the like."

Anthony's expression remained pleasantly remote. His eyes, however, were annoyed. "Perhaps we could find a mutually agreeable time for you to return. His schedule is somewhat freer tomorrow."

"I'll wait."

"If you'll come with me," he said, looking as if he'd swallowed a fishbone, "I'll show you to the executive lounge."

"Thank you."

The lounge, five times the size of the ICU waiting room where she'd spent most of the last week, was furnished with a deep navy carpet, leather furniture, a full bar, a coffee station, and a pool table. Anthony left her to her own devices and, after pouring coffee from a silver carafe into a bone china cup, settled into a chair to listen to an audiobook. She considered calling Emily, but Emily was at work and she didn't want to pull her into this place even by talking about it.

Close to an hour later, Anthony reappeared. "He has five minutes."

"More than enough time." Derian pocketed her phone and left the china cup on the table beside the sofa. She followed Anthony past a series of offices with closed doors to the end of the hall where another admin, male again, sat in an alcove in front of a set of enormous walnut double doors with gleaming brass handles. Anthony slid a security card through an unobtrusive card reader off to one side and, at the discreet sound of a faint buzz, held the door open for her. Martin's office was a suite of rooms larger than many apartments with layers of plush oriental carpets, multiple seating areas, a flagship desk in one corner with views of Manhattan on two sides, and an array of computer monitors on one wall. Anthony slipped out behind them and the doors closed, leaving them alone.

Martin looked up as she crossed the expanse of carpet but didn't bother to rise.

Derian stopped a few feet from his desk but chose not to sit, preferring to look down at him. She hadn't seen him in three years, but he hadn't changed at all. His hair was still jet-black, his face tight and youthful appearing, and even sitting, she could tell he was in shape. He had a passion for handball and played several times a week with his assistants. He still wore his suit jacket, even at his desk, with his tie only minimally loosened. A mantle of power shimmered around him.

"I'm in the middle of a busy morning," Martin said coolly. "I have businesses to run, after all."

"Then I'll get right to the point," Derian said just as coolly. "I'm taking over the agency until Henrietta is back on her feet. I want you to call Donatella and tell her to vacate the office."

Martin laughed and leaned back in his high–backed leather chair.

"Putting aside the fact you have absolutely no experience, we both know that kind of work would strain your…capabilities."

"Business is just a sophisticated game," Derian said, echoing one of Martin's favorite sayings, "and one thing I'm very, very good at is winning games."

"So I'm given to understand. Why would you even want to attempt this one?"

"Because that's what Henrietta wants." She took a chance, knowing her aunt would never leave any eventuality uncovered. "She's made sure I have a holding interest in the company. It's in the paperwork somewhere, and you probably already know that."

"What I know," Martin said, an edge creeping into his voice, "is that you haven't bothered with the business or anything else for years. Henrietta's return is uncertain, and your pretending to be in charge for a week or two is a foolish exercise."

"I'll be here for as long as necessary, and there are plenty of experienced people already present at the agency who know how to do their jobs. Emily May is a senior agent and has worked closely with Henrietta for years. Should I need to consult with anyone, she'll be available."

"Emily May's employment status is uncertain"—he waved a hand—"and given that, the board decided someone with more experience and long-term investment in the enterprise was needed." He smiled, his lips a thin line. "I'm afraid you and Ms. May have a great deal in common. Neither of you is fit to helm the agency."

Derian slid her hands into her pockets and strolled to the windows, putting her back to him. His easy dismissal of Emily, as if she was already headed back to Singapore, infuriated her more than his expected ridicule of her own abilities. "I haven't been very interested in the business, you're absolutely right. But I find that I suddenly have a new appreciation for Winfield Enterprises. Up until now, I've been happy for Aud to represent me at board meetings, but now I find I'd rather do that myself. Of course, it's possible I might not always be in agreement with your position when it comes time to vote."

She didn't have to turn to feel a wave of anger wash over her. She couldn't block him in a vote, but he wouldn't be happy if she took a position against him, especially if she sided with other board members who might disagree with some of his plans. He wouldn't risk that.

"You've got a month, if you last that long," he said. "However, the board has asked for an audit, which will be ongoing. Donatella will oversee that."

"Just make sure Donatella's out of my office before I arrive."

She turned and walked out without bothering to say good-bye.

CHAPTER NINETEEN

Wide-eyed and breathless, Ron burst into Emily's office, caught the door just before it slammed in his haste to close it, and skidded to a halt. "She's here!"

Emily set aside her iPad and stared at him. "Who's here?"

He canted his head in the direction of Henrietta's corner office. "Derian Winfield."

"Derian?" Emily shot to her feet. "Here?"

"In the flesh." Ron eyed her suspiciously. "I think you've been keeping secrets."

"No, I haven't." Feeling her blush deepen, Emily sat slowly and hoped her excitement wasn't evident. Never had she had such a spontaneous thrill just from hearing someone's name. "I had no idea she was coming."

That was certainly an understatement. The last time they'd talked, Derian hadn't said anything about visiting the agency, but then, why would Emily expect her to? They were becoming friends, at least she felt that way, but hardly intimates, and Derian had no reason to discuss business matters with her. Derian was a Winfield, after all, and as much as she resisted accepting the role of heir apparent, that's what she was. For an instant, Emily felt a twinge of hurt, and then brushed it impatiently aside. Business was business, and if Derian was here, that was certainly none of her concern. What mattered was the agency.

"She is Henrietta's niece, after all," Emily said offhandedly, "so it shouldn't be a surprise she's here."

"That's not what you said a few days ago. No interest in the business, I think you said. Plus, why do you look as if it's Christmas morning, and you've got a big present under the tree?"

"I do *not*."

"With a giant red bow and—"

"Stop it." Emily had to laugh.

Ron pulled a chair closer to her desk, plopped into it, and settled in for what looked like a long campaign. "It's time for you to spill it, honey."

"There's absolutely nothing—"

He wagged a finger. "When just the thought of someone makes your eyes light up the way yours just did, you are honor bound to have to tell your friends."

Was that true? She didn't know. She hadn't discussed intimate feelings for someone since she was a teenager, and those wishful relationships had just been crushes. And come to think of it, she'd never really discussed her girl crushes with her friends, especially since her biggest had been on a best friend who was undeniably and irrevocably interested in boys, and only boys. And after that, there hadn't been anything serious enough to discuss with anyone. But what would she say?

"I wouldn't even know where to start," she said, almost to herself.

A sympathetic expression crossed his face. "You could start with how you feel about her."

Emily laughed abruptly. "Wouldn't that be starting at the end instead of the beginning?"

"I suppose it depends on your perspective. Start at your beginning, then."

Something about his kindness and the genuine friendship beneath all his teasing and prodding, mixed with her own confused emotions, prompted her to put into words what she'd almost been afraid to consider. "We've had dinner a couple of times."

"Aha, and where did that happen?"

"Well, I told you about the first time," she said a little impatiently, not at all certain she wanted to go down this path. "At her apartment in the Dakota."

"I've never been in there. Is it as fabulous as they say?"

She laughed. "It is."

"Okay, enough of that—you can tell me all about the décor later. And the next time?"

"I cooked for her," she said softly.

"Wow," he said with a reverent tone. "That's very personal. Just dinner?"

"Yes," Emily said hearing the prim tone in her voice and chiding herself inwardly. Why was she hiding her feelings? "Just dinner and…a good-night kiss." Before he could say another word, she held up her hand. "That's all, just a kiss. And I'm not saying any more about that."

"Oh, you can't be serious. You kissed Derian Winfield? How many times?"

"I'm not giving any details."

"All right," he said musingly, a thoughtful expression crossing his face, "let's discuss the theoretical. Do you want to kiss her again?"

For one of those rare times in her life, words failed her. If she voiced her desires, then what? Would she no longer be able to deny to herself how very attracted she was to Derian? And since when was she afraid to face her own feelings or the realities of her life? She sighed. "I certainly wouldn't mind."

"And how about her? Has she issued any invitations?"

I want to make love to you. Derian hadn't been afraid to say what she wanted—and what did that say? Was Derian so unused to rejection, she didn't mind exposing her feelings? Or had she really been as driven by passion as she'd sounded? Emily remembered the heat of Derian's mouth on her throat and the gravelly desperation in her tone. *God, I want you.* Emily's breathing kicked up again, her blood racing. Hopefully Ron couldn't tell. "I think she's interested also."

"Wow." Ron looked suddenly serious, an unusual expression for him. She'd learned over the years his approach to dealing with almost everything in life was with humor liberally laced with sarcasm. "That's kind of serious. Derian Winfield isn't exactly known for serious."

"If you mean she has a reputation for being a player, I know that," Emily said. "But she's not the person the media makes her out to be. She's kind and generous and sensitive."

"Oh."

"What?"

"You've got a thing for her. I mean, beyond the *she's hot* kind of thing."

Emily made an exasperated sound. "Just because I happen to like someone, and find them attractive, and…" She caught her breath as she heard herself denying again. That wasn't her. "Actually, you're right. I have a big thing for her. She's gorgeous and sexy and pretty much wonderful."

"Well," Ron said with finality, "then I think you should drag her off somewhere and have your way with her. Because I've never heard you say that about anyone before, and opportunity doesn't usually knock twice."

"You know, Ron, everything isn't about sex."

"Of course it is, when everything is said and done. Okay sure, maybe you won't have sex with your best friend, but when you start thinking about your best friend as being attractive and gorgeous and wonderful and sexy, they're not your best friend anymore. They're something else altogether. And, opposite side of the coin, you know, someone doesn't have to be your best friend to have really hot, satisfying sex with them."

"I don't think of her as my best friend," Emily said. "Actually, I think of you as my best friend and I've never wanted to have sex—"

"Okay, let's not go there," Ron said, grinning.

"If she's here, Ron," Emily said, decidedly *not* going to discuss sex with Derian with anyone, "it might not mean anything at all. She's never been interested in the business. It's possible she just came on an errand for Henrietta."

"You think you can find out?"

"I'm not going to use my relationship with her to get insider information. If she's here for anything other than a brief visit, I'm sure we'll all find out at the same time."

"You know, sometimes you're absolutely no fun."

"You might be right." Emily grinned. "But sometimes, I am."

"Well I know one thing," Ron said, rising and starting for the door. "Things would be a hell of a lot better around here if she stayed."

He slipped out the door and Emily leaned back in her chair and closed her eyes. Derian couldn't be planning to get involved at the agency, could she? As much as she wanted to see Donatella dethroned, she wasn't at all sure she wanted to see Derian in Henrietta's place. If she and Derian had to work together, she wasn't sure their personal relationship could go any further. For the first time in her life, her professional goals ran smack up against her personal ones. She'd never had to choose between her goals and her desires, and she wasn't sure what she would do if she had to.

❖

"Hi, Vonnie darlin'." Derian swung around Vonnie's desk and kissed her on the cheek. "You look beautiful as always."

Vonnie jumped up and gave Derian a quick hug. In a low voice, she said, "You're a sight for sore eyes. How have you been? Still my favorite bad girl?"

"So I'm told."

"No, really," Vonnie said gently. "It's been a long time. Too long."

"I've been doing okay," Derian said, stretching the truth a bit. With each passing day she wondered if she'd been doing anything more than killing time—or maybe wasting it, along with her life. "A lot better now that Henrietta is on the mend."

"Don't I know it?" Vonnie glanced behind her at the closed office doors. "Her getting back here can't be too soon for me."

"Donatella hasn't left yet?"

"Not unless she flew out the window on her broom, which wouldn't surprise me at all."

Derian laughed. "Is everything pretty much under control?"

"We've had some concerned calls from clients and publisher reps, worried that Henrietta's absence will disrupt some of our commitments. Everyone knows Henrietta is the power here."

"Just tell anyone who asks it's business as usual and there won't be any changes."

"I wish that were the case, but—"

"Don't worry. Just leave it to me."

"You know what you're up against in there?" Vonnie's brows drew down in worry.

"Hey, I was born for this, remember?" Derian strode to Henrietta's door, knocked perfunctorily, and let herself in. Donatella hadn't changed much since the last time she'd seen her, although she appeared thinner, if that was even possible. Her skin was stretched tight over sharp facial bones, her dark hair sculpted to her skull. She wore gold at her throat and her wrists, her black suit severely tailored to her anorectic frame. Her wide mouth tightened, her voice a hiss. "Derian."

"Hi, Donatella," Derian said easily, shedding her suit jacket and draping it over a clothes tree. She rolled up her sleeves, scanning the room. Henrietta's touch was everywhere—floor-to-ceiling glass-fronted bookcases filled with countless books by authors the agency had represented over the past hundred years, the comfortable seating area where Derian could imagine HW or Emily relaxing with a manuscript, the huge desk from which HW steered the agency. "Did Martin call?"

"He did."

Derian turned and slid her hands into her pockets. "I'll grab a cup of coffee while you gather up your things."

"As I'm sure Martin informed you, we have an audit ongoing which will take some time to complete." If possible, her lips grew even thinner. "Long overdue."

"The business offices are on the third floor. I'll make sure someone gives you a space to work. But I'll be working here."

"Really, Derian," Donatella said condescendingly, "how far do you plan to take this charade? You don't know anything about the business, and even if you did—"

"I've already been this route with Martin, and I don't really have time or the inclination to repeat myself. I plan to run the agency in Henrietta's absence. If you have an issue with that, you can take it to my father." She grinned, the kind of grin that said, *Go ahead, make my day*. "He can take it to the board. I'll be happy to fight it out there."

Martin would not want a public schism. He was chairman of the board, but at least half the members were elected by the shareholders, and he would not tolerate any show of weakness to those who might conceivably challenge him in the future. His image was all important, and he would want to appear unassailable. Derian wondered if Martin had any idea his attempts at training her to win in the business world would one day be used against him. She smiled at the thought.

"Your aunt," Donatella said with a touch of distaste, "has run this business like a charity for far too long. The staff is bloated, half of the clients are marginal producers if that, and the agency's catalog is hopelessly outdated. Nothing short of a complete overhaul will bring this business into the twenty-first century. Do you really think you're capable of that?"

Derian held on to her temper. She didn't mind being insulted, but she wouldn't stand for Henrietta being criticized when she wasn't there to defend herself. "You'd be surprised," she said softly, "at exactly what I'm capable of doing. If you'd like to find out, you can try standing in my way."

Donatella lost the staring contest and rose with a huffing sound. She gathered papers and pushed them into a large black shoulder bag. "This is a ridiculous, childish maneuver that will only compound the problems at this institution. I expect you'll discover you're in well over your head very shortly. Call me when that happens." Her thin smile blossomed crimson, as if infused with fresh blood. "At that point I think the board will be delighted with anything we suggest, so you'll be doing us a favor when you fail."

Derian stepped aside as Donatella stormed out. An unexpected wave of satisfaction rolled through her despite Donatella's prediction. She hadn't expected winning a round in business to be as satisfying as pulling down a large take at the tables, but it was. Maybe she'd been missing out on something all this time.

Donatella was right about one thing, though. She didn't know exactly how to win at this game, and she needed to find out. Henrietta's legacy and a lot of people's futures, including Emily's, depended on her being able to pull this off. She opened the door. "Vonnie?"

Vonnie swiveled in her chair, a pleased expression on her face. "Yes, boss?"

"Derian will do." Derian chuckled. "Where's Emily's office?"

Vonnie's smile widened and she pointed. "Around the corner and down the hall to your right. First door."

"Thanks," Derian said, heading off in the direction Vonnie so kindly indicated for her with a buzz of expectation.

CHAPTER TWENTY

Ron was at the door again. Emily closed her iPad and set it aside with an inward sigh. She was used to people dropping in and could usually work around disruptions, but today, somehow, she couldn't concentrate, couldn't lose herself in the words, and that was so unusual it left her feeling completely off balance. "More news?"

"Depends on what you call news," Derian said.

Emily glanced up quickly, a small gasp escaping before she could catch it. Derian stood in the doorway looking nonchalant and totally at home, wearing a gorgeous dark gray pinstripe suit with dark chocolate stripes, loafers, and an open-collar shirt that matched the subtle brown in her suit. She looked every inch the business magnate she had always said she didn't want to be. "Oh, I thought you were Ron."

"I hope you're not too disappointed." Derian raised a brow. "Do you have a moment, or should I come back later?"

Flustered more by the pleasure spilling over her than Derian's unexpected appearance, Emily searched around for words. The only one that came out was "Yes."

"As in, you're disappointed I'm not Ron, this is a good time, or I'm bothering you and I should come back later?" Derian's infuriatingly charming grin said she knew exactly how Emily was feeling.

How embarrassing.

Gathering her scattered wits, Emily gestured to the chair in front of her desk where Ron had sat an hour before, quizzing her about her feelings for Derian. Suggesting she might want to take Derian to bed. And now Derian, who was most certainly here in an official capacity, was sitting in her office and she could barely put two words together.

Did she need any other reminder of why office romances were a bad idea? "Please, of course, come in. I didn't expect you."

Derian quietly closed the door and took the seat Emily had indicated. "Sorry, my decision-making process has gotten a little turned around lately. By the time I figure out what I want to do, it's past time to do it."

"Please," Emily said, "you don't need to explain anything to me."

Derian crossed her legs at the ankles and managed to look relaxed even while appearing totally in control. "This is your turf, Emily, and we ought to be very clear about that right from the outset."

"It certainly isn't," Emily said, not arguing, but adamant. They needed to be clear about a great many things, it seemed. "If it's anyone's turf—after Henrietta's, of course—it's yours. Is there something I can do to help?"

"How about relaxing? I was hoping you'd be glad to see me."

"I am," Emily said quickly and, smiling ruefully, shook her head. "I really am. I'm sorry. Everything is just a little off track for me these days."

"I understand. For me too." Derian sat forward, her forearms casually resting on her long, lean thighs. "You have me a little off-kilter too."

"Perhaps," Emily said, although Derian looked anything but off-kilter. She looked confident and self-assured. Under other circumstances, Emily might have wanted to hear just how she'd managed to put such a formidable woman off stride, but this was not the place. Warring with her desire to verbally dance with Derian, she finally surrendered to reason. "As unlikely as I find that, we should save that conversation for another time."

"You're absolutely right. And we will." Derian grinned. Emily was interested, she could feel it. And Emily was also totally correct that the office needed to be someplace where business, and only business, was the topic. It was just so damn hard not to flirt with her, when all she thought about was her. "I have evicted Donatella."

"Bless you," Emily said with real feeling.

"I'll take that as a happy thought."

Emily snorted. "You have just made a dozen people very, very happy."

"I doubt anyone downstairs in the business department will like me very much," Derian said. "She's doing an audit and there's nothing I can do to stop it. I sent her downstairs where at least she won't have an opportunity to intrude on your end of things."

"Thank you. Is the audit anything to worry about, do you think?" Emily hesitated, unsure of her ground with a new chief administrator, and added quickly, "Of course, that's not something you need to tell me, but—"

"Emily," Derian said, "we both know you should be sitting in Henrietta's office. A snarl of red tape and some antiquated opinions about lines of succession are the only things preventing it."

"I appreciate you saying that, but neither of those barriers is minor, and besides, it's not entirely accurate. I'll admit Henrietta has intimated that one day, my role in the company might change, but that time isn't now. Certainly not when my status is so uncertain."

"The visa, you mean?"

Emily nodded. "Who knows what will happen with that now."

"Nothing any different is going to happen," Derian said. "I'll look into it and see that it's taken care of."

"Thank you," Emily said, wishing the solution were that easy. But knowing Derian at least wanted to try to sort things out gave her a glimmer of hope. Not time to panic—not yet.

"You're important, Emily," Derian said quietly, her voice filled with conviction, "to the business, and to me."

"I don't know why," Emily said, "but I appreciate your help."

Derian waved a hand impatiently. "As far as the business goes, I'm only doing what makes sense. And personally, well, it makes me feel good to help you out if I can."

"I wish I could return the favor."

"Oh, you can. I just took a look at Henrietta's calendar. It's terrifying."

Emily laughed, the tension draining from her chest. Derian had a way of making the most troubling situations seem surmountable. Derian hid her strength and resolve beneath a layer of nonchalance, but it only took being around her for a few moments, watching her, listening to her, to realize she was a woman who did what needed to be done. "I'm sure Vonnie can help you sort your way through things."

Derian nodded. "I think she's already taken care of a great many things, but there are meetings she said I'd need to take and a big conference in a few days—the BEA?"

"Of course," Emily said. "It's the biggest industry book event of the year. We have appointments already scheduled with authors and publishers on the foreign rights schedule, and a booth that Ron and several of the others will staff. Henrietta and I usually cover the rights appointments."

"So you'll have to hold my hand through that." Derian grinned. "Figuratively speaking, of course."

"I could probably handle the appointments with Bill or one of the others."

Derian shook her head. "I need to actually be involved in the running of the agency. It's the only way I'm going to keep Martin and Donatella from moving back into Henrietta's office. They know I don't know a damn thing about the nuts and bolts, and they're going to be looking for any excuse to force the board to push through a reorganization while Henrietta is absent. We can't let that happen."

"No," Emily said, "we can't."

A part of her felt selfish, knowing she would probably be one of the first staff members to be ousted if there was a reorganization, but more was at stake than just her position or even the security her job afforded Pam. The agency itself was at risk, and she would do anything to protect it. She believed in what they did, and believed that Winfield's century-long contributions to the arts should not be only preserved, but continued. "I'll be more than happy to assist you."

"I'm afraid it might be a little more than assistance, but I'll try not to work you too hard." Derian winced. "I'm going to need a pretty intensive course in how things run around here."

"Whatever you need," Emily said.

Whatever you need. Derian needed things she hadn't even realized she wanted until now. She wanted to prove to her father that she was capable, a word he had always used to remind her she was less than what he wanted in a child, less than the sycophants who followed him around, less than anyone. She wanted to take care of Henrietta, and a big part of that was taking care of the agency and securing Emily's future there. She wanted Emily to look at her as she had a few minutes ago when she'd first walked in—with a flush of pleasure and a quick flash of desire. Everything she wanted was connected, and at the heart of it all was Emily.

"How about we meet after lunch and go over the calendar, so I can get some idea what I'll be in for."

"Two o'clock?"

"That sounds fine." Derian rose. "I think I might actually get to like this job."

As she headed back toward her office, she heard Emily's soft laughter. The sound made her smile.

❖

"You're really serious about this?" Aud said as the waiter at the Old Homestead slid steaks onto the table and misted away as if he'd been incorporeal.

"Of course."

"Dere," Aud said with a mixture of affection and exasperation, "despite the fact that Martin thinks of the agency as Henrietta's pet hobby, it's a multimillion-dollar business. It's not something you can just pick up in a day or two."

Derian cut into her filet and sipped her Scarecrow cabernet. "You honestly think I don't know that?"

"I know you enjoy irritating your father."

Derian smiled. "Am I? Good."

"Honestly, Dere. Are you still seventeen?"

"Is that a nice way of saying I'm being juvenile and irresponsible?"

"No." Aud sighed. "I may be one of the few people who knows you're neither of those things. But what are you really doing?"

"Martin is taking advantage of Henrietta's illness." Derian kept her rage on a tight leash. Aud wasn't the enemy, but it was hard to know she was in Martin's camp all the same. "Don't you find that just a little bit reprehensible? Don't you find it just a little bit hard to continue carrying the standard for him, when he's such a coldhearted bastard?"

"I'm not carrying his standard," Aud said, but she'd flushed and, for just an instant, had looked away.

"Then what?"

"My father has cancer," she said quietly.

Derian put down her silverware and took Aud's hand. "Why didn't you tell me?"

"How could I? You're never here."

"I'm sorry." Derian accepted the blame. Now wasn't the time to argue their long, complicated relationship. Now was the time to draw on the love they'd always shared. "When did you find out?"

"He was first diagnosed with colon cancer seven years ago."

"You didn't tell me even then?"

"I promised I wouldn't. No one knew. He didn't want people to look at him and see a weak man." Aud's eyes clouded and she hesitated, blinking. "As if he was ever that."

Derian pulled out the folded linen handkerchief in her pocket and handed it to her. She remembered doing the same for Emily. "Does Martin know?"

"He's one of the few. He's been decent about it, but I'm not sure what will happen now."

"There's a recurrence?"

"Yes, and it's fairly widespread. There's treatment," Aud said with false brightness, "and of course we're all certain he's going to beat it back this time as well, but—"

"You don't have to explain. Of course you'll be there in any way he needs you." She squeezed Aud's hand. "I'm really sorry. If you need anything, if George needs anything, I'm here."

"Are you, Dere?" Aud smiled sadly. "You're not, really, you know. Sometimes a person needs more than a voice on the phone or a text."

"I'm here now," Derian said, and for the first time, she realized she meant it. Her responsibilities no longer felt like obligations heaped on her shoulders, forcing her to be a person she didn't want to be. She was becoming the person she wanted to be on her own terms. "I plan to stay at the agency as long as I can, because the longer Henrietta takes to recover, the better it will be for her long-term. And if you need me, or your father does, I'll be here after that."

"Why? Why the sudden change?"

"People change," Derian said softly. "Or maybe they just grow into the people they always were."

"How much of this sea change has to do with Emily?"

Derian tensed. "I don't know what you're talking about."

"Don't you?" Aud sighed wearily. "All right, then. We'll save that for another time."

"Actually, I did want to ask you about her." Derian went back to eating, carefully and casually asking, "Explain to me about this whole visa situation and why all of a sudden it's a problem."

"How much do you know?"

"Start at the beginning—small words." She listened carefully as she sipped her wine, her appetite waning as Aud described the miasma of agencies, quotas, applications, approvals, and vicissitudes of the immigration process. In the end she wondered how anyone ever made their way through the system. "So what's the procedure to straighten all this out?"

Aud shrugged. "We file the papers, the applications, and the justifications, and hopefully everything will go through as it has in the past."

"Assuming Martin doesn't get his way and start cutting staff and reorganizing the agency."

"Admittedly, Emily's status isn't as…secure as it might be."

"Is there any way to secure her status for the long term?" Derian filled Aud's glass and her own.

"Well, ideally, she would become a permanent resident, which is another long and less-than-certain process. But even that wouldn't put her in line for taking over the agency, despite what Henrietta wants. You know the unwritten word—family first."

"Martin doesn't care about family," Derian said. "That's just a smokescreen to manipulate me and everyone else."

"Not entirely true," Aud argued. "Part of the strength of Winfield Enterprises is its legacy of being family run. If you really mean what you say about staying, then you should be Henrietta's permanent successor."

"I don't want the job permanently." Derian considered all the permutations Aud had just told her. "Emily needs her green card."

"That would solve a lot of problems, yes."

"Well, then there is a solution. She needs to get married."

"That's the best solution." Aud laughed. "But probably not a timely one, unless you plan on marrying her yourself."

Derian smiled and sipped her wine.

Aud stared. "You can't be serious."

"It would certainly solve all the issues at one time—for everyone. She'd be established here in the country, and she'd be family, so she could take over from Henrietta."

"Really, Derian. That's crazy."

"Why? It's not illegal, and she's already proven she deserves the position."

"What about the small issue of the marriage being a sham?"

"Lots of people get married for lots of reasons, and this is as good as any." Thinking of her parents, she grimaced. "Better than many."

"What about the small matter of love?"

Derian went very still inside, the kind of icy calm she always experienced in moments of highest risk. "Emily's career is her main focus, and you know what the circuit is like. I'd be away frequently. We'd have a very compatible relationship."

"If I really thought you were serious, I'd try to stop you." Aud shook her head. "But even you can't be that crazy."

Derian didn't argue. Aud wasn't the one she needed to convince of her seriousness.

CHAPTER TWENTY-ONE

The downstairs buzzer rang at 6:30 a.m. Someone had buzzed her apartment by mistake. Emily debated ignoring it, but almost immediately changed her mind. Maybe it was an early-morning delivery of some kind. She pressed the intercom button beside the door. "Yes?"

"I come bearing gifts."

A delivery, but not one she'd been expecting.

"Derian?" She didn't really have to ask. She recognized the golden honey-smooth timbre of her voice and recognized the quick upbeat of her heart as well. She glanced down at her fluffy bunny slippers and her sweats and her tank top. "I'm not dressed."

"Oh, then by all means, hurry up and buzz me in."

Laughing, Emily said, "I thought we were meeting at the convention center?"

"I know, but I was awake, and I knew you'd be up. Should I just leave my gifts out here on the steps?"

"Of course not." Emily pressed the foyer door release and contemplated whether she had enough time to change into something—anything—that wasn't this. Too late. Derian must have taken the stairs three at a time, because somehow she was rapping at the door already. Sighing, Emily opened the door and immediately forgot why she cared what she was wearing.

Derian smiled in at her, her dark hair slightly windblown, her darker eyes dancing with mischief and pleasure. She leaned in and kissed Emily's cheek. Her lips were warm. "Hi."

"Uh…hi." Emily held the door open wider and Derian breezed by, full of energy and carrying the scent of spring, brisk and fresh and new. She shed her topcoat and casually draped it over the arm of the sofa. She wore tailored dark pants, a black belt, and a pearl gray shirt. Professionally casual. Gorgeous. Breathtaking.

"You look great."

Derian tilted her head, eying Emily as if she'd never been complimented before. Which was impossible. "Thanks. I've been studying the dress code."

Emily laughed at the outright exaggeration and caught the aroma of something mouthwatering. "What have you been doing so early this morning? Whatever you've got in there smells wonderful."

"City Bakery." Derian carried the bag to the little table in front of the windows and settled easily into the chair, looking totally at home. Her gaze wandered over Emily and she grinned. "You look terrific, by the way."

Emily tried to keep the blush from rising to her face. "I look like I'm in my pajamas, which I am. Thankfully, I have showered."

Derian's mouth quirked. "I thought I smelled something wonderful just now."

"Would you like some tea?" Emily tried desperately to redirect the conversation.

"Sure." Derian leaned back in the chair and stretched out her legs, totally content to simply watch Emily move about her small kitchen with practiced efficiency. She did look great in a pale salmon tank top, red sweatpants that had been washed so much they too were nearly a faded pink, and honest-to-God bunny slippers. How could someone look so sexy and not know it? Watching her was a pleasure, but suddenly she wanted more.

"This thing we're going to," Derian said, hearing the huskiness in her voice, "how important is it?"

Emily paused in the process of pouring steaming water into her teapot and shrugged. "The BEA? For us, it's like the biggest race on the Grand Prix circuit."

Derian frowned. "Really."

"Really." Emily carried the robin's-egg blue teapot, cups, and matching sandwich plates to the table on a hand-painted tray picturing a weeping willow beside a sparkling waterfall and set it down. "Why?"

Derian caught Emily's hand, pulled her onto her lap, and nuzzled her neck. "So it would be a bad thing if we blew it off."

Emily stiffened for an instant, surprise giving way to a swift surge of desire. She'd already wrapped her arms around Derian's neck before she realized what she was doing. And by then she didn't care to consider anything but the urge for Derian's mouth on her skin. She tilted her head to give her throat, stroking Derian's nape as she thrust her fingers into her hair, wanting nothing more than for Derian to continue her slow course of kisses down her neck, for Derian's hands to slide under her T-shirt and over her bare belly and breasts. God, she wasn't wearing underwear. "Derian. We have to go to the meeting."

"Uh-huh." Derian pressed her cheek to the creamy, soft skin of Emily's chest and wrapped her arms around Emily's waist, closing her eyes and breathing her in. "How late can we be?"

"We have appointments first thing."

Derian rubbed her cheek over the swell of Emily's breast. "Every other second—no, *every* second—I think about being with you, like this, of kissing you slowly, everywhere, and undressing you, filling my hands with you."

"No one has ever said anything like that to me before," Emily said with a sigh. She cradled Derian's cheek and raised Derian's head from her breast. Dark, enticing shadows swam in Derian's eyes, beckoning her, promising her pleasure and discovery. Emily kissed her, craving the taste of her, yearning for the heat she knew would flood her. Derian groaned deep in her chest, a primal, possessive sound Emily loved. She loved the power she had to make Derian hunger as she hungered. Desire flared, pulled from deep inside where some ancient, primitive voice echoed *yes*. Yes and yes and yes. Distantly, her mind reverberated with *no, no, no*, but her mind was no match for the sensations swirling through her. The excitement, the wonder, the aching clawing need. "Oh God. We have to stop, but you feel so good."

"Kiss me again," Derian whispered, words she'd never said in her life. She slid a hand beneath the back of Emily's tank, smoothing her fingers up and down the faint ridge of her spine, molding Emily's body closer to hers. She could feel Emily's breasts, soft and full, pressing into her chest and slipped her hand around to cup the warm yielding curve of her. Instantly, Emily arched with a small cry of surprise. A lightning spear of desire shot through Derian's depths and Derian closed her hand without thinking.

"Oh yes." Emily gasped and pressed her hand over Derian's,

aching need blinding her to everything. The room disappeared, her past fell away, her future was only the want in Derian's eyes. "That feels so good. You make me feel so good."

Derian groaned again. "I want more. I need more. I need you naked."

"I want you too, you must feel it." Emily shuddered. "Not...now."

"When?"

"I can't think. I have to think."

"Why?" Derian pressed her face to Emily's breasts, her chest heaving, and the hand around Emily's breast trembled. "I want you so much."

Emily couldn't recall why not. "We don't have much time. If we hurry—"

Derian growled and shook her head. "I'm not rushing. Not with you." She looked up, grinned. Emily's lips, flushed and red, parted. Her eyes glinted with hunger, hunger that answered Derian's. She looked sexy and dangerous. "I need a lot of time to do what I'm planning to do."

"Slow is nice," Emily murmured, skimming her fingers over Derian's mouth. She wanted her mouth. She wanted her mouth *everywhere*. "But honest to God, I wouldn't mind fast right about now."

Derian laughed. "There's my bad girl."

Emily grinned. "You definitely have the wrong idea about me."

"Oh yeah? I don't think so. Everything about you amazes me." Derian wrapped both arms around her and tugged until Emily straddled her lap. She kissed her mouth, moved to her throat, and explored her breasts through the thin cotton of her tank, brushing her mouth over the hard points of her nipples. When she pulled one into her mouth, cotton and all, Emily arched, pressing tight into her lap, her head thrown back, her breasts mounding beneath her tank. Derian's vision swam and longing pushed the breath from her chest.

Keeping Emily steady with an arm wrapped around her waist, Derian pulled up Emily's tank and caressed her breasts and her belly and angle of her hip. Emily rocked in her lap, a seductive invitation for more. Derian murmured against her skin, "You're sure about the time thing?"

"Believe me, I wish I weren't." Emily struggled for breath. "But if we miss any of our appointments, Henrietta—"

"Stop!" Derian groaned. "Way to put out the fire, baby."

Laughing, Emily caressed Derian's face, both hands gently outlining her cheeks and the angles of her jaw, finally sliding down her neck and under the collar of her shirt. Derian had never been touched with such care, or such desire. She sighed, content despite the simmering tension making her insides roil. "I love the way you touch me."

"I'm so glad." Emily kissed her again, for herself, for the pleasure of the softness of Derian's mouth and the way the briefest contact filled her with longing and delight. She kissed her for the low groans torn from Derian's chest, for the tightening of Derian's hands on her hips, for the quickening of Derian's pulse beneath her fingertips. She kissed her for the sheer and simple joy of it. "I don't think I could ever get tired of touching you."

"I'm dying to give you the chance to find out."

"I wish I didn't have to do this." Emily kissed her lightly, and with more strength than she'd ever known she possessed, braced both hands on Derian's shoulders and carefully climbed off her lap. Her legs were shaking. Everything inside her quivered. She hadn't been kidding. She wouldn't have minded fast at all. If Derian touched her right now, she was pretty sure she would come. But if Derian wanted slow, then they'd do slow, sometime. If she didn't think about it, if she didn't give in to the tiny kernel of panic that kept threatening to swell into reason and make her run, far and fast. If she didn't think about what they were doing or what it might mean.

Derian frowned. "Whatever you're thinking about, stop."

"What do you mean? I wasn't really thinking of anything." Emily stepped back and busied herself pouring the tea. "How could I be? You tend to make me brainless."

"No," Derian said quietly, opening the bakery bag. "A minute ago you weren't thinking at all, and you wanted me. Then you started worrying. Don't do that."

"I don't know if I can stop," Emily said carefully, taking two plates from the tray and setting one in front of each of their places at the table. She sat across from Derian, grateful not to have to stand any longer when her legs still threatened to desert her. "I'm a planner. I'm not spontaneous. I like to know the consequences, or at least the possibilities, before I rush into something."

"I didn't get you cookies, but I thought you might like scones."
Derian placed a cinnamon scone with a swirl of white frosting on the
top in front of Emily.

"It's perfect. Thank you."

Derian fixed her with her heavy-lidded, languorous gaze. "Don't
overthink your feelings. There's some things you can't know until they
happen. You can't call the shot until the card is played. Sometimes you
just have to gamble."

"I'm not much of a gambler."

"Sure you are. You took a chance coming to this country, you took
a chance contacting Henrietta, and you took an even bigger chance
setting your stakes at the agency. You're winning all of those. Trust
your instincts. You're a winner."

"There isn't a single thing about going to bed with you that
resembles any of those choices." Emily broke off a piece of scone. It
was delicious, but after Derian's kisses, not enough to satisfy.

Derian grinned. "I'm very glad to hear I have more appeal than
Winfield's. I'd like to think I'm a lot more exciting."

"Oh, I think I can safely say that you are." Emily took a breath.
"I'm not really sure we should go any further, though."

"Emily, that ship has sailed."

"Oh, baloney," Emily snapped.

"Baloney?"

Emily waved a hand. "Nothing has sailed anywhere until we—"

"When," Derian said comfortably, popping a piece of carrot
muffin into her mouth. "When we make love."

"Are you always so damn sure…never mind, I know you are."
Emily blew out a breath. "But things have changed at the agency.
You're there now, you're in charge. You're my boss."

"Oh, baloney." Derian tamped down a wave of irritation. She
couldn't discount Emily's feelings, as ridiculous as she found that
whole argument. If it was important to Emily, it had to be important to
her. "First of all, I'm not your boss. I'm Henrietta's temporary stand-in,
and you are more *my* boss than the other way around. Everyone knows
it."

"Derian, you've been at the agency half a week. You catch on
quickly. And even if you were an utter failure, you're still Derian
Winfield, Henrietta's niece, and you are very much everyone's boss."

"Is that how you think of me?"

Emily sighed. "I'm trying to."

"What's stopping you?"

"You. You confuse me. I have trouble thinking clearly when I think about you."

Derian grinned that self-satisfied grin. "Good." She glanced at her watch. "I guess we should probably get going if we're going to make those appointments."

"The problem isn't going to go away," Emily said, taking her tea with her as she rose. "I'll be ready in just a few minutes."

"The problem isn't a problem unless we make it one," Derian called after her. "Do you think you could wear the slippers?"

Emily muttered something under her breath Derian couldn't catch, but the intention was clear. Derian laughed. She'd never met a woman who could make her laugh as easily as she could make her insane with desire. Emily was unique. She wouldn't let a tangle of government red tape or her father's ego threaten Emily's happiness, especially not when she could do something to solve the problem.

CHAPTER TWENTY-TWO

The Town Car let them off at the corner of Thirty-Fourth Street and Eleventh Avenue in Hell's Kitchen behind a long line of double-parked cabs disgorging people in droves. Sidewalks and crosswalks were packed with people converging on the Javits Convention Center, a sprawling modern glass and concrete building four stories tall and as many deep, that extended for six blocks along Eleventh. Rows of hot dog and pretzel vendors were setting up on the curb and, given that the sky was overcast and threatening rain at any second, the ubiquitous vendors selling umbrellas from the back of vans had arrived as well. A carnival atmosphere prevailed despite the menacing skies.

"Looks like opening day in Cannes," Derian remarked, resting her hand gently in the small of Emily's back as they wound their way through the crowds.

"Prepare yourself for something very different," Emily said, laughing.

"Oh, don't worry, I have." Derian imagined a long day of networking, the very idea of which made her want to head in the opposite direction. But she'd have Emily for company, and that made the dreariness more than tolerable. She was actually looking forward to the event.

When they made it through the long row of glass doors into the foyer, Derian drew a sharp breath. She'd known what to expect, but the assault was always the same. Huge spaces filled with people, banks of escalators going up and down, signs everywhere, and an overwhelming sense of disorientation. Even casinos had more orderly layouts than this place. Sweat gathered on the back of her neck. The initial panic was always the same.

"We just have to pick up our badges." Emily, her voice bright with excitement, pointed to the registration area and a long row of booths in the far right corner.

"I don't think I've ever seen anyone so excited to be going to a conference," Derian said, hurrying to keep up with Emily, who cut through the crowds like a cab on Seventh Avenue.

"Oh," Emily said, arrowing in on her target, "this is a lot more than a conference. This is…everything—it's what we're all about. Not just what's new in books, but how we make them, who's reading them, and where the industry is headed."

"I'm afraid I'm going to need an interpreter," Derian said, "because I feel like a stranger in a strange land."

Emily grasped her arm. "Don't worry, you have a seasoned guide. The first time I attended with Henrietta I was the same way."

"I doubt that—at least you speak the language."

"You will too, soon. Until then, I'll be your backup."

"It seems like you've been doing that for me since we met." Derian grimaced. "I'm usually not quite so useless."

Emily paused and the crowd flowed around them, leaving them standing like a tiny island in a sea of frothing humanity. "You are less in need of aid than any person I've ever met."

"Thanks, but I owe you—"

"No, you don't. Caring is not something that comes with a price on it."

"It is where I come from," Derian said softly. "With everyone except HW. And now you. It will take some getting used to."

"Work on it, then. Because I'm not going to stop."

Emily spoke quietly, but her words carried deep into Derian's soul. She wished they were anywhere but in a crowded convention hall right that moment. The desire to kiss her was a physical ache. "That's good to know."

"I want you to promise me something," Emily said.

"Anything."

"That you'll stop looking at me like that for the rest of the day."

Derian grinned. "That's going to be very difficult for me to do, but I'll try."

"Thank you," Emily said, her voice a warm embrace. "Now come on. The *W*s are at the far end." She slid her hand behind Derian's elbow, unobtrusively leading her past the snaking rows of people queued up in front of overhead signs. "Let's find your line."

When Derian got at the end of the line Emily indicated, she said, "I better wait here for you. If I try finding you, I'm likely to get turned around and end up wandering in here for forty years."

"No, you wouldn't." Emily smiled. "If you did, I'd find you."

"Good to know." Derian wasn't used to anyone helping her out in these kinds of situations, but then she never let on how hard some things were for her.

"I'll be right back, and then we'll do a little reconnoitering," Emily added. "This place is a big city, and it takes a little getting used to it."

"I'm game," Derian said. "Go ahead. I'm good."

"I know." Emily hurried to the appropriate row to pick up her badge, hating to leave Derian and feeling foolish for worrying at the same time. Derian was perfectly capable. She traveled the world, made her home in more cities than Emily ever hoped to visit, and wasn't going to be overcome by the chaos of a convention center. As much as she knew all of that, she still hated to leave her. She wanted to be with her, not because Derian needed taking care of, but because she enjoyed being near her more than anything she'd ever experienced. She loved talking business with her, loved playing verbal games with her, certainly loved kissing her, and just found the world a brighter, more exciting place when she was with her. She loved—

"Can I help you?" A cheerful middle-aged man with a badge around his neck that said he was a volunteer smiled at her from behind the registration counter.

"Oh!" Emily wondered how long she'd been standing there. "I need to pick up my registration materials. Um, Emily May."

"Certainly," he said and began riffling through a long box of name cards. "Here we are."

"Thanks." Emily took the package automatically, not listening to his well-practiced rundown of what she could find inside the bag. Her thoughts were filled with Derian. She turned away to make room for the next person and made her way back to Derian. She didn't see her at first and her heart leapt anxiously. *Don't be silly, she's got a cell phone. She's not going to get lost. All you have to do is call her.*

Emily reached for the phone and then she saw her, leaning back against a pillar, her registration bag dangling from one hand, observing the crowd around her, a calm steady presence amidst the noisy jostling masses. A sensation of relief and something far greater settled into the center of Emily's chest. Derian turned her head, and despite the dozens of people still milling back and forth between them, looked directly at her. Their gazes caught, and Emily recognized the tide rising within her. Oh no, how had this happened? Shouldn't she have known, shouldn't she have recognized it far before this? She loved everything about Derian Winfield, everything Derian made her feel, everything Derian made her dream. Everything Derian made her desire. All because she was falling in love with Derian Winfield.

Derian's gaze pulled her through the crowd as if she'd reached out and taken her hand. Emily made her way to her, the sea of faceless people parting under the strength of their invisible connection.

"All set?" Emily tried for a casual tone she was far from feeling.

"Perfect."

Derian's hand was on her back again, a familiar movement Emily realized she'd come to love, like all of Derian's other little casual touches that to her felt possessive and incredibly intimate. Oh, this was so, so not good. And yet so exactly what she wanted.

"Lead on, Tour Guide," Derian said teasingly.

"Right." Emily gathered her wits. "Right. We need to be—hold on"—she dragged out the thick program guide and searched the index—"third floor, section A-1028." She dropped the book back into her bag and checked her watch. "We'll have half an hour before they open the doors to the general attendees. Come on, we've got a lot to do."

"We do?"

"Yep." Emily grinned. "We get first crack at all the swag. Let's go."

"Swag?" Derian kept pace with Emily's unerring twisting, dodging path through the crowds. She was clearly an expert at this. Only half joking, she said, "Don't leave me."

Emily laughed and glanced over her shoulder, jumping onto the escalator to the next level. "I wouldn't think of it."

At the top, they stepped off into an enormous space filled with aisle upon aisle of booths and books. Books everywhere—piled on tables, stacked on the floor, shelved behind counters, and overflowing from open cartons. There must have been five hundred booths and five hundred thousand books. The aisles were still relatively clear of people, with only handfuls scurrying up and down doing final setup. Big signs hung above the aisles with white letters and numbers like street signs. Derian's chest tightened as she took in the foreign space and struggled to make sense of it. "I'm afraid you're going to have to take me wherever we need to go. You can just leave me there while you do…whatever."

"Absolutely not." Emily took her hand. "You'll be fine. Just stay with me."

"Try getting rid of me," Derian said.

"Besides, you're elected to do the carrying. Here."

"Uh…" Derian stared at the shiny multicolored bag with the cartoon image Emily handed her. "You want me to walk around carrying a bag with Captain Underpants on it?"

Emily laughed. "Those are in incredible demand and will be gone in half an hour. Whatever you do, don't put it down anywhere." As she spoke, she was dropping books into it.

"Are we stealing these?" Derian asked.

"No," Emily said, handing her another bag, this one thankfully unadorned except for a publisher's logo. "These are all advance reading copies. They're free."

"Why?" Derian grabbed a handful of Hershey's Kisses from a bowl on a counter in front of a booth displaying computers running some kind of cataloging software.

"Marketing." Emily smiled and accepted a catalog from a book rep as they passed by the next booth. "Librarians and booksellers are the largest segments of attendees. They'll be looking for new titles to order in the upcoming year. Most of these booths are publishers, promoting their forthcoming catalogs. There'll be a row of printers—not as many as there used to be, now that everything has gone digital—and companies selling software to handle metadata and royalties and whatnot."

"Okay, I need a crash course, that's pretty clear," Derian muttered. "But first I'm gonna need more coffee."

Laughing, looking young and happy and energized, Emily nodded. "We'll have plenty of breaks between appointments. We've got three days to get you properly initiated."

"I'm sorry I'm not going to be much help." Derian grimaced and glanced around, realizing she had no idea which direction they'd come from or how to get back there. "And I'm something of a liability on top of that."

"You absolutely are not," Emily said fiercely. "Don't ever say that again."

The force of her words washed over Derian like a flurry of kisses. Her belly warmed and she had to remind herself about her promise of business only for the rest of the day. "I like it when you champion me. You make me feel special."

"You are," Emily said, still in battle mode. "And you are not the first person to feel lost in this place. I'm just used to it."

"I'm okay," Derian said, realizing she was. She'd find Emily if they got separated. One way or the other, she'd find her again. Emily kept her centered. "Come on, we've only got fifteen minutes left and there must be a few thousand more books you need to get."

"At least."

"Wait—what about those comics." Derian pointed to a kiosk. "Can we get them?"

"Of course. Any preference?"

"Superheroes are always good. And paranormal. I don't suppose there'd be any Patricia Briggs?"

Emily grabbed copies and dropped them into Derian's bag. "There might be some of Briggs's graphic novels over at Dynamite."

As she spoke, Emily scanned the huge signs and kiosks and posters. "I think they're down this way." She grabbed Derian's hand and tugged her in that direction. "Briggs is signing this afternoon, so they might not have anything available yet."

At nine o'clock, a voice over the PA system announced the doors would be opening momentarily.

"That's our cue," Emily said. "We should grab some coffee, find our table, and get out of the way of the hordes."

Derian shifted the bags into a more comfortable position on her shoulder. She figured Emily was exaggerating, but she was wrong. A minute later a tsunami of people poured off the escalators, flooding the aisles, rushing everywhere, filling bags with books and pens and bookmarks and free promotional items. "This place is a madhouse."

Emily laughed, clearly delighted. "And everyone thinks book

people are stodgy. You don't want to get in the way of someone trying to get an advance copy of their favorite author in this place. You're likely to get run down."

"All we need are the hot-dog vendors and the carnival will be complete," Derian said.

"Oh, they'll be at the far back of the room. And I like hot dogs, so you can get me one later."

Derian smiled. "My pleasure."

And it was. Being with Emily gave her the inexplicable desire to hunt and gather and take care of her. Emily might not need her to do any of those things, but Derian planned on doing whatever she could to be sure Emily's future was secure.

❖

Derian made it to the hospital a few minutes before visiting hours ended, rapped on the partially open door, and walked into Henrietta's room. HW was the only patient in there and was sitting up in bed with the newspaper spread out on the bedside stand in front of her. Some of her color had returned, but she looked thinner and, for the first time, older. Her fragility sent fear through Derian's chest. "Sorry it's so late, but I just wanted to stop by and make sure you weren't driving the nurses crazy."

"I've been behaving but they still won't let me have my computer."

"Good."

Henrietta set the paper aside. "How did the appointments go?"

"Emily was happy. She seemed to think several of the deals were strong ones."

"What did you think of the process?"

"It was a lot like a card game, not quite as interesting but—I could see the appeal."

Henrietta laughed. "You're right—a good negotiation is always a bit of a game."

Derian paused, noting an extra IV pole. "Is it my imagination, or is there more equipment in here today than yesterday?"

"Oh, just some extra medication they added."

"Why?"

"Nothing serious, just a little blood clot. The medicine will take care of it."

Derian grew very still. "Blood clot? Where?"

"My right leg," Henrietta said with a huff of disgust. "Apparently it happens when you don't get up and move around enough. Although how I'm supposed to do that—"

"Okay, I got it." Derian kept her voice calm. "How come no one called me about it?"

"It's not like there was anything you needed to do," Henrietta said. "It was far more important that you take care of business and not be distracted. I'm perfectly capable of making my own medical decisions now."

"I want to talk to the doctor." Derian turned to go.

Henrietta caught her arm. "He's not going to tell you anything that I haven't already told you. I need a course of anticoagulants—heparin—and then some oral medication after I get home. It's not a major setback."

"Are you telling me the whole story?" Henrietta was perfectly capable of downplaying the seriousness of the complication, but going head-to-head with her was not something she wanted to do.

"Absolutely."

"Okay, but I'm still going to talk to him tomorrow."

"Of course you are," Henrietta said fondly. "So tell me all about today."

Derian recounted everything she could remember about the meetings with the foreign rights agents. "Emily is writing everything up for you because she knows you'd want to know. But you have to promise to let us handle it."

"How is that going? The two of you at the agency?"

"I'm surviving, but I'm pretty much useless." Derian hadn't told her about Donatella and didn't intend to.

"I doubt that. You're quick when you put your mind to it. And Emily knows what she's about. The two of you should be able to handle anything."

"Emily could handle anything without me," Derian said.

"Everyone needs a sounding board, Derian. And given the circumstances, Emily needs your support."

"She has it," Derian said. "And the sooner we get things straightened out, the better."

"As soon as I'm up and around—"

Derian shook her head. "No deal. You're not going back to work, HW. Not until the doctors say, and until then, I'm in charge."

Henrietta's brows shot up, and the old fire kindled in her eyes. "Really? A coup, is it?"

Derian grinned. "You might think of it that way."

Henrietta leaned back against the pillows, looking tired, but satisfied. "If I'd known I'd have to have a heart attack to get you into the office, I might have contemplated it previously."

Derian leaned over and kissed her. "I'm sorry. If I'd known you needed me, I would've come."

Henrietta stroked her cheek. "I know that, and you did come. I've always known that too."

"It's good to be here." She never thought she'd say that, but then she never thought she'd want a lot of things she suddenly found she couldn't stop thinking about. "I should let you get some sleep."

"Don't forget you have the National Book Awards coming up," Henrietta said.

Derian winced. "Yeah. I saw that on the schedule. I don't suppose—"

"Emily will need company—it's always easier to network that way."

"Oh." Derian thought for a second she saw an amused glint in HW's eye, but then it was gone. Any excuse for a night out with Emily was fine with her, even a stuffy awards ceremony. "Right. I'm looking forward to it."

"I'm sure." Henrietta laughed. "I can't wait to hear all about it."

CHAPTER TWENTY-THREE

Emily was dressed and ready to go way too early. To keep from checking her makeup for the tenth time or looking in the mirror again to be sure her dress fell just right and not too low between her breasts, she went to the window to watch for Derian. She couldn't pretend she didn't feel like a high school girl waiting for her prom date, even though she'd never actually gone to the prom. She'd missed those things after the accident. Refusing to allow the past to intrude on a night she'd been anticipating for weeks, she let those memories drift back to where they belonged.

She was dressed to the nines and going out to a gala with a handsome woman, and she intended to enjoy every minute of the evening, even if she was the only one who thought of it like it was a date. Derian undoubtedly thought of the National Book Awards as a necessary evil of her temporary job, but she'd agreed to attend with the same willingness she'd tackled all the other new responsibilities at Winfield's. She'd settled in remarkably well at the agency, and despite not having any formal training in literature, she had an innate appreciation for what worked and what didn't. Derian seemed to enjoy their business discussions as much as Emily and had a natural affinity for the production side of the business, being exceptionally good with numbers. Emily laughed to herself. No surprise there.

Helping Derian learn the agency didn't feel like work at all. She looked forward to every day, with their morning meetings, their after-lunch conferences, and the impromptu moments when Derian would drop by her office to ask her a question or discuss something that had come across her desk. Derian wasn't trying to replace Henrietta, but she was learning what made Winfield's tick. Unlike Donatella, Derian appreciated Henrietta's vision, the heart of it all, and that mattered more than anything.

A black Town Car slid to the curb and Emily's pulse soared. She was used to that reaction by now, since every time she saw Derian, exhilaration rushed through her. She loved simply looking at her, the way she moved with a graceful, confident stride, the way her brows drew down just a little when she was deep in thought, the lazy way she sometimes watched Emily that made Emily feel incredibly sensual.

Emily had only had a glimpse of her when Derian stepped from the car before she disappeared onto the stairs, but a second was enough to put her heart in her throat. For tonight's formal event, Derian had chosen a dark suit with a classically tailored jacket and notched lapels, fitted trousers, and a pale gray silk shirt—sleek and elegant, like her.

Feeling only a teeny bit foolish, Emily waited next to the intercom for the buzzer. As soon as it sounded, she said, "I'll be right down."

"Let me come up," Derian said. "I'm your escort, remember?"

Emily laughed. "I think I can manage the stairs."

"No doubt, but a lady should be handed into her carriage in the proper fashion."

"All right." Still laughing, Emily released the inner door and, when the knock sounded, took a deep breath and told herself not to think, just to enjoy the night. She opened her door and Derian's gaze swept over her.

"You look incredible." Derian folded Emily's hand in hers and kissed her knuckles. With her head still bent low, she murmured, "You take my breath away."

"You make me feel amazing."

Derian looked up, her eyes glinting. "I've been looking forward to this, and you are the reason."

Smiling self-consciously, Emily grabbed her small clutch from the table by the door and stepped out, closing it behind her. "I happen to know the National Book Awards is not exactly high on your list of events to attend. But I really hope you enjoy it."

Derian slid her hand behind Emily's elbow and walked close beside her down the hall. "You'll be there. How can I not enjoy it?"

"After the twentieth conversation about market trends and

predictions of doom for the demise of the entire industry, you might change your mind."

Derian held the door for her. "Who said I was going to be listening to any of that? I'm an expert at appearing to be interested and nodding at all the appropriate places while contemplating the next race."

"Your skills will come in handy tonight, then." Emily firmly told herself not to think about when Derian might be off to the next stop on the endless racing circuit. Henrietta was home from the hospital, but thus far they'd all managed to keep her away from Winfield's. Derian wasn't leaving yet, and tonight was just for tonight. She'd think no further.

After they settled into the backseat of the car, Emily gave the driver the address. Derian sat close, her arm stretched out behind Emily, the fingertips of her left hand resting on Emily's bare skin. She hadn't worn a wrap and now she was doubly glad. The weather had finally cooperated, and the evening promised to be one of those rare spring nights that felt like summer and held its warmth into the late hours. Derian's fingertips on her skin warmed her all the way through, or maybe Derian's touch was just a reflection of the heat that had been building inside her for days.

"We'll have about an hour to mingle before the event starts," Emily said. "I suspect everyone is going to want to meet you, so be prepared."

"My loins are girded," Derian said dryly.

"Well, try not to draw your sword unless absolutely necessary."

"I promise, no bloodshed." Derian's hand moved slowly up and down Emily's arm. "Besides, I'll have you to think about, and nothing could possibly bother me while I'm doing that."

Seated at a large round table near the front of the banquet hall with eight other Winfield people, platters of hors d'oeuvres, and open bottles of champagne, Emily found her pledge to concentrate on business getting more difficult by the second. Usually she loved events like this one. She enjoyed networking, taking the temperature of the industry, watching the maneuvers of the power people who were part of the living machinery of the publishing industry. And she truly appreciated the work of the authors being fêted, even when, like tonight, none of Winfield's were on the stage. She thought several of the authors they represented had deserved to be finalists, but awards were always less about quality and far more about politics. After all, they were determined by individuals who, no matter how well-informed and knowledgeable, still had personal agendas, biases, and favoritisms. Still, one always wanted one's work to be appreciated, and as long as recognition was formalized this way, she was as competitive as anyone else in the business.

Tonight her attention was split between the stage and Derian. She couldn't seem to stop stealing glances at her, and every time she did, all she wanted was to be alone with her. As the various awards and categories were announced and awards given, Derian leaned closer.

"How many of Winfield's authors have been shortlisted?"

"Quite a number," Emily said quietly, "but not as many as should be, in my opinion."

"You'll have to tell me some other time how this all works."

"We'll have a breakfast postmortem."

"Tomorrow works for me."

Derian chuckled, a low seductive sound that slashed through Emily like lightning, making her forget everything that was happening in the moment. Impulsively, she said, "For me too. I always love to start the day with a business discussion."

"That's the best offer I've ever had," Derian said. "How soon can we get out of here?"

Emily was thankful the lights were turned down low in the room and no one at their table was close enough to hear their conversation or notice her response. She wasn't in the mood for pretending she didn't know what Derian was talking about. She was in a very different mood altogether.

"We have to stay to the end of this," she whispered. "But I did happen to come by a very nice bottle of wine I thought you might like to share afterward."

Even in the dim light she could see the predatory glint leap into Derian's eyes. She loved knowing she brought out the hunter in her and, ridiculously breathless, reveled in the wild surge in her depths.

"I would love nothing more." Derian leaned closer until their shoulders touched. "Waiting is exquisitely painful."

"I know." Emily turned back to the stage, clapped in the appropriate places, and tried without success to concentrate on the rest of the ceremony. She caught Ron glancing their way more than once and envisioned another social cross-examination from him in the near future.

As soon as the last award had been bestowed, the lights came up and the audience began to disperse. The award recipients gathered by the stage for photographs with their respective agents and publishers and those who waited to congratulate them.

"Now?" Derian leaning closer, her mouth almost brushing Emily's ear.

"Yes," Emily said, grabbing Derian's hand and pulling her away before they could get caught up in the aftermath conversations. "Now."

❖

The car was waiting and they rode in silence, Derian's arm once again around Emily's shoulders, their bodies touching. Emily leaned in to Derian, anticipation electrifying every sensation. The warm air caressing her skin made her long for Derian's hands to do the same. By the time they arrived and climbed the stairs hand in hand, she ached. She let them into her apartment and switched on a table lamp that gave just enough light to fill the room with a pale glow.

"This should be ready now," Emily said, pointing to the merlot she'd left open to breathe on the counter.

"Emily," Derian whispered, catching her in a gentle grip and turning her around.

Caught in the undertow of Derian's gaze, Emily stilled.

"What about you?"

Ready? Oh yes, she was ready. For what, beyond needing to touch and be touched, with this woman, by this woman, she didn't know. And didn't care. All was now. "Yes."

Derian's kiss began with a slow, commanding press of her mouth, one hand on the back of Emily's neck and her arm around Emily's waist. Emily knew this kiss, remembered it in her bones. She went into

Derian's arms easily, naturally, sliding both arms around her shoulders. The kiss went on forever while they swayed together, everything receding from her awareness but the taste of Derian's desire, and her own restless hunger. When they broke apart, she was gasping. She wanted another kiss, she wanted the unknown that lay beyond it. She tightened her hold on Derian, brushed her lips over Derian's throat.

"Have I mentioned I love your kisses?"

"I don't believe so."

"I do—and I'd like more."

"Tell me we can have the wine in bed," Derian said, her voice a low growl. She brushed her fingers through Emily's hair, exposing her neck as she kissed the angle of her jaw, her throat, the hollow above her collarbone. Her grip was possessive, demanding. "Please."

Emily closed her eyes and let her head fall back, content for Derian to feast. Her breasts ached to be caressed, her flesh craved to be owned. Her belly was tight, the heat between her thighs spreading like wildfire. "Yes."

"Where?"

"This way." Emily caught Derian's hand and led her into the bedroom. The tall windows let in enough light to see by, and she turned, gripped Derian's jacket, and pushed it from her shoulders. "I've dreamed of seeing you naked."

"Haven't you already?" Derian let Emily strip the jacket down her arms and reached for the buttons on her shirt.

"Well, I have *seen* you naked," Emily said, brushing Derian's hands away to continue opening the buttons herself. "The dreams were more about where and how and what we'd be doing."

"I hope the reality—"

Emily kissed her into silence. Derian stood still, letting her have her way, and the thrill of possession broke over her. Never had she imagined such pleasure. Her hands trembled with the power as she pushed the crisp edges of Derian's dress shirt open and kissed the hollow of her throat. "Oh, believe me, the reality is far, far better."

"For me too," Derian murmured, a note of wonder in her voice.

Emily slid the cuff links from Derian's sleeves and reached blindly toward the bedside table to set them down, never stopping her soft kisses down the center of Derian's chest as she bared pale, smooth skin. She loved this soft glide of Derian's skin under her lips, loved the heady sweet scent of her. She pushed Derian's shirt off and pulled the sleek silk she'd worn underneath upward, and then there was only the rise of Derian's breasts beneath her mouth and the honeyed wonder of her skin.

Derian groaned. "We need to do this lying down."

"I know." Emily's breath fled as Derian unzipped the back of her dress, slid the fabric down her shoulders, and lifted her breasts free of the material. She pushed into the heat of Derian's hands, kissing the sweep of Derian's breasts, just glancing her nipples. "I can't seem to stop touching you."

"Then don't. Whatever you want, it's yours."

Derian unbuckled her belt and shed the rest of her clothes. Emily let her dress fall to the floor in a pool around her feet and started to remove her undergarments.

"Wait." Gloriously naked, and completely unself-conscious, Derian knelt. "Let me do this."

Emily braced her hands on Derian's shoulders and looked down, watching Derian's hands move on her body. Her thighs quivered. Her vision clouded. "Hurry."

Derian laughed softly. "Not tonight."

"Whatever you want," Emily whispered, catching her lip between her teeth as Derian pressed a cheek to her stomach and slid a hand up her back to release her bra. Derian stroked her hips and hooked her thumbs under the scrap of lace she'd so carefully chosen, knowing Derian would see them.

"These are pretty," Derian breathed against the sheer fabric. She looked up and grinned her arrogant grin. "For me?"

"Mmm." Emily raked her fingers through Derian's hair, words having abandoned her to the primal language of desire. Derian's fingers lightly trailed across the delta of her thighs, stroking her through the silk. Emily's hips lifted to her touch. "Derian, take me to bed. I want you on top of me."

The plea in Emily's voice broke Derian's patience. She surged to her feet and, circling an arm about Emily's waist, half carried her the few feet to the bed. Reaching down with her free hand, she tossed the covers roughly aside and guided Emily down. When she slid on top of her, their legs entwining and Emily holding her tight, Derian hungered with an ache that threatened never to be satisfied. Stripping away the last shimmer of material between them, she filled her hands with Emily's warm flesh, tasted her, drank of her, gloried in her. She didn't hurry, kissing and caressing her breasts, her stomach, the insides of her thighs. She lost herself in her and still the hunger roared.

"I want you so much." Derian braced herself on one arm, watching Emily's face. "I want to make you come."

"So, so good." Emily arched beneath her touches, electric with desire. "Take, touch me."

Derian stroked between Emily's thighs, and Emily's eyelids fluttered. Emily's lips parted, her unfocused gaze sought Derian's, and her body tightened. Derian kissed her gently and slid deep inside her. Emily's cry against her mouth filled her with a primitive surge of triumph. She stroked in time to the lift and fall of Emily's hips, and when Emily covered her hand to guide her, her heart nearly stopped. Chained by desire, she willed herself to Emily's call.

"You're going to make me come," Emily exclaimed, part shock, part pleasure.

Derian stilled, every sense focused on feeling her, hearing her, seeing her come apart with pleasure. When Emily gave herself over, the moment was forever and swifter than a heartbeat. So powerful, so exquisitely perfect.

"More," Derian whispered and slid down to take her into her mouth. Emily's hands came into her hair and she surged into Derian's mouth. Derian teased her, stroked her, took her to the edge and over again. Emily's wild cry rifled down her spine, fired her blood. She wanted never to move, but the pull of Emily's hands on her shoulders drew her upward and then somehow she was on her back.

Emily straddled her thighs and leaned down to kiss her, her hair a soft curtain around Derian's face. She clasped Emily's hips, guided her back and forth in a slow roll against her as they kissed. Emily came again in short, ecstatic thrusts against Derian's stomach. Derian rose up and cradled her in the curve of her body. She kissed her, stroked the damp hair from her cheek. "You're amazing."

Emily laughed weakly. "I think that's my line."

"No line," Derian whispered, kissing her closed lids, her mouth, her neck. Emily made soft contented sighs, caressing Derian's breasts and belly. Derian shuddered. "And you're pretty much driving me crazy."

"My turn," Emily said in a throaty commanding tone. She pressed her hand to the center of Derian's chest and pushed her down. Still curled beside her, her hair spread out on Derian's chest, she kissed her throat and stroked her chest and belly and cupped between her thighs.

"I love the way you touch me." Never had Derian wanted so much to be taken.

Emily gave another of those contented sounds, her mouth traveling over Derian's breasts as her fingers closed around her and tugged in slow, sure motions. Derian gritted her teeth, incredibly close but willing herself to hold on. Somehow Emily knew just how fast and how far to take her, until every muscle was poised to explode, and then she'd let her down just enough to keep her on the brink. Once, twice, three times she brought her within a heartbeat.

And then Derian begged. "Please, don't stop this time."

Emily gathered Derian close, her mouth a breath from Derian's. "I won't."

Emily kissed her then, a kiss to steal her breath, a kiss to steal her reason, a kiss to steal her old life and take her to a place she'd never been. Derian came hard, she came helplessly, trembling in Emily's arms.

CHAPTER TWENTY-FOUR

Derian woke at dawn with Emily spooned against her, back to front. Her arm was around Emily's waist, her cheek nuzzled against Emily's nape. Chestnut hair twined across her face. The oddest sensations, contradictory yet forged into a single flame, fired her blood. Contentment, warm and soothing, along with banked desire, edgy and wanting. Kissing the back of Emily's neck, she lightly stroked Emily's breasts and abdomen, fingers drifting lazily. Pieces of the night played through her mind—Emily moving beneath her, sharp cries of pleasure, pleas for more and again. Emily riding her, stroking her, taking her— surely and without reserve. Derian's clit pulsed and she groaned, sliding a hand between Emily's thighs. She was warm and wet.

Emily gave a pleased murmur and pressed her hand over Derian's, rocking her hips into the curve of Derian's body. Derian's contentment rapidly gave way to consuming craving.

"That's a nice way to wake up," Emily said drowsily.

Derian kissed a spot below Emily's ear she'd discovered the previous night that Emily liked very much. The swift gasp of breath encouraged her to keep going, turning Emily gently onto her back to claim her mouth. She eased on top of her, keeping her weight on her arms, and indulged herself.

Emily nipped at Derian's earlobe. "If this is what you're like in the morning, I'm very glad you stayed."

"It's a new experience for me," Derian said, making her way down Emily's neck to her breasts. She rubbed her cheek against Emily's rapidly hardening nipple. "And one I like very much."

Emily loved the weight of Derian's body over hers, the sensation one of equal parts owning and being owned. Stroking both hands over Derian's shoulders and down the arch of her back, she clasped Derian's hips and wrapped her legs over Derian's. Their bodies fit together as if they'd joined a thousand times, but the excitement racing through her was as great as the first instant they'd touched. "I'm afraid you may have unleashed a demon."

Derian chuckled and slid a little lower. "I certainly hope so."

Thought fled as Derian's mouth awakened her. Emily gripped the sheets when she could no longer reach Derian, her body open and vulnerable and alive with anticipation. Derian's groan, a low rumble of possessive pleasure, shot through her, stirring her even more than the impossible glory of Derian taking her with her mouth and hands. How could every move be so perfectly timed, unerringly stroking and pushing her to places she had never realized she could go?

"I love touching you," Derian muttered. "You feel so damn good."

The words, as powerful as Derian's touch, thrilled Emily to the core. Derian's delight in her was as wild and wonderful as the orgasm unfurling inside her. She cried out, her back arched, her legs taut, and felt Derian's fingers entwined with hers. She held on to the slender tether while her body, her very essence, took flight.

"I can't keep coming like that," she gasped at last. "I'll disappear."

"Oh no, you won't." Derian kissed her and sent another aftershock spinning over her. "I won't let you."

Emily drifted and almost fell asleep, until a hard, hot body pressed against her. She dragged herself back to reality and opened her eyes. Derian lounged beside her, her head propped on her elbow and a supremely self-satisfied smile on her face.

Emily laughed. "Have I ever mentioned you're the most arrogant woman I've ever met?"

Derian kissed her lightly. "I'm wounded."

"You're wonderful." Emily lightly scraped her nails down the center of Derian's abdomen.

Derian's eyes grew smoky. "Only if you think so."

Emily pushed Derian onto her back. "I do, but don't let it go to your head."

"Right now, I'd agree to anything." Derian's voice was husky, her muscles twitching wherever Emily teased.

"Really?" Emily had never imagined the thrill of possessing a woman, of filling her hands with beauty and passion and vulnerability. She snugged between Derian's thighs and, starting with her breasts, worked her way slowly down the center of her bowstring taut body, kissing and nipping and sating her every urge.

Derian groaned, determined to let Emily take what she wanted and praying she could last. The waiting was excruciating. The sounds torn from her throat were unlike anything she'd ever heard before. When Emily's lips closed around her, white lightning burst inside her head, incinerating every thought. A second later, she was lost.

"I'm sorry," Derian finally said, aware her cheek had somehow come to be nestled against Emily's breast. "I'm not usually so quick off the block."

Elated, Emily kissed the top of her head. "I thought it was unbelievably sexy."

Derian tilted her head, caught the gratified smile. "You seem to do very unexpected things to me."

"Do I," Emily said with a low purr. "Good things?"

"Fabulous things."

"Mmm. That's handy, since I really want to do it again."

Derian laughed and started to sit up.

Emily's arm tightened around her shoulders. "Stay a minute. I like you there."

Derian stilled, unused to being held by women. She wasn't used to being possessed, and she damn sure wasn't used to being controlled in bed. Until Emily. Giving Emily whatever she wanted, including her body and her will, had suddenly become her greatest pleasure. She sighed. Why fight what felt so damn good? "I would be happy to stay here the entire day, but I want to go with Henrietta to her rehab appointment."

"You have to go—or else she'll browbeat them into shortening her program. Besides, it's a workday and I should get going too." Emily rested her cheek against Derian's head. "Although I don't know how I'm going to concentrate on any of it. I can't seem to think of anything except…"

Derian finally had enough energy to sit up and dragged Emily into her lap. "Except?"

Emily kissed her. "More."

"There's always more."

"I'm very glad to hear that."

Derian nuzzled her throat. "How about now?"

"Oh, that's nice. A nice thought, I mean." Emily laughed. "And if you keep doing that, you're going to get me started again."

Undeterred, Derian muttered, "I'm afraid that's not going to make me want to stop."

Halfheartedly, Emily gripped her hair. "Later?"

"When?" Derian said instantly. The idea of being apart from her was strangely disturbing. She didn't want to stop touching her. Hell, she didn't want to let her out of her sight. She had no idea what to make of that.

"Come to dinner," Emily said. "We still haven't had the red."

"I'm sorry if we ruined last night's bottle."

"I stoppered it. Not form, I know, but it will probably be fine."

Derian frowned. "When?"

"When you fell asleep."

"I can't believe I didn't feel you get out of bed."

Emily kissed her lightly. "You were sleeping pretty heavily. By the way, I like watching you sleep."

"Uh...okay. Good, I think."

"Mmm. Very good." Emily hopped out of bed, just managing to escape Derian's grasping hand. "Stop."

Derian groaned.

"If I stay, I'm going to want you inside me again, and you need to waylay Henrietta before she makes some kind of end run."

"You're really trying to kill me, aren't you?"

"I know you're tougher than that." Emily leaned down, her breasts brushing Derian's shoulder, and kissed her. "You can always join me in the shower."

"Not if you want to go to work anytime soon. Like in the next week." Derian grabbed Emily's hand. "I'll be thinking about tonight all day."

"So will I."

❖

Emily was determined to get some work done, even though she couldn't stop thinking about the night before. She thought she'd known what it was like to make love with a woman, but she hadn't even begun to fathom the addictive, exquisite exhilaration of bringing Derian pleasure. She loved knowing Derian desired her, loved running her hands over Derian's body, loved answering Derian's need. She loved seeing her passion reflected, her hunger met and matched. All she could think was again. Again. Again. Again.

"Hello-o-o," Ron called from the doorway.

With a start, Emily said, "Oh. Hi."

"For a second, I thought you were sleeping, but your eyes were open." Ron came in and dropped into his usual pose in the chair, elbow on knee, chin in his hand, studying her. "Tell me everything about last night."

Emily's face flamed. "Last night? Weren't you there?"

Ron made a *pfft* sound. "I don't mean the awards. What about all the rest—insider gossip, you know, the good stuff. You must have gotten something juicy."

"Oh," Emily said, struggling furiously to focus. "Yes. No. I mean, yes, I went. But you know how it is. The usual suspects, the usual topics of discussion. Nothing really new."

"How disappointing." Ron flopped back and sighed. "Not much surprise with the winners either. I don't know why I keep hoping every once in a while they'll actually pick the best book instead of the most politically advantageous one."

Emily laughed. "Yes, well, we'll probably have world peace at any moment too."

Ron snorted. "How did Derian behave?"

"Derian?"

"Yes, you know the one I mean, Derian Winfield, our boss? The woman glued to your side all night long?"

"Oh, Derian. She was fine."

"I think you'd better elaborate," Ron said slowly, his eyes narrowing. "Because something obviously happened. You seem a little dazed and confused."

Emily glanced at the open door. She didn't want to have a personal conversation about Derian in the office, and she didn't want to tell Ron she'd slept with her either. She wasn't falling back on false modesty, she wasn't that precious. But Derian was their boss, even if just temporarily, and it didn't look good for either one of them if people knew. She wasn't as concerned about her own reputation as much as she wanted to protect Derian's. She already knew most people thought Derian was a self-absorbed player, and she knew that was far from the truth. Unfortunately, false impressions were often the hardest to change. She looked at Ron. "Derian was absolutely fine."

"And that's it?"

Emily smiled. "That pretty much covers it."

"You'll tell me the rest one day soon, right?" Ron asked knowingly.

"When the time is right," Emily promised, although she had no idea when that might be. Or even how she would know. She'd vowed not to think beyond the moment, which twenty-four hours ago had seemed like a reasonable decision, but that was a promise she was finding harder to keep by the moment. Any relationship with Derian could only be temporary. Now all she had to do was convince herself of that.

CHAPTER TWENTY-FIVE

Derian settled onto a couch in the family area adjoining the gym, replete with treadmills, exercise benches, workout mats, and stationary bikes, where Henrietta was starting her rehab program. She could see HW, decked out in matching sweatpants and sweatshirt with NYU emblazoned in big bold letters, through the windows that spanned the top half of the wall separating the two rooms. Compared to many, no, *most* of the other rehab patients, HW looked hale and hearty. No one who didn't know her would realize her steps were slower than her usual near-running pace, or that she was a little unsteady getting up from a chair. Her voice probably sounded normal to other people, but to Derian's ear she was a bit on the quiet side. All things considered, though, her aunt looked great. The doctors had cautioned Henrietta at the last visit not to push too fast just because she seemed to be recovering very quickly. Henrietta, of course, countered that her job was a desk job and was no more strenuous than sitting at home. Derian, who'd insisted on going with her, had pointed out HW was rarely behind her desk but more often running off to meetings, conferences, and power lunches. Fortunately, the doctors hadn't been that easily hoodwinked and had instructed Henrietta to stick to the rehab schedule.

HW wasn't supposed to be back in the office full-time for at least another six weeks, but Derian doubted they'd be able to prevent her from working part-time for much longer than another two. She wouldn't mind when Henrietta moved back behind the desk where she belonged, and doubly glad that someday Emily should rightfully take that seat. Her brief stint as the interim CEO had been more than enough to convince her she wasn't cut out for helming the ship. As to what she was cut out for, she didn't know and, before now, she'd never really cared to try. She'd avoided making any kind of long-range plans since she'd graduated from college. Her only goal then had been to put as much distance as possible between Martin and herself as quickly as possible. That hadn't required much in the way of thought, another thing she'd tried to avoid as much as possible. Being without a purpose was not the Winfield way, which was probably exactly why she had chosen that lifestyle.

She hadn't been idle, but she hadn't been living a conventional life either. Sure, she'd profited by putting her money behind the right racing teams, investing wisely, and having a natural affinity for winning at the tables. Those successes hadn't been planned so much as fallen into. Being able to look at things from a distance now, she realized she'd spent all her life trying to be anything but a Winfield and doing anything that wasn't the Winfield way. Sometimes, maybe, she'd gotten in the way of her own satisfaction without realizing it. Working at the agency had been a surprise—especially when she'd discovered she enjoyed being part of the team. Now that her tenure was ending, she was unexpectedly disappointed to be leaving. True, not seeing Emily every day was a big part of that, but she'd miss the spirit and passion of the place too.

A nurse walked Henrietta back into the waiting area and Derian got to her feet. "Tired out already?"

The nurse looked aghast, but Henrietta merely laughed. "I could go a few more rounds but my therapist called it quits." She thanked the nurse and took Derian's arm. Her grip was strong and firm. "Are you taking me to lunch? That's within the bounds of the program, isn't it?"

Derian laughed. "It's not a prison sentence, HW."

"You should try it sometime and see what you have to say after a few days."

"Point taken." She'd ordered up one of the company cars and it was waiting in the entranceway when they walked out. "Anyplace special you'd like to go?"

"Fortunately, I'm still allowed to eat. Let's do Junior's."

"I'll call and get us a spot."

They arrived at the diner a little before the lunch hour and secured a booth in the window. After they'd ordered, Henrietta sipped her orange juice and regarded Derian with a speculative gaze. "I think it's time for you to tell me what's really going on at the agency, don't you?"

Derian swallowed the mouthful of coffee she'd just taken and tried not to cough. Somehow, HW always knew what was really going on. She'd known about Derian and Aud getting involved in high school almost before Derian had figured it out, and had merely told them to exercise caution around Martin, who had a remarkable penchant for narrow-mindedness.

"I guess there's no use in my trying to bluff my way out of this, is there?" Derian said.

"See the bet or fold your cards."

Derian laughed. "Everything at Winfield's is fine. I wasn't lying about that. There have been some…incursions from the enemy camp, but we're handling that."

Henrietta tapped her glass with a nail, a thoughtful expression on her face. "Donatella Agnelli."

"How the hell did you know that?"

Henrietta smiled thinly. "Because Donatella is Martin's hatchet woman. When he wants something nasty done, quickly and lethally, he sends Donatella. Did she try to gut the place?"

"She might have, but we put a stop to it."

Henrietta's eyebrow arched up. "We?"

"Emily and I have kept her out of your office." Derian grinned, feeling the same thrill she did when she'd just won big on a long shot. "Donatella has been overseeing an audit, but nothing is coming of it. Your books are good, and your bottom line is well within range of other agencies."

"But nothing like what your father would like to see."

Derian lifted a shoulder. "It's not Martin's business, is it."

"No, but he'd like it to be. Actually, he'd like to destroy it just for spite, because it was what I always wanted and something our father valued." Henrietta sighed. "What Martin can't control, he seeks to destroy."

"The agency is safe. I promise."

"And what about you? How are you holding up under Martin's guns?"

"He didn't draw much blood this time."

"I'm sorry. He's a fool."

"I'm learning not to expect him to change." Derian realized the most powerful antidote to her father's criticism was her own sense of accomplishment. For the first time, the sting of his disregard no longer made her want to grab the first plane to anywhere else. "And I'm okay with that."

Henrietta squeezed her hand. "Then you truly have won."

Derian wasn't sure about that, but she figured she might be on the right track at last. And right now all she really wanted to think about was her dinner date with Emily.

❖

Emily wiped her hands on a dish towel and hurried to the door. She checked the peephole and quickly pulled the door open. "Hi! You're early."

"Your downstairs neighbor let me in. I assured her I wasn't a burglar."

"You do have the look of a scoundrel about you," Emily said, leaning up to kiss Derian quickly but firmly. "Come in."

"I'm a little early, but I was just hanging around the office, and I thought I'd much rather be hanging around here." Derian lifted the bottle of wine she had tucked under her arm. "In case the other one didn't survive."

"Thanks. I'm afraid I'm still in the prep stage, and"—Emily frowned, indicating her jeans and T-shirt—"I'm not dressed."

"I was kind of hoping for the bunny slippers." Derian set the wine on a nearby table and pulled Emily close. She kissed her, one hand settling low on her back, her fingers dipping beneath the waistband of Emily's jeans. She loved the feel of that little dip at the base of her spine, so soft and sensuous. "You look terrific. Don't change a thing."

Emily wriggled closer. "I'm not having dinner with you wearing a *Star Wars* T-shirt."

Derian grinned. "I like it, but I would've put you in the *Star Trek* camp."

"I'm one of those rare individuals who's never chosen sides. I think they're both incredible for different reasons." Leaning back, Emily spread her palms over Derian's chest, flicking open the top button of her shirt to kiss the hollow of her throat. "You, now, you're definitely *Star Wars*. Speed and derring-do, a raider in the sky."

Derian laughed and walked Emily over to the sofa. "Do you have anything on the stove?"

"Not yet, I was still chopping—" Emily gave a little squeak when Derian dumped her onto the couch and then lost her voice when Derian stretched out over her. Somehow they managed to wrap themselves around each other on the narrow space and then Derian was kissing her and Emily was grabbing on to every part of her, desperate to touch every inch, to pull her inside, as deep inside her as she could.

"I missed you," Derian growled against her throat, one hand sliding under her T-shirt, stroking down her belly, and fumbling at the button of her jeans.

"Let me help," Emily gasped, suddenly desperate to be naked, to have nothing between her and Derian's hands. She tore open her jeans and pushed them down her legs, kicking them off while trying to keep Derian on top of her, not caring how ungraceful she looked as long as Derian never moved. Derian's mouth was on her throat, her teeth lightly scraping, sending shivers of heat down her spine and fireworks bursting between her thighs.

"Oh my God." Blindly, Emily found Derian's hand and pressed it between her thighs. "Inside. I want you inside."

Derian knelt between Emily's thighs, stroking her breasts and her belly and finally filling her. Her eyes burned, feral and magnificent, stark and famished. For her. For her.

"Hurry." Emily gripped Derian's wrist and lifted to take her deeper. When Derian leaned down and kissed her, she exploded.

"Okay, so fast is good too," Emily murmured into Derian's neck.

"Fast is pretty fantastic."

Emily squinted, focused finally. Derian lay beside her, holding her. "You still have all your clothes on."

"You have a *Star Wars* T-shirt. I'm underdressed."

Emily laughed, a little wildly, still trying to put the pieces of her sanity back together. "I never wanted anything the way I want you."

"I can't seem to stop touching you."

Emily stretched and murmured contentedly. "That's very good, then. I would like it, though, if we took your clothes off now so I can feel your skin. Love your skin. It's so hot."

Derian grinned against Emily's rumpled hair. Hot skin. Why did she think that was the most exciting thing she'd ever heard? "I missed you all afternoon. Why did you have to have meetings scheduled back to back?"

Emily tilted her head and kissed Derian's chin. "Oh, you know. Business? You remember the agency."

"Oh. That. Vaguely."

"I *did* have a very hard time thinking about work." Emily opened the buttons on Derian's shirt. Finding the skin she'd been hungering for, she ran her tongue in circles around Derian's nipple. Derian's fingers threaded into her hair and pressed her face closer to her breast.

"I like it when you do that," Derian whispered, her limbs shifting restlessly.

Emily intended never to stop, but first she needed more. She slipped off the couch and knelt beside it, opening Derian's belt and trousers. "Sit up."

"Emily," Derian groaned, swinging her legs to the floor. "I—"

"Off." Emily gripped Derian's trousers and tugged, pulling them down and away. She knelt between Derian's legs and kissed Derian's inner thighs, slowly working her way higher until Derian's thighs tightened and her hips lifted from the couch.

"Emily," Derian warned, "I'm close."

Emily splayed her fingers over Derian's tense stomach and took what she'd been aching for all day. The sweet heat of Derian's surrender pierced her, impaling her with awe. She stroked and caressed and drew her deeper until she felt the telltale tightening everywhere. At the last second, she slipped inside her and Derian convulsed, a hoarse cry of surprise and pleasure torn from her throat.

"So beautiful," Emily whispered, her cheek pressed to Derian's thigh. Derian's fingers played in her hair, her breathing harsh and unsteady.

"I never had anyone own me the way you do," Derian said.

Smiling, Emily kissed her stomach and climbed up beside her on the sofa. She pulled Derian down, and they tangled together again.

"I never knew I had so much craving inside me," Emily said. "It's a little maddening."

"I know." Derian kissed her. "Maddening and amazing and something I never get enough of."

Emily tapped her fingers on Derian's hip. "Although if we keep putting off dinner, we might die of starvation."

"Never." Derian wrapped a hand around Emily's nape, holding her close. She wasn't ready to let her go. She couldn't think of anything she wanted beyond lying right where she was. She sighed.

"What?" Emily asked, in no hurry to get up. Derian had a way of making her forget everything she needed to do.

"I got a call this afternoon from some nervous investors. I need to show up before the race in Rio. Sponsor-type stuff."

Icy tentacles slithered through Emily's chest. "Oh. When?"

"The day after tomorrow. I tried to put it off, but—"

"No, of course you can't. You've been away for quite a while now," Emily said, starting to sit up. She couldn't be this close to her and know that she was leaving. She was more than half-naked, she was exposed and feeling incredibly vulnerable, as if her skin were peeling away. At any moment she was afraid she might start bleeding. She had to gather her strength, somehow re-erect her shields. She ran both hands through her hair and tugged as she untangled her curls, the tiny spears of pain clearing the fog of sex and false security. Jumping up, she searched on the floor for her jeans. She couldn't be naked any longer. "I should do something about dinner."

"I know I might be leaving you in the lurch at the agency, but I took care of one problem." Derian got up, grabbed her pants, and shook out the wrinkles in a quick, automatic move.

"Oh?" Emily said, trying to think of what to do with her hands. She couldn't touch her right now. She couldn't bear to touch her and want her and know that she'd be leaving soon. Of course she'd always known that, expected it, but hadn't let herself think about it. Just the night, just the now. She'd made that deal with herself, hadn't she? She couldn't go back on it now. She couldn't expect it to be any different than what it was. She'd never lied to herself. She wouldn't start now. She backed up.

"I got rid of Donatella. As of tomorrow, she's gone." Derian pulled on her trousers but didn't bother to button her shirt.

Derian was so damn casual about her body, about everything, and Emily had always known that too, hadn't she? Sex was just another form of conversation for Derian. Nothing wrong with that at all. And she'd given Emily something precious, something far beyond pleasure. Derian had given her the knowledge of what she'd been living without, and what she refused to do without someday. Someday, when she could bear the hunger again.

"How did she take it?" Emily asked, amazed at how easily she could talk about something that mattered not at all while everything that did slipped away.

Derian grinned and poured wine from the open bottle on Emily's kitchen island into the glasses Emily'd left on the counter. She handed one to Emily. "I told her she'd had enough time with the numbers. I'd gone over the books myself in the last couple of days, and there was nothing there to find. Winfield's bottom line was far more than acceptable."

"That's great news." Emily sipped the wine, found it tasteless.

Derian leaned against the counter, drinking wine and looking completely composed, not bothered in the least that she'd soon be leaving. "I don't think she expected me to understand any of the numbers, but when I made it clear that I did, she pretty much ran out of ammunition. Her slings and arrows bounced off at that point."

"I owe you a great debt," Emily said.

Derian shook her head. "No, you don't. If I'd been in the picture all along, my father probably wouldn't have tried to take over as soon as Henrietta gave him an opening."

"Nevertheless, everyone at the agency appreciates everything you've done."

"I've enjoyed it. Working with you was a special bonus." Derian set her glass down. "Henrietta has agreed, at least for now, not to fight her rehab regimen. It'll be a few weeks before she can even work part-time. I'll be back—"

"We'll be fine," Emily said. "You've interrupted your schedule, your life, for all of us, not just Henrietta. You've done enough."

Emily tried to slip by her to hide in the kitchen. Just putting a counter between them would help, but she didn't make it. Derian pulled her closer until she was almost standing between Derian's legs. She couldn't be this close to her and not put her hands on her. She clenched her fists at her sides. Please, she needed a little bit of distance, just so she could think again.

"There's something else I wanted to talk to you about," Derian said.

Business, that would be good. If they could just get back to business. "Oh?"

"I think I found a solution to all our problems," Derian said. "Your visa, keeping Martin away from the agency, and taking care of the long term."

"It sounds like a miracle cure," Emily said.

"It might be," Derian said, laughing. "I think you and I should get married."

Emily stared, the cold enveloping her completely.

"It's perfect, really," Derian said, reaching back for her wineglass. "No one could argue about succession. You'd be a permanent resident, you'd be an insider—family, and you'd be the logical one to take over after Henrietta."

"And what would you get out of it?" Emily asked, thankfully having recovered her powers of language. Her mind seemed to be working although she'd lost all feeling below her shoulders. She was actually numb. "Besides annoying your father, that is."

Derian frowned. "My father? What does he have to do with this?"

Emily managed to extract herself and backed up until they were no longer in contact. That helped bring some sensation back into her body, and what followed was anger. No, not anger, fury. "I can't imagine he'd be very happy to discover that you'd outsmarted him at one of his own games. He's wanted to dismantle the agency or, at least, take control of it, and since you'd never shown any interest in it, he had the perfect opening. And then you outsmart him by marrying someone who, I imagine, he wouldn't approve of, and making it impossible for him. You win."

Derian frowned. "It's not about winning some game with my father."

"Isn't it? Then what is it about? This arrangement you're suggesting."

"It's a sensible solution," Derian said, caught off guard by Emily's accusations. She wasn't trying to get back at her father. "I was trying to help you and Henrietta."

"Help? By committing yourself to a marriage of convenience."

Emily felt just a little bit crazy. "God, I've become a character in one of my manuscripts."

"Marriage of—no, that's not what I'm suggesting."

"Then what are you suggesting, Derian? We've had the marriage conversation already, remember? You're not interested in marriage. It doesn't fit with your lifestyle. Why would you do this?"

"Because—" Derian stumbled over the swirl of emotions tangled in her head, thrown by Emily's anger, struggling to sort out feelings she'd never faced before. Trying to see the future she'd never envisioned. "I want you to be able to stay—isn't that what you want?"

"For Henrietta. For the agency." Emily nodded, the numbness receding. Only her heart remained frozen. Not for her. Of course, not for her. Derian didn't love her. She took a deep breath. "I appreciate your offer. It's very kind of you."

Derian's brows drew down. "Kind? It's not about being kind—"

"Yes, that's exactly what it is. That, perhaps, and some misplaced guilt about not being here sooner."

"Guilt." A muscle in Derian's jaw tightened. "Because I ran out on my family, you mean. Because I didn't fulfill the Winfield legacy."

"Before we say things we might regret," Emily said very carefully, fighting desperately for solid ground while a tornado of hurt and self-recrimination whirled inside her, "I think we need to reassess exactly what we're doing."

"Reassess," Derian said, her eyes narrowing. "That sounds like a business proposition."

"Yes, well, we're talking about business, aren't we?"

"Not exactl—"

"And I think it would be best if we keep our relationship on professional terms from now on." There, she'd done it, what she should have done from the beginning—erected some boundaries in her relationship with Derian, for her own self-preservation.

"And if I don't agree?" Derian's eyes were molten.

"I'm afraid you don't have a choice."

"You're wrong about that," Derian said on her way out the door. "I'm no longer part of the Winfield Agency as of right now, so our professional relationship, if that's what you'd like to call what we've been doing, is officially over."

Emily slumped against the counter, staring at the closed door and trying to convince herself she'd just made the only decision she could. She believed that, she really did, but doing the smart thing didn't mean it didn't hurt. How far would she have to go to silence the craving for the sound of Derian's voice and the touch of her hands? She had no clue, but she at least knew where to go first.

CHAPTER TWENTY-SIX

Derian only knew one way to handle confusion and anger and disappointment—she moved on to the next stop on the revolving stage of her life. Head down, cutting her way through the early evening sidewalk strollers with the ease of years of handling casino and racetrack crowds, she pulled up the number on her phone of her favorite travel agent, one of several kept on retainer by the corporation to handle all the upper-level management travel needs, including hers.

"Monica? Derian Winfield."

"Yes, Ms. Winfield. How can I be of assistance?"

"I need to be in Rio by this time tomorrow."

"Just a moment." Monica sounded as if the peremptory request was just another ordinary item in a day's work, which Derian guessed it was. She imagined Monica must go everywhere with a mobile, because no matter what time of day or night she called her, Monica always took care of her.

"I can get you on a direct flight from DC at six ten a.m. You'll fly the corporate jet to Reagan National. Shall I send a car for you at four?"

Derian hesitated. She needed to go—she'd been putting off Antonio, her business manager, for weeks. If he said she needed to put in an appearance to woo some nervous investors before the next leg of the circuit, she believed him. She had nothing pressing at the agency—nothing she couldn't have Vonnie delegate with a quick phone call. After all, Emily could have been doing her job all along, and she'd planned to have Emily step in while she was away. At the moment, talking to Emily and pretending everything was business as usual felt like more than she could handle. She ruthlessly pushed aside the quicksilver flash of pain when she imagined Emily at the office, looking beautiful and sexy as only she could in casual business clothes. Looking beautiful and sexy no matter where she was or what she was doing. "Yes, have me picked up at the Dakota."

"Very good—shall I arrange a wake-up call when the driver is en route?"

"That would be fine." She didn't have much to pack. Once she'd left, the Dakota staff would take care of disposing of the few things in her kitchen, sending any clothes she left behind out to be laundered, and cleaning the place.

"I'll reserve your usual suite at the Copa?"

Suddenly weary just thinking about the high-octane world she'd be jumping back into the next night, Derian sighed. Maybe the nonstop parties masquerading as business meetings would be just what she needed to quench the seething unrest souring her stomach. "Sure. Thanks."

"Of course, Ms. Winfield. Have a good flight."

"Good night." Derian shoved her phone into her pants pocket and tried not to think about the hash she'd made of the night. Since kicking herself was a physical impossibility, she'd just keep walking until she burned off some of the anger. Nothing had turned out the way she'd expected, and she still couldn't figure out where things had gone so wrong. She mentally replayed the conversation with Emily—hell, all their conversations—wondering how she'd misread the signals so completely. One minute they'd been closer than she'd ever been with anyone, not just physically, but in every way, and the next she'd felt like she'd been talking to a stranger. Emily had actually suggested Derian's proposal was meant to manipulate Emily into doing something just so Derian could gain an advantage over Martin. Pain knifed through her chest. That Emily could imagine Derian was like him—a manipulator, someone who used people as weapons against one another—hurt far more than all the insults Martin had ever hurled her way.

Martin was the last person in the world she wanted to be like, and if that was how Emily saw her, a game player on the grandest of scales, then she'd been a fool to think Emily would want…anything…with her. She couldn't even claim her tarnished reputation, deserved or not, was at fault for Emily's impression of her. She'd revealed more of herself to

Emily than to anyone in her life, even Aud, and that hadn't been enough to matter. She slowed, let out a deep breath. She should have known she couldn't change who she was like she changed her clothes, no matter how much she might've wanted to. She *had* been living off her inheritance and her name, she *was* a player, just as Emily had intimated, and wanting to be someone else didn't erase that. Wanting Emily to see her as more than that wasn't enough to make it so.

And feeling sorry for herself was just another form of self-indulgence. Emily had seen what she'd momentarily forgotten—she'd chosen her path a long time ago. She hadn't wanted the Winfield legacy and had made herself into the woman everyone thought her to be.

Derian stopped at the corner and glanced around. Nothing looked familiar. She checked the street signs and couldn't decipher which direction they were telling her to go. A cold sheet of panic sliced between her shoulder blades. She'd done this before. Countless times when she'd been very young. Found herself in a place she hadn't expected to be where everything looked foreign, as if she had stepped through an invisible curtain into another universe. Alone, and unable to find the way home.

But she wasn't ten anymore. She took a breath, pulled out her phone, and punched in a number.

"Hey, Dere," Aud said, sounding uncharacteristically subdued when she answered. "Is this a friendly call or business? Because I'm wrapping up for the day and I've had business up to my a—"

"I'm a little bit lost." Derian laughed wryly. In more ways than one. "Turned around. Street signs say…um, West Third and Mercer. And I could use a drink."

A beat of silence. Then Aud's brisk voice. "I'm closing my computer right now. I'll grab a cab and be there in ten minutes. Is there a bar somewhere that you can see?"

Derian scanned the streets, stepping out of the way of a vendor pushing a cart full of T-shirts toward the open van pulled up to the curb. "There's one on the corner, neighborhood-looking place. Tony D's."

"I'll find it. Ten minutes. Okay?"

"Yeah, thanks."

The tavern, lit only by the neon beer signs hanging on the walls at irregular intervals, was a single room about the size of Derian's living room at the Dakota. A big plate-glass window looked out on the sidewalk, a scarred bar down one side, a handful of small mismatched tables pushed against the opposite wall. A sign pointing to restrooms in an alcove at the back. A few men and women occupied stools at the bar, most hunched over their glasses in silent communion. Derian found a seat at the far end and ordered a draft. The sharp yeasty bite felt good going down. The last of the panic washed away as she finished it off and signaled for another. Right now, she was tired of thinking about who she was and how much of her father might be in her.

The barkeep slid a bowl of nuts in front of her.

"Thanks." She wasn't hungry, but she ate them automatically, the same way she drank the beer.

Aud slid onto the stool beside her. "How far ahead of me are you?"

Derian shot her a sideways glance. "Not very. This is my second."

Aud waved to the bartender. "Dry martini, two olives." She grabbed a handful of nuts, turned sideways until her knees rested against Derian's thigh, and ran a hand down Derian's back. "So, how the hell did you end up here?"

"Went for a walk."

Aud laughed. "From where?"

Derian clenched her jaw. "I was in the neighborhood."

"Okay, fine."

Derian registered the hurt in Aud's voice and shook her head. "Sorry. I dragged you down here and you came without a second thought, even though I haven't been much of a friend."

"Oh, Dere," Aud said, "that's not true. Just because I wanted you to stay here with me and you couldn't doesn't mean you weren't a good friend. I haven't reached out to you either. I've been too pissed at you for leaving me."

"Running away, you mean."

"Hey, sometimes we have to run in order to survive."

"Maybe you can't outrun who you are," Derian said.

"Bullshit. Martin was poison to you." Aud sipped her martini. "Wow, this place is a find. Best martini I've had in forever. So, why are you here? It's not Henrietta, is it?"

"No, she's fine. Making great progress."

"What the hell happened?" Aud finished her cocktail and asked for another. "If it's not Henrietta, and you haven't had another run-in with Martin—"

Derian snorted. "Martin and I have nothing left to say to each other. We both know where we stand, and nothing will change that."

"Then it has to be a woman, and that being the case, I'd say it's Emily May."

"What makes you think that?" Derian tensed at the mention of Emily, wanting to protect her even though Emily could do that perfectly well herself.

"I've seen you two together, more than once, and I don't think I've ever seen you look at a woman the way you look at her. Like she mattered." Aud ran a fingertip around the wide-open mouth of the glass. "She looks the same way at you."

"Apparently, looks are deceiving." Derian laughed at the lie. She'd always wanted to use that excuse when others judged her on appearances, but in her case it wasn't true. "We had a thing, and that's over now."

"A thing. A thing as in you've been sleeping together."

"That's generally part of a thing, yes."

"Really, Derian, Henrietta's protégé? Do you have to follow your clit everywhere it leads?"

"According to popular opinion, yes." Derian didn't even mind the verbal assault. She didn't feel it, really. She was strangely numb.

Aud rolled her eyes. "So…what? You broke it off and things got messy?"

"Actually, that's not the way it went. Emily changed the game."

"She put you on the street? Well, that must be a first."

"Thanks," Derian said dryly.

Aud sighed. "Hey, all right, I'm being bitchy. I'm sorry. What happened, exactly?"

"I told her I thought we ought to get married, that that would solve her visa problem and take care of the agency going forward." Derian finished her beer and thought about another. She wasn't driving anywhere, hell, she couldn't really even walk anywhere. She pointed a finger at her glass and the bartender magically whisked it away and set a fresh, foaming draft in front of her. "Apparently, my offering to help her out with something we both knew she wanted was manipulative. She suggested that my motivation was to piss off my father."

"Well, wasn't it? Sort of? Because it certainly would make Martin crazy."

"No," Derian said. "Sure, anytime I manage to get to him is a good day, but that's not why I said it."

"Then why in the world did you? Marriage is a serious thing, Dere. It's a legal commitment, at the very least, and usually a lot more. Honestly, what were you thinking?"

The numbness dropped away like ice shattering under a too-heavy tread. Anger came roaring back, scalding and indiscriminate. "I was thinking that Henrietta needs Emily not just now, but to pass on her life's work. I was thinking Emily loves this place, deserves her job, and needs to know she's not going to be sent back to Singapore after everything she's put into getting where she is now because of a bureaucracy that doesn't deal with individuals, only quotas and categories and groundless prejudices. I thought I was offering help."

"What about you, Dere? What were you thinking about you in all of this?"

Derian stared, the heat dissipating as fast as it had flared.

"How many women have you slept with?"

"What?" Derian might have trouble navigating in new places, especially when she was emotionally unsteady the way she had been earlier, but the rest of her mind worked perfectly, and she wasn't following Aud. "What does that have to do with anything?"

"Go ahead, answer the question."

Derian laughed despite herself. "I don't know. A lot. Why?"

"Because you don't know anything about women at all. I'm sure you're fabulous in bed, but do you have any idea what makes a woman tick?"

"Well I should, I am one." Derian stopped, admitting she rarely thought about why she did what she did, beyond the one primal motivating force in her life. Escaping Martin. Escaping the constant rejection. Getting away from the thousand cuts that were bleeding her to death. "You're saying I'm insensitive and self-centered."

"No," Aud said softly, "I'm not, because I know you're not. But has it occurred to you that marriage is something that most women— hell, maybe most people, I don't know, I can't speak for guys—think about, maybe even dream about, their whole lives? It's not a business decision, Derian."

"It often is, and you know it," Derian said. "Besides, Emily is all about her profession. She's not looking for a romantic relationship. We talked about it."

Aud's eyes widened. "The two of you talked about getting married?"

"Not exactly," Derian said, exasperated. "We talked about the future, you know, what we wanted and didn't want. We both pretty much said marriage wasn't for us."

"Pretty much..." Aud laughed wryly. "Oh, Dere. You mean marriage isn't for you. I bet Emily is all about her job right now. I get that. Me too. But that doesn't mean that somewhere down the road she didn't see that for herself."

"Well, there won't be any down the road at Winfield's if she's back in Singapore."

Aud gave her a long look. "That's what this is about, isn't it. You don't want her to leave."

"That hardly makes any difference, since I'm leaving myself."

Aud stiffened. "Are you? When?"

"Soon." As soon as she could.

"For how long?"

"I don't know how long, a couple weeks probably. Henrietta is doing really well, and as long as she keeps to her regimen, she'll be back before too long."

"And does Emily know this?"

"I mentioned it, yes."

"So you announced you were leaving in the same breath as you suggested the two of you get married?" Aud said dryly.

Derian flushed. "Not quite like that, no. I don't know. We didn't actually get to the planning part. What are you getting at?"

"That maybe you don't know the woman you're sleeping with as well as you think."

Derian rubbed her face. "Well, she certainly knows me."

"Don't be so sure." Aud leaned over to kiss Derian on the cheek. "Maybe you're the one who doesn't know you."

CHAPTER TWENTY-SEVEN

Derian landed in Rio in the late afternoon. She hadn't slept the night before or on the plane, and the buzz of being beyond tired ran through her. She wasn't looking forward to navigating another unfamiliar place—but then it looked like she wouldn't have to. An Asian woman bearing a sign with her name on it waited near baggage claim. She didn't look like anyone from the hotel or travel agency, unless their reps were wearing Prada and fifty thousand dollars' worth of diamonds these days.

Derian held out her hand. "Hello, I'm Derian Winfield."

The woman, somewhere in the range of thirty, extended a manicured hand. "I'm Mingzhu Tan, from Beijing Aerotech. Please call me Ming."

"Ah," Derian said, putting the pieces together. She'd met with the tech's CEO six months before when the rising tycoon first showed interest in investing in American sports teams. "And how is Mr. Yee?"

"Very well, thank you. We're so happy to have this opportunity to meet with you."

"As am I," Derian said automatically. She'd danced this dance dozens of times in the past and wondered if she hadn't inherited far more of Martin's business shrewdness than she wanted to admit. Right now, the last thing she wanted to be thinking about was Martin. Every time she thought about him, she heard Emily's subtle accusation that she was motivated by her need to best him. She shook off the memory. "I appreciate you meeting me."

Ming smiled slowly. "Of course, we are pleased to offer you any courtesy we can."

Derian had a feeling those courtesies might extend far beyond a ride from the airport, and felt not the slightest twinge of interest. What she wanted was a long shower, a longer drink, and something, anything, to occupy her mind. A liaison with a strange woman, however, was not on that list.

She collected her luggage and carried it out to the waiting car. The trip to the hotel was mercifully short and she didn't have to do more than make casual passing conversation with Ming. When the limo pulled up in front of the Copa, she shook Ming's hand and bowed. "You were very gracious to take the time to meet me."

"We are staying here as well," Ming said, again with a smile that could be an invitation but stopped short of being insistent. If she was disappointed that Derian didn't request to meet at another time, she didn't show it. "My suite is 407. Please ring me if I may be of service."

"I'm sure I'll see you again, and please give my regards to Mr. Yee."

Derian picked up her key from the express check-in wall and headed directly upstairs. The hotel bar would undoubtedly be filled with people she wasn't in the mood to talk to just yet. Her suite was another large, fully appointed trio of rooms with the requisite balcony, this one overlooking the Copa beach. A cool ocean breeze cut the shimmering heat enough to make sitting outside look inviting. Still jittery, like a car with the idle revving too high, Derian took a shower and ordered up a bottle of champagne. In briefs and a short-sleeved shirt, she settled on a lounger on the balcony and let the alcohol slowly dull her nerves. Watching couples amble across the white glittering sand, she glanced at the empty recliner beside her. Loneliness was not a sensation she generally dwelled upon, but she couldn't help wishing Emily was there with her. An evening spent over a quiet dinner and a late-night stroll on a moonlit beach, Emily's hand in hers and Emily's warm laughter washing over her, struck her as more satisfying than anything she'd ever done. She'd never wanted that with any other woman, and she wouldn't be finding it anywhere she went tonight.

Derian dropped her head back and closed her eyes.

When she woke, the last red-gold rays of a brilliant sunset slanted across the ocean and draped her body in fiery shadows. She had to be at the sponsor's reception in half an hour. She took another shower and, after the cold water drove the alcohol fumes from her brain, dressed and joined the familiar crowd in the ballroom on the mezzanine. The room was exactly like a hundred others she'd been in—huge gleaming chandeliers, tall columns flanking both sides, ornately painted ceilings, and an army of waiters with silver trays and a thousand flutes of champagne. Plus the bars discreetly spaced at intervals around the perimeter.

Derian took a glass of champagne she wasn't interested in drinking and made a mental note of the time. An hour was about all she could take. Ming nodded to her from across the room. Derian made the rounds, shook all the right hands, and made her business manager happy by wooing potential new partners. As soon as she could, she slipped away and ordered a car to take her to a hotel in a less popular part of the city. Gambling was illegal in Brazil, but that didn't mean there wasn't any. You just needed to know where. She settled at the baccarat table and played all night.

When she returned to the Copa at noon the next day and finally fell asleep, she still couldn't leave Emily behind. Her dreams were a dark chaotic tangle of lost opportunity and fruitless searching for something just beyond reach.

❖

"Okay, thank you, everybody." Emily grabbed her iPad, quickly rose as the rest of the staff gathered up their things, and escaped into the hall. She'd barely reached her desk when Ron slipped in behind her and closed her office door.

"If I didn't know better, I'd think you were a ghost," he said in way of greeting.

"I don't have any idea what you're talking about."

"How about you've been hiding out here for the last week, and avoiding me."

"I haven't been hiding or avoiding," Emily said, although she doubted she sounded convincing. She was terrible at lying.

"If you don't want to talk about it, that's too bad," Ron said. "Because whatever it is, I can tell you're miserable."

"I'm not miserable," Emily lied again. She dropped into her chair and tried to ignore her iPad and the picture she'd seen just that morning on Flipboard of Derian and a beautiful woman getting into a limo outside the Copacabana Palace. A minute passed and she straightened up. Ron was still in the same place, hands on his hips, the look on his face suggesting he wasn't leaving anytime soon.

"You might as well sit down if you're not going to leave."

He took his customary seat and regarded her with a sympathetic smile. "Sometimes it helps to talk."

"And sometimes there's nothing to say."

"It's Derian, I already know that. You've been miserable since the day she left."

"Coincidence."

"Really, and I look like I was born under a mushroom?"

"Ron," Emily said gently, "I don't want to talk about Derian."

"Fair enough, then how about talking about you? We can pretend that the other party is…Woman X."

"Oh, and that's going to work well."

"All right, you *don't* talk about her, and I'll just guess." Ron took a deep breath and tapped his chin. "Okay, you're harboring a secret crush on Woman X, and now that she's gone, you regret that you didn't jump her the way I told you to."

"This is not going to work."

He waved a hand. "Okay, let's try that again. You did jump her, like I told you to, but in an uncharacteristic Derian Winfield fashion— whoops, sorry—Woman X declined your offer." He frowned and shook his head. "Really, though, I never took her for a fool, so even I don't believe that one."

"Ron," Emily said in a threatening tone.

"No, I've got it. You did jump her, she accepted, and she was absolutely terrible in bed."

"Derian is wonderful in bed," Emily said, almost amused when Ron's mouth dropped open. If she'd had any fiber of her being left that wasn't miserable, she might have laughed too. "I don't remember who jumped who, but believe me, there was nothing to complain about."

"I'm sorry," Ron said. "You don't strike me as the one-night stand type, and I know Deri—"

"No," Emily said, "you don't know. No one does. Derian is nothing like her reputation."

"You're right, sorry. She made a really good impression with everyone while she was here. But you knew it was only temporary."

"Oh, I did. Unfortunately, I seem to have forgotten that somewhere in the process of taking off my clothes."

Ron laughed wryly. "I've been there and done that. Are you sure it's just temporary?"

"She's gone, isn't she? And there was never any discussion of it being any more than that, unless you count the part where she asked me to marry her."

Ron stared. "You're not serious."

"Actually, I am, and this does not go any further than here. I mean it."

"I swear." He crossed his heart. "Derian Winfield asked you to marry her? And you said, what, no thanks?"

"What do you think?"

"I'm missing a few steps. Like the whys and the wherefores."

Emily sighed. Maybe if she said it all out loud she'd stop torturing herself with the endless replays. Maybe she'd convince herself she'd been right in sending Derian away. "Derian thought it would solve everyone's problems—I'd become a permanent resident, and voilà, no more visa problems. I'd be in a position one day to ensure that Winfield's continues with its mission, and presto, Henrietta's legacy is preserved. All that and Derian manages to not only infuriate her father but gain the upper hand in their long-standing private battle." She dusted her hands. "Everything taken care of all neat and tidy, as long as you don't consider the fact that she and I would be legally bound to one another."

"Well, you're already having sex."

"Are you going to sit there and tell me that's all that matters?"

He grinned. "It's a good start."

"It is, I won't argue that. But it's not a reason to get married."

"There are lots of reasons to get married, including the fact that you like someone, you have terrific sex, and it's sensible. They don't call it a contract for nothing."

"It's not enough for me, especially when—" Emily looked away. Especially when she wanted much more than a contract with Derian.

"Uh-oh."

Emily smiled sadly. "Yes, uh-oh indeed."

"Does she know?"

"Of course not."

"Maybe you should've told her."

"No. That's not fair."

"Honey," Ron said gently, "love isn't about being fair or unfair. It's about being honest."

"There's nothing dishonest about keeping one-sided feelings to oneself."

"When you see her again, you should reconsider."

"By the time I see her, it won't matter any longer."

Emily's phone rang and she grabbed it like a lifeline. Please let there be some problem she needed to take care of. She didn't want to talk about Derian—it took all her energy not to think about her.

"I think you better come down here," Vonnie said ominously.

"Oh no, tell me Donatella hasn't slithered back in."

"See for yourself."

Emily jumped up. "I have to go."

"This isn't over," Ron said.

Emily shook her head. "I'm afraid it is."

❖

"What is it?" Emily whispered as she approached Vonnie's desk. The door to Henrietta's office was slightly ajar and she really didn't want to go in there and see Donatella where Derian should be sitting.

"Go on in," Vonnie said with an air of resignation.

Emily steeled herself and pushed ahead.

Henrietta sat behind her desk, looking just as she had the last time Emily had seen her there.

"What are you doing here?" Emily blurted.

"The last time I checked, this was still my office."

"You're supposed to be home recovering."

Henrietta gave one of those peremptory motions of her hand, less a wave and more an incision, cleaving air. "I promised my doctors I would not come into the office *to work*. There's nothing wrong with my brain, and if I'm sitting at home I can be looking at my computer, which is probably a lot better for my overall state of health than staring at daytime television. Have you actually looked at what's on there recently?"

Emily grinned despite herself. She was just so glad to see Henrietta with color in her face and fire in her eyes again she couldn't be angry with her, even if she was still too thin and just a bit fragile looking and should not be there. "Television in general is not something I usually have time for."

"Then consider yourself better off for it." Henrietta speared her with a hard look. "How much does Derian have to do with how unhappy you look right now?"

"Absolutely nothing," Emily said instantly. Whatever had gone so terribly wrong between her and Derian was entirely between them. "Derian was a tremendous help and the entire staff is appreciative."

"I see," Henrietta said, looking as if she really did see but was kind enough not to probe any further. "I want you to take a few weeks off. Go home, see your sister."

"I can't go now," Emily said. "You're not coming back to work—"

"I can handle from home whatever Vonnie and Ron can't deal with, until you get back." Henrietta looked at her watch. "Now that's settled, you have a meeting with Audrey Ames in the conference room in five minutes."

"I do?"

"She's taking over the matter of getting your immigration status straightened out. After you meet with her, go. You shouldn't have any trouble with reentry now."

Emily's heart stuttered. Of course. If her work visa was not renewed, she couldn't leave the US. She knew of plenty of people who lived and worked in the US for years without a proper visa, but they couldn't leave to see family overseas, not if they wanted to come back.

"All right, yes. Thank you." Emily rose, suddenly so tired. "You'll go home too?"

"I will. And, Emily? It's going to be all right."

Emily didn't see how, as she went off to meet with Derian's best friend.

CHAPTER TWENTY-EIGHT

"Morning," Emily said as she walked into the conference room where Aud waited with a laptop open before her and a yellow legal pad by her right hand. Aud's navy suit jacket with matching trousers and an open-collared pale blue striped shirt looked more stylish than standard business garb on her willowy frame.

"Hi." Aud smiled, looking tired beneath her flawless, understated makeup. "Sorry I didn't get this scheduled with you ahead of time. Henrietta called and issued a priority edict."

"That's fine." Emily settled across from her. "Henrietta took us all by surprise today."

"At least she's feeling better." Aud leaned back. "So—today is just a review so I can be sure you understand the protocols and what we'll be doing to get you squared away."

"I thought—sorry, I'm not sure of the etiquette here, but I didn't think you were part of the agency's legal team."

"Technically," Aud said, not appearing put out by the question, "Winfield Enterprises' legal department represents all the divisions. The agency usually works with just one or two of us, but Henrietta requested me. Are you okay with that?"

"Of course."

Aud gave her a long look. "Actually, Henrietta intimated Derian was behind it."

Emily's face grew hot. So much for keeping her relationship with Derian private. All she had to do was hear her name and she telegraphed exactly how she felt about her. "Ah, that's kind of her."

Aud laughed. "Derian is many wonderful and infuriating things, including kind, but I don't think that's what motivated her this time. She knew I'd give this more than just the normal business-as-usual attention."

"Personal attention."

"Yes."

Emily studied the beautiful, sophisticated woman. She seemed exactly the kind of woman Derian would choose for a friend, or a lover. Had Derian discussed their relationship? And if she had, what did it matter. "I appreciate that."

"We're friends, Derian and I," Aud said quietly, as if answering some unspoken question.

"But you're in love with her, aren't you?" Emily asked, much preferring straightforward conversations to roundabout word games. And being on a level field with Aud, if all that meant was being honest, seemed important now that they were to have more than a passing acquaintance. Derian was part of their lives—even if Derian was part of her past now. The feelings remained, and she didn't want to hide them.

Aud gave a short, hard laugh. "My whole life."

"Does she know that?"

"Oh, I'm sure she does. And she loves me, in her way. In the only way she can." Aud shrugged, her expression amused and a little sad. "We can't help who we love, or who we don't. Derian isn't in love… with me."

"I'm sorry, it's none of my business."

"Isn't it?" Aud said lightly.

"No. Especially now, but really not ever. Derian's relationships are not my concern."

"Really? If she was my lover, I'd put a big sign around her neck— no trespassing."

Emily laughed and shook her head. "She's not my lover."

"Maybe, maybe not. But she wants to be sure you're here when she gets back."

Emily ignored the quick fluttering of her heart. Aud didn't know that. Neither did she, and she couldn't let herself get drawn into false hope. She'd had years of wishing reality could be changed and wouldn't be crippled by futile longings again. "I'm glad you're handling this."

Aud leaned forward, pulling the laptop into range. "All right then. Let's see about getting your immigration situation straightened out."

Emily listened, provided what information she could, and tried not to panic. Aud knew what she was doing—everything would work out. It had to.

"That's it for now," Aud said after half an hour. "I'll be in touch as soon as we start filing the preliminary forms. I'll push it as fast as I can."

"Thanks."

"I can't promise we'll get this sorted out anytime soon. Immigration laws are changing just about every minute, and with the way things are in Washington—everywhere across the country, really—regulations are getting tighter. Added to that we've got three federal agencies involved—Customs, Homeland, and Labor—and none of them speak the same language or to each other. But since you're already here and established, and paying taxes…" Aud smiled. "That always helps. I'm hopeful this will be taken care of before it becomes a serious issue."

"You mean before I have to leave."

Aud nodded. "Perhaps you should reconsider Derian's offer. That's a surefire way to cut through all the red tape."

Emily snorted. "She told you about that, did she? Her plan for me to be a mail-order bride?"

"She mentioned it, and I might've suggested it was a crazy idea at the time. But it's not illegal, especially since the two of you do have a relationship. You'd hardly be a mail-order bride."

"It's a ridiculous idea. I wouldn't chain her to a meaningless relationship."

"And what about yourself?"

Emily stared at the lines of script on the yellow notepad. She couldn't even pretend Derian didn't matter.

"No, I didn't think it would be meaningless." Aud rose and efficiently gathered up her notes. "I'll do my best to see that you stay."

Emily stayed behind, waiting for the rapid-fire events of the morning to settle. Henrietta was right, as usual. She needed to get away for a little while, and now was the perfect time for her long-delayed visit with Pam. Maybe when she wasn't coming to the agency every day, she wouldn't be reminded Derian wasn't there any longer. Mentally she laughed at her own self-delusion. Nothing would make her stop thinking of Derian. Was Aud right—had Derian reached out from afar to make sure someone who really cared would help her now?

Derian had tried to help her too, and even though her solution wasn't something Emily could live with, she at least ought to thank her. She owed her that.

❖

Derian collected her winnings and wended her way through the gaming tables to the bar for a drink before heading back to her hotel. At three in the morning, most everyone was at the tables, and the bar was almost empty except for a brunette in a red sheath dress at one end and two men at the other. Derian slid onto a stool halfway down the bar and nodded to the bartender in a crisp white shirt and black bow tie. "Macallan, neat."

A minute later, the bartender placed a tumbler of scotch onto a square white coaster on the polished black marble-topped bar in front of her. "Thanks."

The brunette eased onto the adjacent seat. "You don't remember me, but I was at the Speed-Pro company party the other night."

"I remember." Derian had a good memory for faces, and she'd noticed the brunette in a low-cut black dress that had showcased her killer body. She remembered the burly older man whose arm she'd clung to as well.

"I don't recall seeing you with anyone." The brunette's voice was a low, smoky purr.

"I'm not here with anyone."

"Neither am I." At Derian's slightly raised brow, she laughed. "Oh, I am married, but my husband prefers to spend his time at the tables. We have an understanding, in case something like that matters to you."

Derian savored her scotch. "I appreciate you telling me. It makes things easier, but I'm not looking for company."

"Everyone's looking for company of one sort or another." The brunette signaled the bartender and he placed another martini in front of her. "Whether we know it or not."

"You might be right," Derian said. "I should have said I'm not looking for anyone's company but one particular woman's."

"I see. Someone special."

Derian turned the glass in her hands, Emily's face all she could see. "Very."

"Well, how about another kind of company, then. For a little while."

"I'm Derian Winfield," Derian said, offering her hand.

"Veronica Riley."

"Nice to meet you, Veronica."

They shared another drink, and Derian offered to see Veronica back to her hotel.

"That's kind of you, but I'll be fine."

"Thanks for the company, then."

Veronica smiled and Derian walked away. As the cab brought her back to her hotel through the dark, quiet streets an hour before dawn, the restless unease of the last few weeks settled between her shoulder blades with an insistent throb. She'd done what she'd come here to do. Her business was finished, and what remained held no promise of pleasure. Time stretched out before her like a prison sentence, but she didn't have to accept the verdict. Maybe she'd left this life behind before she'd even returned. She just hadn't known it.

When she walked into her suite, the red light on her phone was blinking and she pushed the button for her messages. Emily's voice stopped time—stopped everything as Derian concentrated on the lift and fall of her voice, shuddered as warmth coursed through her. She steadied herself with a hand on the back of the sofa. What had she said? The words hadn't registered. Derian played the message again, and then again just to hear her voice. Emily was thanking her for being so kind, so helpful? That was all Emily had heard?

Derian closed her eyes. What an idiot she'd been.

Chapter Twenty-nine

Emily kissed Pam's gaunt cheek and reflexively tucked the colorful plaid blanket around her thin shoulders. "It's almost time for your dinner. I'll be back tomorrow. I love you."

She nodded to Yi Ling, gathered her purse and jacket, and walked outside. She paused in front of the residential center to breathe in the cool night air and shake off the sadness. She loved seeing her sister, but this city, this country, was not home to her anymore. She missed her apartment and her friends at the agency and her work and her life. She sighed. And she missed Derian. She hadn't heard from her, and she hadn't expected to, but a little part of her had hoped.

There was that word again. Hope. She couldn't shake it—not when it came to Pam, and not, it seemed, when it came to Derian. She joined the crowds on the sidewalk and walked back to her hotel. By the time she got there the sadness had dissipated along with the sun. In another few minutes twilight would give way to evening. Too keyed up to go inside after a day spent talking to a sister who might or might not have known she was there, she strolled aimlessly along the edge of a small park across from the hotel. All she had to look forward to was another evening with a solitary meal and a book. Something she usually looked forward to on vacation, but this time, her solitary pleasures were not enough to satisfy.

Emily stopped abruptly and stared, giving herself a second while her breath stuttered in her chest to be sure her imagination hadn't blindsided her.

Derian sat on a bench just inside the park, arms stretched out along the top, a slow smile on her face. Emily took a second to steady herself before walking over to her. If she let her heart lead the way, she'd be racing. And she didn't want to be wrong, couldn't bear to be wrong.

"Hello, Derian. I didn't expect to see you."

"I got your message. Sorry I missed your call. I wanted to say thank you."

Emily laughed softly, teetering on the brink of fleeing and touching her. Derian was really there, in the flesh, of course she was. "Most people would've just called me back."

"I did." Derian tilted her head to meet Emily's eyes. She looked tired, smudges under her eyes, and so incredibly beautiful. "You weren't at the agency."

Emily gestured to the bench. "May I?"

"Yes."

Emily sat and immediately felt the tips of Derian's fingers touch the back of her shoulder. Even through her jacket, the contact was electric. Familiar heat rushed through her. Oh yes, she was real all right. "I'm on vacation."

"I know, Ron told me."

"He didn't know where I was staying."

"Monica—my travel agent—is a wizard. Hope you don't mind me showing up."

"No, of course not." Of course not? How about, Oh my God, I've been so miserable since the moment you left. Can you just please not move for about a century. "I thought you were in Rio in the midst of business and…whatnot."

"I'm done with whatnot." Derian slipped her fingers from cotton to the bare skin at Emily's nape. She couldn't resist touching her any longer. The connection was like coming home, and the coiled tension inside her unwound and faded away. The ache that had tormented her for days dissolved in the welcome in Emily's eyes. "I had to see you. I missed you."

Emily's breath caught. "Derian."

"Emily…" Derian leaned closer and kissed her. "I made a mess of things the last time we talked."

Emily slid her hand onto Derian's leg, stroked up and down her denim-clad thigh. "No, you didn't. Well, maybe, but so did I. I know you were only trying to help. That's why I called, to thank—"

"No, no." Derian grimaced impatiently. "I was, trying to help, I mean, but that's not really what was going on. You were right about that."

"No, I wasn't." Emily needed her to believe this. "I meant what I said on the phone. I know you're not your father, and I know you weren't trying to use me to get back at him."

"Thank you. I need you to believe that."

"I do." Emily sighed. "How long are you here for?"

"Until you get tired of me."

The words pierced with the sweet blade of hope Emily couldn't allow herself. "I have another ten days."

"My reservation at the hotel is open-ended."

"You're staying here?"

"Yes. But if you don't want to see me, I'll leave."

Emily cupped Derian's cheek. How could she even think that? "Of course I want to see you. I hope…I hope at least we're friends."

Derian turned Emily's hand over and kissed her palm. "I don't want to be your friend, Emily." She met Emily's gaze. "I want to be your lover."

Emily summoned every ounce of will. Derian was going to break her heart, and she'd never recover. "I can't, Derian. I—"

"You really aren't going to tell me it's because of the business, are you?"

Emily shook her head. No more time for hiding the truth. "No, it's not that. I—"

Derian gave an impatient growl and, still holding Emily's hand, slid gracefully onto her knees in front of Emily.

A few people passing by paused to stare.

"Derian, what are you doing?"

"What I should've done before."

Derian's eyes gleamed and sent Emily's heart racing.

"I love you," Derian said, her voice strong and pure. "I want to be your lover and your mate, your friend and your spouse. I want you to marry me, Emily. Will you?"

Emily's heart said *yes, oh yes, yes*. The words would not come out. Derian was watching her, clear-eyed and intense. "I wasn't expecting this." She laughed shakily. "I might need a few minutes."

"How about you think about it over dinner? Long enough?"

"I love you," Emily said, unwilling to let Derian be the only one taking a chance. "I have for a long time."

Derian grinned. "Me too."

"I'm just not sure about all the rest."

"That's okay. I am."

Emily laughed. "You can get up off your knees now."

"I like it here."

Emily freed her hand from Derian's grasp and framed Derian's face. Leaning over, she gave her a proper kiss, slow and deep, that helped fill the emptiness she'd been carrying inside her since the moment Derian walked out of her apartment. When she drew back she whispered, "I love you."

Derian somehow managed to flow to her feet and pull Emily up with her, catching her in the circle of her arms. "Tell me we can have dinner in my room and you'll think about being mine."

"Yes, all right," Emily said, "I'll think about it."

Derian kissed her and murmured in her ear, "Tell me again you love me."

"I love you," Emily whispered.

❖

"I never want to live without room service." Derian tightened her hold around Emily's middle and kissed the back of her neck.

Emily wiggled her rear a little tighter into the curve of Derian's hips, found her hand, and drew it to her lips for a kiss. "Did we eat?"

Derian chuckled. "Not yet. But we can whenever we want."

"I don't ever want to move."

"Then we don't have to. There's nowhere else I want to be." Or anything else she'd rather be doing. Lying with Emily, loving Emily, filled her with quiet contentment and excitement that never relented. "You're everything I want, and I want you endlessly."

"I'm so glad." Emily gave a little groan, rolled onto her back, and pulled Derian's head down to kiss her again. "I love being yours."

Derian leaned on an elbow and stroked Emily's warm, pliant body. She couldn't stop touching. Couldn't get enough of her. Knew she never would. "Are you? Mine?"

"I am." Emily's smile was small and, for just a second, a little sad.

Derian's middle clenched. "Does that make you unhappy?"

Light leapt in Emily's eyes. "Oh no. Never, not for a second."

"But there's something, isn't there?"

Emily laughed, a little tremor in her voice. "I'm just being me. I'll miss you when you're gone."

Derian frowned. "Where am I going?"

Emily grinned, the sadness vanishing in the face of so much joy. She had fallen in love with a woman who lived on the edge. She would cope. "Oh, you know, race cars, fancy casinos, and…all of that."

"There is no more all of that, only you." Derian pushed up on the bed and pulled Emily into her arms. "Clearly, I have not done a good job of this proposal business."

"You did a perfectly wonderful job. I will never forget you, on your knees in the park, or the things you said."

"Good, because I meant all of them." Derian brushed Emily's hair from her neck, kissed the tender spot below her ear, drew her in. Emily's scent flooded her with the essence of belonging. "You're the only woman in the world I want, the only thing I need. I love you. I need you, I need to be with you."

"Derian…" Emily put her lips to Derian's throat where she could feel her pulse race, taste the life and power of her, bask in the preciousness of being so close. "I love you too, with all my heart. And I want you to be happy. I want you to live the life you want to live, and it's not back in—"

"It's with you, Emily. Where you are, that's where my life is."

Emily swallowed hard, wishing that little logical part of her brain would shut up and let her just believe in this fairy tale. But she loved Derian too much to let her give up the things that mattered to her. "I'll always be there for you, I promise. I'm a one-woman woman, and you have my heart."

"Then why don't you believe that you are my heart?"

"I would like nothing better than to go to sleep with you every night and wake up next to you every day," Emily said, giving voice to the dream. "But not if it means caging you in, making you unhappy."

"It won't. I want that too. Every day for the rest of my life." Derian kissed her. "So if it's all right with you, I'll be heading home with you. And staying."

"I would love that, but what will you do?"

"I'll have to travel sometimes for racing business, sure, and I'll hate every second away from you. But I can cut down my personal appearances so I won't be away very often."

"Maybe," Emily said slowly, a new, breathtaking image of the future forming, one she believed was not a dream, "I can come with you sometimes."

"I'd love that." Joy erupted in Derian's chest. "Whenever, wherever you want to go. I'd love for you to come."

"As long as you promise no celebrity photos."

Laughing Derian nuzzled her neck. "Can't promise that—you'll look gorgeous on camera."

Emily pressed against her. Beautiful is exactly how Derian made her feel. "What will you do the rest of the time?"

"I thought I'd get a little more involved in the business. I have a seat on the board I've never bothered with. I'm good with numbers, and I have accumulated a great many international contacts." She shrugged. "It might even be fun."

Emily rolled her eyes, the idea of high-powered business dealings her farthest idea from fun. But Derian had a knack for it, and it was, after all, her legacy. "What about your father?"

"For all he's constantly criticized me for not taking part, he probably won't like it." Derian grinned and kissed Emily. "And you were right about one thing, I enjoy irritating him. So that's a bonus."

Emily laughed, lightness flooding her heart. She couldn't fight what she wanted so much. Love was about believing, about taking the gifts that were offered and rejoicing in them. "I want us to be together always."

Derian grinned. "Are you going to marry me, then, because I want us to get married." She kissed Emily quickly before a question or protest could form on her lips. "Not because of Henrietta, not because of the agency, not even because of your visa. I want you to be mine and I want everyone to know it. I want us to have a life together, to make life what we want it to be, together. And...I want everyone to know I'm yours."

Emily slid her hand into Derian's hair and gave a little tug. "That means only mine. All mine. You understand that, right?"

"I've been all yours since the first kiss. All I think about is you, all I'll ever want is you. For better or for worse."

"For today and tomorrow," Emily whispered.

"For all the tomorrows." Derian rolled over, slid a leg between Emily's thighs, and kissed her throat. "Did you just say yes?"

"Yes, God, yes." Emily arched her back and wrapped a leg around the back of Derian's calf. "You make me feel so good."

"Yes, what? Yes, Derian, I will marry you…" Derian swirled her tongue around a very firm nipple. "Or yes, Derian, I want you to make mad, passionate love to me forever and ever."

"Both." Emily clutched Derian's shoulder. "You are so arrogant. God."

"You like me that way."

"Yes, I do. Now, show me just how good you really are."

Laughing, Derian trailing kisses along the curve of Emily's breast and down her belly, slipping a hand between them to stroke and tease. "I can't stop wanting you."

"Don't, don't ever." Emily's mind was fragmenting, words deserting her. She rocked to the rhythm of Derian's caresses and, when a shock wave jolted through her, grasped Derian's arms. "Hold me. I'm coming."

Derian gathered Emily up just as Emily cried out against her shoulder, catching a bit of skin and muscle in her teeth. Derian, already breathless and blinded by Emily's beauty, groaned at the unexpected possession. So damn good. The tension spiraling between her thighs erupted. "Oh yeah."

Weakly Emily shoved at Derian's shoulder. "Done. Done, done, done. Go 'way."

Laughing, Derian rolled onto her side and pulled Emily against her. "You just need a little food, and you'll recover."

"I may never get out of this bed."

"Fine by me, but all the same, I'll call for room service."

Emily held on to her a little harder. "Not just yet."

"Hey, are you okay?" Derian brushed a wisp of a tear from Emily's cheek. "What's wrong?"

"Absolutely nothing. Everything is right. I love you so much."

"I love you. I can't wait for you to be all mine."

"I already am," Emily said with absolute certainty. "But I still plan on marrying you just as soon as we can arrange it."

"So is this like a pre-honeymoon, then?" Derian kissed her.

"Whatever you like. But you really will have to feed me soon, if you want to keep celebrating."

"Calling right now." Derian lunged for the phone.

"And, Derian?"

"Hmm?"

"When room service comes? Don't forget to put some clothes on. Because from now on, the only one who's ever going to see you naked is me."

Derian laughed, already relishing the idea of being all Emily's. "There must be a robe around here somewhere."

About the Author

Radclyffe has written over fifty romance and romantic intrigue novels, dozens of short stories, and, writing as L.L. Raand, has authored a paranormal romance series, The Midnight Hunters.

She is an eight-time Lambda Literary Award finalist in romance, mystery, and erotica—winning in both romance (*Distant Shores, Silent Thunder*) and erotica (*Erotic Interludes 2: Stolen Moments* edited with Stacia Seaman and *In Deep Waters 2: Cruising the Strip* written with Karin Kallmaker). A member of the Saints and Sinners Literary Hall of Fame, she is also an RWA/FF&P Prism Award winner for *Secrets in the Stone*, an RWA FTHRW Lories and RWA HODRW winner for *Firestorm*, an RWA Bean Pot winner for *Crossroads*, and an RWA Laurel Wreath winner for *Blood Hunt*. In 2014 she was awarded the Dr. James Duggins Outstanding Mid-Career Novelist Award by the Lambda Literary Foundation. She is a featured author in the 2015 documentary film *Love Between the Covers*, from Blueberry Hill Productions.

She is also the president of Bold Strokes Books, one of the world's largest independent LGBTQ publishing companies.

Find her at facebook.com/Radclyffe.BSB, follow her on Twitter @RadclyffeBSB, and visit her website at Radfic.com.

Books Available From Bold Strokes Books

Best Laid Plans by Jan Gayle. Nicky and Lauren are meant for each other, but Nicky's haunting past and Lauren's societal fears threaten to derail all possibilities of a relationship. (978-1-62639-658-6)

Exchange by CF Frizzell. When Shay Maguire rode into rural Montana, she never expected to meet the woman of her dreams—or to learn Mel Baker was held hostage by legal agreement to her right-wing father. (978-1-62639-679-1)

Just Enough Light by AJ Quinn. Will a serial killer's return to Colorado destroy Kellen Ryan and Dana Kingston's chance at love, or can the search-and-rescue team save themselves? (978-1-62639-685-2)

Rise of the Rain Queen by Fiona Zedde. Nyandoro is nobody's princess. She fights, curses, fornicates, and gets into as much trouble as her brothers. But the path to a throne is not always the one we expect. (978-1-62639-592-3)

Tales from Sea Glass Inn by Karis Walsh. Over the course of a year at Cannon Beach, tourists and locals alike find solace and passion at the Sea Glass Inn. (978-1-62639-643-2)

The Color of Love by Radclyffe. Black sheep Derian Winfield needs to convince literary agent Emily May to marry her to save the Winfield Agency and solve Emily's green card problem, but Derian didn't count on falling in love. (978-1-62639-716-3)

A Reluctant Enterprise by Gun Brooke. When two women grow up learning nothing but distrust, unworthiness, and abandonment, it's no wonder they are apprehensive and fearful when an overwhelming love just won't be denied. (978-1-62639-500-8)

Above the Law by Carsen Taite. Love is the last thing on Agent Dale Nelson's mind, but reporter Lindsey Ryan's investigation could change the way she sees everything—her career, her past, and her future. (978-1-62639-558-9)

Actual Stop by Kara A. McLeod. When Special Agent Ryan O'Connor's present collides abruptly with her past, shots are fired, and the course of her life is irrevocably altered. (978-1-62639-675-3)

Embracing the Dawn by Jeannie Levig. When ex-con Jinx Tanner and business executive E. J. Bastien awaken after a one-night stand to find their lives inextricably entangled, love has its work cut out for it. (978-1-62639-576-3)

Love's Redemption by Donna K. Ford. For ex-convict Rhea Daniels and ex-priest Morgan Scott, redemption lies in the thin line between right and wrong. (978-1-62639-673-9)

The Shewstone by Jane Fletcher. The prophetic Shewstone is in Eawynn's care, but unfortunately for her, Matt is coming to steal it. (978-1-62639-554-1)

Jane's World by Paige Braddock. Jane's PayBuddy account gets hacked and she inadvertently purchases a mail order bride from the Eastern Bloc. (978-1-62639-494-0)

A Touch of Temptation by Julie Blair. Recent law school graduate Kate Dawson's ordained path to the perfect life gets thrown off course when handsome butch top Chris Brent initiates her to sexual pleasure. (978-1-62639-488-9)

Beneath the Waves by Ali Vali. Kai Merlin and Vivien Palmer love the water and the secrets trapped in the depths, but if Kai gives in to her feelings, it might come at a cost to her entire realm. (978-1-62639-609-8)

Girls on Campus, edited by Sandy Lowe and Stacia Seaman. College: four years when rules are made to be broken. This collection is required reading for anyone looking to earn an A in sex ed. (978-1-62639-733-0)

Miss Match by Fiona Riley. Matchmaker Samantha Monteiro makes the impossible possible for everyone but herself. Is mysterious dancer Lucinda Moss her perfect match? (978-1-62639-574-9)

Paladins of the Storm Lord by Barbara Ann Wright. Lieutenant Cordelia Ross must choose between duty and honor when a man with godlike powers forces her soldiers to provoke an alien threat. (978-1-62639-604-3)

Taking a Gamble by P.J. Trebelhorn. Storage auction buyer Cassidy Holmes and postal worker Erica Jacobs want different things out of life, but taking a gamble on love might prove lucky for them both. (978-1-62639-542-8)

The Copper Egg by Catherine Friend. Archeologist Claire Adams wants to find the buried treasure in Peru. Her ex, Sochi Castillo, wants to steal it. The last thing either of them wants is to still be in love. (978-1-62639-613-5)

Capsized by Julie Cannon. What happens when a woman turns your life completely upside down? (978-1-62639-479-7)

A Reunion to Remember by TJ Thomas. Reunited after a decade, Jo Adams and Rhonda Black must navigate a significant age difference, family dynamics, and their own desires and fears to explore an opportunity for love. (978-1-62639-534-3)

Heartscapes by MJ Williamz. Will Odette ever recover her memory, or is Jesse condemned to remember their love alone? (978-1-62639-532-9)

Built to Last by Aurora Rey. When Professor Olivia Bennett hires contractor Joss Bauer to restore her dilapidated farmhouse, she learns her heart, as much as her house, is in need of a renovation. (978-1-62639-552-7)

Girls With Guns by Ali Vali, Carsen Taite, and Michelle Grubb. Three stories by three talented crime writers—Carsen Taite, Ali Vali, and Michelle Grubb—each packing her own special brand of heat. (978-1-62639-585-5)

24/7 by Yolanda Wallace. When the trip of a lifetime becomes a pitched battle between life and death, will anyone survive? (978-1-62639-619-7)

Murder on the Rocks by Clara Nipper. Detective Jill Rogers lives with two things on her mind: sex and murder. While an ice storm cripples Tulsa, two things stand in Jill's way: her lover and the DA. (978-1-62639-600-5)

Salvation by I. Beacham. Claire's long-term partner now hates her, for all the wrong reasons, and she sees no future until she meets Regan, who challenges her to face the truth and find love. (978-1-62639-548-0)

Trigger by Jessica Webb. Dr. Kate Morrison races to discover how to defuse human bombs while learning to trust her increasingly strong feelings for the lead investigator, Sergeant Andy Wyles. (978-1-62639-669-2)

A Return to Arms by Sheree Greer. When a police shooting makes national headlines, activists Folami and Toya struggle to balance their relationship and political allegiances, a struggle intensified after a fiery young artist enters their lives. (978-1-62639-681-4)

After the Fire by Emily Smith. Paramedic Connor Haus is convinced her time for love has come and gone, but when firefighter Logan Curtis comes into town, she learns it may not be too late after all. (978-1-62639-652-4)

Necromantia by Sheri Lewis Wohl. When seeing dead people is more than a movie tagline. (978-1-62639-611-1)

Fortunate Sum by M. Ullrich. Financial advisor Catherine Carter lives a calculated life, but after a collision with spunky Imogene Harris (her latest client) and unsolicited predictions, Catherine finds herself facing an unexpected variable: Love. (978-1-62639-530-5)

Dian's Ghost by Justine Saracen. The road to genocide is paved with good intentions. (978-1-62639-594-7)

Wild Shores by Radclyffe. Can two women on opposite sides of an oil spill find a way to save both a wildlife sanctuary and their hearts? (978-1-62639-645-6)

boldstrokesbooks.com

Bold Strokes Books

Quality and Diversity in LGBTQ Literature

Drama

SCI-FI

E-BOOKS

MYSTERY

EROTICA

YOUNG ADULT

Romance

W·E·B·S·T·O·R·E

PRINT AND EBOOKS